Harriet was still on her knees, clutching the scrap of paper, tears of desperate disappointment running down her cheeks, when she heard the sound in the next room. *Someone was there! Someone who had obviously been listening and waiting!*

There was only one doorway. Whoever was in there had to come through this room to get downstairs. . . .

Harriet looked at the dark doorway. "Who is it? Who's there?" she whispered. There was no answer, only another furtive sound. "Who is it; tell me!" She shouted passionately.

A tall figure appeared at the door. There was a faint silver shine from the long thick hair. The face was strange, beige-colored, horrible.

"Why, it's me, my dear," came the throaty voice that she had last heard on the telephone that morning. "Weren't you expecting me?"

Other Ace Books by Dorothy Eden:

Listen to Danger

Dorothy Eden

ace books
A Division of Charter Communications Inc.
A GROSSET & DUNLAP COMPANY
1120 Avenue of the Americas
New York, New York 10036

I

ON THAT DAY life had been going on apparently as usual in the red-brick block of flats situated attractively in a quiet London square. Obviously it was only people with good incomes who could afford to live there, and enjoy the view from their windows of the winter-gray trees in the gardens, the mists growing blue over the lime-green lawns, and the rows of pastel-colored houses opposite.

Although a few yards away the traffic in High Street roared past, the sounds were muted here, and everything seemed leisurely, tradesmen's vans pulling up and uniformed delivery men getting out, a milk cart going past with a gentle tingling of the bell around the horse's neck, a laborer sweeping up leaves in the gutter, and of course, the coming and going of tenants from the flats, some expensively fur coated, a great many with small pampered dogs on leashes, the occasional nanny pushing a shiny black perambulator, and the occasional char-woman, with shabby coat and string bag, departing after her morning's work.

It would seem that in these quiet surroundings life was comparatively smooth and pleasant for the tenants of Manchester Court. But, as always, that was a fallacy. The human element, the small private longings, the lonelinesses, the impotence against fate, was no more in subjection here than in the poorest tenement area.

There was the young widow, Harriet Lacey, who was having another domestic crisis. Nannie Brown was leaving because, in her own words, she "could not do with Jamie's naughtiness any longer," and Harriet had the prospect of finding yet another woman, kind and reliable, with whom to leave Jamie and the baby Arabella while she went to rehearsals, and later to evening and matinée performances. This filled her with despair. What was she doing wrong with Jamie and why was he being so naughty? He missed his father of course. At first she had known his wild intractable moods were a subconscious protest over the fact that his father had mysteriously disappeared, and at the time there had been no way of explaining to a three-year-old why he would never come back. But Joe had been dead nearly two years now. Instead of passing, Jamie's naughtiness had become a habit. And lately, much to the disapproval of Nannie Brown, he had formed strange friendships, not only with the blind man in the flat immediately beneath Harriet's flat, but with that strange old woman, Mrs. Helps, mother of the flats porter, who lived in the basement and made wigs.

Sometimes life with two young children and a career to which she obstinately clung seemed to Harriet to be too complicated. . . .

Nor was life easy for Flynn Palmer. He had partially accustomed himself to his blindness. In a physical sense, at least, he was able to cope, and day by day things were becoming simpler. But the hard core of bitterness and refusal to resign himself to such an enormous handicap remained. He was no longer suicidal. Instead, he gave vent to his feelings by lashing out at everyone who annoyed him, or seemed even more stupid than the average human being. That idiot girl who had made a forlorn attempt to be his secretary had been one of them. Her grating voice, with its attempt at gentility, had driven him mad, and when, in this voice, she had read aloud some of the more tender passages in his great-grandfather's letters he had torn his hair and cried out in rage. It was not surprising she had told him that she just couldn't work for him, she had tried, she was that sorry for him, but he was quite impossible.

After her departure the flat had seemed heavenly quiet. But the fact remained that now he had no one to help him with his work, and his great-grandfather's letters, that goldmine of literary treasure onto which he had stumbled when sorting out an accumulation of family possessions shortly before the accident that had caused his blindness, were going to remain unedited. Unless he found another secretary, of course, and at present he shrank from such a task. To be sure, both Zoe and Jones were helpful in trying to find someone. But Zoe admired brisk overpowering efficiency, and Jones's taste in women was not his most reliable quality. He was inclined to dwell lingeringly on their physical appearance, until Flynn had to remind him acidly that it was no use his getting a secretary for her looks since he wouldn't see them anyway. Whereupon Jones exclaimed, 'Oh, sir!' in a shocked, remorseful voice, and the hot rage rose in Flynn because of the man's obvious pity.

Pity, pity, pity . . . He would not tolerate it. Its slimy softness had lapped over him ever since his accident. From doctors, nurses, relations, servants, and, most intolerably of all, from young attractive women. It seemed inescapable.

When he was able to do more for himself, he would live alone, like a hermit. Or perhaps he would allow the occasional visits from that odd, forthright, stubborn little boy, Jamie, who treated him as an equal, and never questioned his disability. So long, of course, as Harriet, his mother, another pitier, kept away. . . .

If life was complicated at present for Harriet and Flynn, it had never been simple for the old lady, Mrs. Helps, who lived in the basement flat, and kept house for her tall, good-looking son, Fred, who was doing his first steady job for a long time as porter of the flats. It was so wonderful to be in a nice place of her own after the makeshift rooms in which she had lived during what she called Fred's wild life. Now at last she had plenty of room for her wigs and her dummy heads. She had also kept her clients, in spite of her many shifts and the shame of that year while Fred was in prison. But now it seemed Fred intended to go straight. He was proud of his smart, dark green uniform which he put on in the afternoons; he liked opening the door with a flourish to people coming in, and smiling at the pretty well-groomed women. He even, he told his mother, intended to look seriously for a girl to marry, which probably would mean that the old lady, with her macabre luggage, would have to move again. But she was not worrying about that so long as Fred settled down. She was so afraid that in spite of the comfort here, and the owner of the flats not minding that she plied her strange trade in the basement, there would be too much temptation for Fred. Seeing other people with plenty roused some meanness in him, and he had to say, "Mine, too." But perhaps he had grown out of that phase. His good sense would tell him not to risk losing a job like this. In the meantime she kept out of sight as much as possible, because Fred told her to. It was not that he was ashamed of her exactly, but she was chronically untidy, and Fred's good-humored remonstrances made no difference. On her the neatest dress seemed to become vague and shapeless, and she was much attached to an old gray woolen scarf without which she always caught bronchitis. Also her preoccupation with other people's hair left her with no particular interest in her own.

So she sat all day in her dark room, rather like a large gray spider, her thin fingers cleverly shaping gray, black and auburn strands of hair, her background the faceless dummies standing or lying like so many dismembered heads, in odd corners of the room.

If only Fred would go straight, and find himself a nice girl. . . .

Jones, too, Flynn's neat, quiet and nicely-spoken manservant, had his personal troubles, or rather one trouble, his wife Nell, who had been an invalid for nearly ten years. He had to do a job where he could be home at nights. During the day he engaged a nurse-companion, but apart from being unable to afford to have anyone living in, there was no room in the tiny flat anyway. Since Nell's illness he had had a series of jobs, barkeeper, shop assistant, hotel porter, and finally this one as valet to the blind man, Fred Palmer.

To date, it was the best job he had had. The pay was good, the hours regular, he could get home to Nell punctually at seven each evening, and years of caring for his wife had made him patient and understanding, which was necessary in working for

Mr. Palmer, with his sudden violent tempers.

Really, Jones told himself, things were not too bad at present. Life was not exciting and full of promise as he had once thought, it was merely a rather dreary matter of building bridges from one trouble to the next. But one managed.

There was one other person who was ill at ease that evening. That was the girl, rather plump, with long, thick light brown hair and china blue eyes who walked past Manchester Court looking at it contemplatively.

Millie longed to work in the West End. This square, with its spacious gardens, its balconied houses, its air of ease and luxury, impressed her favorably. She had meant to get a job in a shop, of course. Actually, she would have liked that best. But stronger than her desire to sell expensive perfumes or expensive artificial jewelry was her desire to get away from the overcrowded house in Bethnal Green. And all those kids. Her own brothers and sisters, certainly, but giving a girl no privacy nor realizing she wanted it. And Mum and Dad looking over every boyfriend she brought home, and making caustic comments. No, her idea was a life of her own, and the best way to start acquiring that was to get a living-in job in some nice West End house of flat. After that, well—Millie flicked her heavy locks and tossed her head. A girl only had to have a chance, hadn't she?

She hadn't actually looked after other people's kids before, but there was nothing she didn't know about kids, and she liked them well enough. She could play with them or be firm as the occasion demanded. It might be rather fun wheeling one of those posh prams with fringed hoods into Kensington Gardens and making acquaintances. It was no trouble to Millie, friendly and gregarious, to become acquainted with people. It had been a good idea to come over and take a look at this place before answering the advertisement. She was shrewd in that way. She looked before she leaped. Of course, the mother of the two children, "a boy of five and a baby of fifteen months," the advertisement had said, might be one of these rich idle fault-finding types. But she liked the look of the square and the block of flats. There was no harm in taking a look at this Mrs. Lacey, also.

Though what Mum would say when she knew Millie was leaving home was another thing.

Millie giggled and tossed her hair again. Really, at eighteen, it was more than time she asserted herself. She would say she was nineteen. . . .

Resolutely she walked to the telephone box in the square.

That was the first of the series of telephone calls to Harriet's flat that was to become first an excitement, then a slowly mounting horror. . . .

II

THE TELEPHONE rang just as Harriet came in. It was curious that, even now, after nearly two years, her heart still gave a small excited leap at that sound. Joe had always announced his return this way. The urgent shrill of the bell had become a symbol to her. So that now there was always that split second transformation from joy to a disciplined despair before she could pick up the receiver and speak.

At this moment she was exhausted after a long and particularly trying rehearsal. She wanted to put her feet up and have a long cool drink at her side. All the way home she had daydreamed about such a felicitous state of affairs, the children in bed, the flat tidy, a pleasant girl in the kitchen getting the evening meal. And then, of course, came the forbidden part of the dream, the familiar step at the door, the so-longed-for voice. . . .

Some day, Harriet told herself, she would really sit down and cry for Joe. She would no longer blink back tears on buses, in restaurants, at the door of her flat, inhabited only by children and servants. Some day, when there was time and privacy. In the meantime, one must go on. Answer the telephone now, since Nannie Brown did not appear to be going to do so.

Letting her bag and gloves fall on the hall table,

Harriet picked up the receiver. A high girlish voice said,

"Is that Mrs. Lacey?"

"Yes, this is Mrs. Lacey."

"I'm ringing about the job you advertised, looking after your ki—I mean, children."

Harriet winced. The cheerful Cockney voice was not part of her dream of the ideal nursemaid. Arabella was just learning to speak and one did not particularly want her first vowels distorted. On the other hand, the owner of this blithe voice sounded young and full of vitality. Hadn't she resolved to have no more middle-aged or elderly women who could not cope with Jamie's irrepressible energy? Harriet glanced over her shoulder into the living room and saw its depressing state of untidiness, toys littering the carpet, cushions mussed, one of Arabella's discarded crusts on the piano, Arabella's outdoor clothes flung on a chair. Repeatedly she had told Nannie Brown to keep the children and their clutter in the nursery, but the woman had said feebly that Jamie always insisted he liked this room better, and Mrs. Lacey knew very well that her son was impossible to manage. Even as Harriet rapidly reflected on all this, Nannie Brown, dressed in hat and coat, appeared, her elderly face puckered and obstinate.

"Just a minute," Harriet said quickly into the telephone. She listened to Nannie Brown's urgent voice.

"I'm on my way home, Mrs. Lacey. I can't stand any more. If I've told Jamie once I've told him a dozen times he's to stay in the flat, but one might as well speak to that chair!"

"Where is he now?"

"I really cannot say. He might be with Mr. Palmer,

or he might be with that dreadful old woman in the basement. I won't be responsible for him any longer. Some tragedy will happen to him and I'll be to blame. I can't stand it, Mrs. Lacey. I'm not young enough, and even if I were, that child—" The woman shrugged helplessly and made for the door.

"Arabella?" Harriet asked.

"Oh, she's in bed asleep. She's all right. If it was only her I wouldn't be leaving you."

Harriet looked at Nannie Brown's elderly, prim and disapproving face, and wondered briefly how she had ever come to engage the woman. Of course, it had been the old story, the difficulty of getting anyone at all. Suddenly, the cheerful young voice on the telephone seemed full of promise.

"Don't worry, Nannie. I quite understand," she said swiftly. "You get away home. I'll find Jamie and cope."

The door closed behind Nannie Brown, and Harriet spoke crisply into the receiver. "I'm so sorry to keep you waiting. Now will you tell me your name and how old you are."

"I'm Millie Green, and I'm nineteen."

"Have you had any experience in looking after children?"

"Not out at work, but I've got six brothers and sisters at home."

The girl giggled, and Harriet winced again. Then she thought of Nannie Brown, too old and ineffectual, and of the difficulty of getting any answers at all to advertisements for domestic help.

"I think you'd better come and see me, Millie. Where are you?"

"I'm in Kensington, Mrs. Lacey."

"That's fine. Then perhaps you could come in, say, half an hour?"

"Yes, I can do that."

"That's excellent. Flat 14 on the top floor. In half an hour."

Harriet sighed as she put the telephone down. The girl sounded young, lively, good-humored. Apart from her Cockney voice and her habit of giggling, she might be an ideal nursemaid. One should not have this depressed feeling of failure before one has even seen the girl.

The flat was empty now, except for Arabella tucked in her cot in the nursery and smiling with uncritical affection as Harriet went in. To this child of hers Harriet always felt a vague unexplainable guilt. Was it because Joe had died before he knew of her conception? Arabella's chief beauty, beyond her baby chubbiness, was her head of red-gold curls, Harriet's own hair in its new baby-fine state. Joe had always hoped that one day they would have a daughter with Harriet's hair and now the daughter was here, but Joe didn't know, and had never known. Somehow it had seemed to deprive Arabella of an identity. She was like a guest who had arrived embarrassingly late for a party. Harriet adored her, and yet felt guilty. It was a curious thing.

"Hello, darling," she said brightly. "Time you were asleep."

Arabella cooed contentedly. Harriet saw, propped on the table, one of Mrs. Blunt's cryptic notes. These notes were usually scattered prominently about the flat, and were obviously written as the thoughts came into Mrs. Blunt's head. This one read, "Arabella sick on carpet, it won't come out."

Harriet saw the depressing stain, and sighed again. What had made Arabella sick? Why hadn't Nannie Brown told her, or coped in time? This spasmodic housekeeping, picking up where Mrs. Blunt and a succession of nannies left off, could not go on indefinitely. But what other prospect was there?

Perhaps this girl Millie—Harriet's thoughts broke off as the telephone rang again.

A frantic chuckling greeted her as she answered it. Finally Jamie's voice emerged, "It's me, Mummy. Guess where I am."

"Wherever you are," Harriet said sternly, "You're to come home this minute. I thought Nannie forbade you to leave the flat."

"Oh, her!" said Jamie, with scorn. Then he added excitedly, "Mummy, I rang you all by myself. Flynn said I could."

"Flynn! Oh, Jamie! Didn't I tell you you were not to go worrying Mr. Palmer."

"I don't worry him," said Jamie. "I help him. He needs a sekkertery."

"So you are busy at the typewriter!" Harriet said scathingly. "Jamie, I insist—"

It was no use insisting anything, for she heard Jamie saying in his shrill, uninhibited voice, "Over there, Flynn. Over there!" and the receiver crashed heedlessly down.

She would have to go and get him. It was not fair of Flynn Palmer to allow him to stay when he knew she disapproved. Flynn always said that Jamie was not a nuisance, and he liked his company occasionally, which must have been true. For Flynn did not bother to disguise either hostility or dislike if he felt them. Becoming blind, with tragic suddenness, seemed to have removed any inhibitions he might once have had about behavior, and now he was pleasant, distantly polite, prickly, or downright rude, as his mood dictated.

Harriet liked him best when he was rude. At least then he was honest and one knew where one stood. She was sorry for him, desperately sorry for him. He was only thirty, and his blindness had deprived him of a career as one of the most promising young politicians. But there were other ways of living in darkness. Flynn Palmer still had a great deal: a comfortable income, a faithful and competent man-servant, his deep interest in music and literature, and plenty of friends, particularly good-looking young women, particularly Zoe.

It was a pity one did not like Zoe. She had been remarkably faithful to Flynn, because she was a very attractive girl, and could not lack admirers. But it was now nearly two years since the accident that had killed Joe and left Flynn with his eyesight permanently affected, and during that time Zoe had stood by him loyally and possessively. Possessively? That was not a kind word. But there was no other with which to describe Zoe's air of ownership of Flynn, his flat, his work, and his man-servant Jones.

It seemed certain that they would eventually marry. Harriet did not know why this fact worried her. Flynn had been merely a chance acquaintance of Joe's. It had been one of those quirks of fate that that night in Boston they had both been at the same party, and Flynn, discovering that they were staying at the same hotel, had offered Joe a lift home. Joe was to have flown back to England the next day. Instead, in the accident that had been the fault of a reckless cab driver, Joe lay dead and Flynn seriously injured.

It could have happened to anybody. But Flynn, with his tortured conscience, had sought out Harriet when he at last returned to England and tried to make what amends he could.

Harriet had tried often to forget that meeting. It had been such a desperate failure. She had been so rigid with grief about Joe, so determined not to break down in front of this stranger whose own face was tightly controlled and somehow anonymous behind the dark glasses, that she must have seemed unfriendly and antogonistic. She had not meant to be. But the whole thing had been such anguish, and she had wished that Flynn's conscience had not brought him to her.

The accident had not been his fault. It had been fate. It had been meant that at twenty-six she was to be a widow expecting a child which would have no father. At that time she had not told Flynn about the expected baby. And later that was to be still another intangible hostility between them. Because Flynn, who blamed himself for depriving her of a husband, had somehow decided that he had an indirect responsibility for her and her children.

That was how she had come to live at Manchester Court.

Joe's parents had not approved of his marriage to an English girl. They had had someone lined up for him in Boston, and it had come as a deep shock to them when he had met and married Harriet all in the space of a few weeks. They had not come to the wedding in London. They had made the excuse that Joe's father, an eminent Boston lawyer, had an important case he could not leave, and his mother was not strong enough to make long journeys alone. But Harriet had known that they were bitterly disappointed, and even her subsequent meeting with them could not break down their hostility.

After Joe's death they had naturally drawn a little closer. They had insisted on making an ample allowance to Harriet and the children, but Harriet, unable to forget the unhappiness they had caused Joe and herself in their brief marriage, refused to use the money for herself. The children, yes. They had a right to it. She would see that they had a good home, and later went to good schools. But for herself, she would be independent. She went back to her career as an actress, with its bittersweet memories of her first meeting with Joe after a show one night when he had waited for her at the stage door.

There was no tall, pleasantly ugly young American waiting at stage doors for her now. Instead, in her life, there was a blind man, Flynn Palmer, who persisted in trying to make amends for a quirk of fate, and had recently enabled her to rent the attractive flat on the top floor of the block in which he had lived for a long time.

The flat, after her trying for months to find the right one, was pure bliss. She had not been so sure about wanting to live as a neighbor of Flynn's.

But this, too, had been better than she had expected, for Flynn did not encroach on her life. He seemed to be making courageous efforts to adapt himself to his new life, Zoe was constantly with him, and he was unexpectedly tolerant about Jamie's uninhibited visits. The accident was fading into the past, and they were just people, with their own particular problems and small happinesses, living in the same building. One was neighborly, that was all. Flynn had Zoe, with her pert sophisticated prettiness, to care for him. Harriet had her children and her work. Sometimes, lately, it had even been a little difficult to conjure up Joe's face out of the empty air. . . .

Looking up at the clock, Harriet made frantic efforts to tidy the flat. This new girl, Millie Green, might be exactly right, and she didn't want her put off by untidy rooms and an atmosphere of haphazard housekeeping. In the kitchen she found another of Mrs. Blunt's notes. "It's time the curtains were sent to the laundry. Shall I do this?" Harriet picked up a pencil and scrawled "Yes." Mrs. Blunt was a treasure. Her plain, kind face was as round as a full moon, rosy and smiling; her prominent, pale blue eyes missed nothing but were uncritical. If Millie did seem a little young, one would know Mrs. Blunt was there a good part of the day to keep an eye on her.

When, a little later, the doorbell rang and the girl, rather plump, with profuse blonde hair, stood there, Harriet hesitated almost imperceptibly before asking her to come in.

She would put her into a uniform, she thought quickly, as she noticed the girl's exaggeratedly long bulky sweater, her too tight skirt, and her high-heeled open-toe shoes. She would also persuade her, diplomatically, to have her hair cut shorter.

Apart from that, the girl smiled in a friendly way, and her eyes were very bright, as if she were excited. She looked kind and pleasant. Those were the important characteristics with children.

"Come in, Millie," she said, leading the way into the now tidy living room. "Sit down. Tell me about yourself. Where is your home, and do you feel happy about taking a living-in position?"

Millie said breathlessly that she lived in Bethnal Green and the house was far too small for their big family. It would be lovely to have a room of her own and live in the West End. Yes, she was good with children, although she didn't stand too much nonsense.

"I'm afraid you'll find my little boy a bit of a

handful," Harriet said wryly. That was a definite understatement, but time enough to find that out when she had met Jamie and decided to like him. If one liked him his extreme naughtiness was not so upsetting. It would not drive one to hysteria as it had done Nannie Brown. But one could not expect everyone's heart to melt with tenderness at the sight of Jamie's ugly, obstinante little face, just because it bore such a resemblance to the photograph of the man on Harriet's dressing table.

"My young brothers are like that, too," Millie said cheerfully.

"Jamie has been difficult since his father died," Harriet explained. "He'll get over it. He's felt deserted, and it's so hard to explain those things to a child. He needs firmness, but kindness, too." She looked at Millie's eager face thoughtfully. Yes, the girl would be kind, she was sure of that. "Arabella is no trouble at all."

Millie's curious eyes slid around the room.

"This is a lovely flat," she said. "It's a lovely building, too. I didn't know where to come, but the porter showed me. He was ever so helpful." Her eyes gave a momentary gleam, and Harriet had another abrupt misgiving. Fred, the porter, was a handsome young man with a roving eye, and Millie, at nineteen (did she say she was nineteen?—she looked younger), with that thick, loose hair and her bright, rather vacuous eyes, gave every promise of being fair game.

But would that necessarily affect her efficiency with the children? And what was one to do if one didn't engage her, with Nannie Brown gone, and no one here tomorrow except Mrs. Blunt?

Because there was really no alternative, Harriet made an abrupt decision.

"Could you start at once, Millie?"

"You mean now, Mrs. Lacey?"

"No, tomorrow. You'll have to tell your mother, won't you, and bring your things."

Millie nodded eagerly. "Can I tell her I've got the job?"

"Well, we can try, can't we? You may not like the children, or they may not like you. But I think they will." Harriet gave her warm charming smile. "Don't bring a lot of clothes with you, because I'd like you to wear a uniform. It's neat, and it will save your things."

"Oh," said Millie, giggling a little, "I love a uniform. It's ever so smart."

Suddenly Harriet knew that the girl was thinking of Fred downstairs in his smart green coat, and again she had a feeling of uncertainty and misgiving. But what of it? The girl was bound to flirt. All pretty nursemaids did.

Nevertheless, as she said goodbye to Millie, the feeling of relief she should have had because her domestic troubles were resolved were absent.

Once more she was prodded by the feeling that she should swallow her pride and let Joe's parents keep her as well as the children, that she should give up her career and devote all her time to Jamie and Arabella. Was it really pride that forbade her to? Or was it selfishness? The hard, exhausting, fascinating life of the theater had been the thing that had saved her during these last two years, and now she was afraid to be without it. Afraid lest her darkness should be greater than that of Flynn Palmer's.

It was always with reluctance that she rang Flynn's doorbell. But Jamie had not come home, and she had to get him. He really was a wretched child.

If it were not for him she would almost never have to see Flynn, living in his luxurious flat, piecing together his life, with the help of a good income, a devoted man-servant, and the faithful Zoe. She could give him nothing but a renewed sense of guilt for Joe's death. It was better that she kept away.

But her obstinate self-willed son and the blind man had found some curious bond of friendship. So here she was once more, waiting for the door to open and to hear Flynn's voice, "Is that Harriet, Zoe?"

It was Zoe who opened the door. Her long green eyes flicked over Harriet in the instant before she smiled and said, "We thought that would be you. Jamie is the most determined stayer I've yet met. God help him when he gets to the party age. He'll have to be thrown out."

"Darling!" That was Flynn's voice from the next room. "Tell Harriet to come in and have a drink."

The inevitable polite invitation. Harriet was aware that she had stiffened slightly, and also realized once more that Zoe did not like her. Heaven knew why. She was not dazzlingly beautiful; she was a widow and the mother of two children. As an actress she was capable and charming, but not brilliant. Also, Flynn, the man Zoe loved, treated her with a casual friendliness that could not under any circumstances be worthy of Zoe's jealousy.

Nevertheless, the girl, beneath her brittle wittiness, was not friendly. Harriet wondered if Flynn knew that. But even if he knew, why should he care? It was of no importance.

"You'll excuse me," said Zoe. Harriet noticed that she had a scrap of organdy apron tied around her slim waist, and there was a minute blob of flour on one cheek. "I'm cooking something rather special for dinner. One has to watch it like a hawk. Jones has gone early because his wife isn't well, and what with answering doorbells and telephones I'm afraid something tragic is going to happen in the kitchen. Do go and talk to Flynn. Poor darling, he gets bored when I'm cooking, and then says the rudest things about the food, just to get his own back."

Zoe vanished into the kitchen. She was not yet married to Flynn, but the atmosphere was purely domestic. Did she do this deliberately to make Harriet feel an outsider? Harriet, chiding herself for over-sensitiveness, went across to the living room.

"Come in, Harriet. I'm sorry we kept Jamie so long, but he was helping me."

"That's very charitable of you," Harriet said in her low, warm voice. "Knowing Jamie, I'm not sure—"

"I was helping!" Jamie interrupted indignantly, getting up from the floor where he was surrounded with what looked like a pile of old yellowed letters.

"Actually that's quite true," Flynn affirmed. "Those are part of a collection of family letters I discovered when one of my old aunts died. I had been planning some day to publish them, particularly the ones written by my great-grandfather. I'd actually made a start on them, but then my secretary left. If she hadn't done so I'd have sacked her anyway. She had a very deliberate, genteel voice. If you can imagine love letters read aloud in that sort of voice—well—"

Harriet saw the quick impatience on his face. Once, she reflected, it had probably been a pleasant ordinarily good-looking face with a high forehead, well-marked brows, a mouth ready to smile. Now it was thin, taut, too prominently boned. Behind the glasses it had a look of watching and assessing.

"How very interesting!" she said. "So that's what Jamie meant when he said he was being your secretary. And how, may I ask, is his reading?"

"I'm not reading them, I'm sorting them," Jamie corrected. "That's right, isn't it, Flynn."

"That's right, Jamie."

"But how can you trust a five-year-old with what may be a valuable manuscript?"

"Jamie is quite trustworthy."

Harriet did not miss the rebuke. So Flynn Palmer thought she did not trust Jamie enough, her five-year-old, noisy, irresponsible, disobedient son who could not be depended on for one moment, and who was the reason for the departure of no less than four nannies. Because Jamie behaved himself reasonably well with Flynn, Flynn thought he knew all about him and exactly how he should be managed. Harriet flushed with resentment.

This she tried to conceal, because another thing about Flynn was his uncanny ability to divine a mood or the nearest shade of feeling in one's voice. That was a part of blindness, of course, and was necessarily more acute in a man who already had a brilliant brain. From the beginning of their acquaintance, partly from pity and partly from a reluctance to become sentimentally involved, she had followed a course of the strictest neutrality.

She changed the subject by saying, "I've just engaged a new nursemaid for the children. She's young and pretty, and I think will be much better than poor old Nannie Brown, who really was past looking after children."

"What's her name?" Jamie asked.

"It's Millie, darling. And she likes little boys, she says."

"She won't like me." Jamie's voice was half bravado, half plain fact. He found, Harriet realized, a kind of dark glory in being disliked. Already he was scowling with the effort of thinking what new pranks he could get up to.

"Come along, old man," Flynn said. "It's rather a thing to be liked by pretty girls. You ought to try."

"They're all wet," Jamie said succinctly.

Flynn smiled broadly. Harriet found herself once more with that fleeting desire to have seen his eyes and what expression they would have had. She had never seen them. But then neither had he ever seen her. Nor displayed any slightest curiosity in her appearance. . . .

She was the widow of the man for whose death he felt responsible. An impossible situation.

"Jamie, we must go. I've left Arabella alone. Thank you for being so patient with him, Flynn."

"Not at all. Jamie, have you clipped all those letters together?"

"Yes."

"Not quite all," said Harriet. "Here's one on the chair."

She picked up the creased sheet covered with sprawled writing, black against the yellowed paper. A sentence leaped to her eyes. Involuntarily she began to read.

"What is it, Harriet?" came Flynn's inquisitive voice.

"Only one letter Jamie missed."

"Never mind. Jones would have found it. He never destroys anything."

"You never told me the letters were like this!"

The slight breathlessness of her voice made him tilt his head into a listening attitude.

"Read it," he said.

Slowly Harriet began to read aloud:

"When you left me at the gate yesterday I turned to watch you go back down the avenue. It was raining, you remember, and you had pulled your hood closely over your head, so that, hurrying along, you were suddenly anonymous, indeed, you were any small anonymous woman hastening to what? A warm fireside, a house full of people to welcome you, a lover? It was as if you had vanished into an unidentifiable multitude of people, and I was left completely alone. Oh, my darling, never cover your head with a hood again. Leave out just one strand of hair, just one beacon to light me back to you. . . ."

Harriet stopped. She was aware of the man, with his familiar listening attitude. She knew he was waiting for her to continue. But she could not. She was remembering the feel of Joe's fingers in her hair, and hearing his voice, bluff, a little shy, "If we ever have a baby daughter, darling, you must spare her some of this stuff. . . ." She was trying desperately not to cry.

"Well—" came Flynn's voice, at last.

"You—you didn't tell me they were love letters like that."

"I said they were worthy of publication. Actually, most of them are not love letters. They're angry tirades against politics, war, the Inland Revenue, the Prime Minister. Great-grandfather was anti everything—except love, of course."

"Flynn, you must do something with them!"

"That's what I'm trying to do."

"You must—" Harriet was suddenly aware that Zoe was standing at the door watching them. She did not know how long the girl had been there, whether she had heard the whole of the letter or seen Harriet's shamed efforts not to cry. She was still wearing the absurd, fetching apron. She was a little flushed from the heat of the kitchen and looked beautiful. And full of antagonism. That was so plain that even Flynn, his head turned away, must have sensed it.

But all she said was, "I'm finding a new secretary for Flynn. Darling, will you be ready to eat in ten minutes? Harriet, we'd love to have you stay."

"No, no, I can't of course. Jamie must go to bed, and I've left Arabella alone. Jamie, darling, say good-night to Flynn and come along."

It was easy to go. She was only eager to be upstairs in her own flat, no longer the momentary subject of Flynn's speculation and Zoe's hostility.

Nevertheless, when Jamie, with less fuss than usual, was in bed, the flat seemed very quiet, very empty. She found the supper Mrs. Blunt had left for her in the refrigerator, decorated with its printed instructions. "This needs heating for thirty minutes. Oven about 350." It was not the elaborate meal Zoe was preparing downstairs, but it didn't matter, for she scarcely tasted what she was eating. Neither did the lines of dialogue in the script propped beside her plate make any sense to her.

She was seeing instead the scrawled black lines on that yellowed sheet of paper. *You were any small anonymous woman hastening to what—a warm fireside? A house full of people? A lover?*

III

Millie was very excited indeed. She thought Mrs. Lacey was sweet, so young and attractive, and her a widow, poor thing. She wasn't afraid of not being able to cope with the children. Find her the small boy whom she couldn't manage. She was still thinking of that pretty little bedroom with radio and all, just for herself.

Mum would be mad about her leaving home, of course. But even Mum at her most intimidating could be managed. And managed she must be, for Millie was determined to go and live in Manchester Court. She had made up her mind as soon as she had seen Mrs. Lacey and the lovely flat and all. Though at that stage, if Mum had been awfully difficult, she might have given up the idea.

But something had happened as she left the block of flats that had completely made up her mind so that it would never be changed. She had had a conversation with Fred, the handsome porter, and she thought she had fallen in love at first sight.

It was absurd, really. Fred had merely told her where to find Mrs. Lacey's flat, as she went in. Although she had noticed him favorably then, with his broad shoulders, his wavy hair and his bright brown eyes, she hadn't expected him to look at her particularly. The thing that excited her so much was that he had. For as she came out after her interview he had come up to open the doors of the lift for her, and had smiled, flashing his white teeth and said conspiratorially.

"Get the job?"

"How'd you know I was after a job?"

"I knew the other was leaving, so I put two and two together." Again came the flashing smile. "I told myself Mrs. Lacey would like a nice-looking girl like you."

His brown eyes were full of admiration. They flicked over Millie in an experienced way.

"You're a smooth one, aren't you?" she murmured.

"Not me, miss. I just like to help. That's what I'm here for. I'd like to see Mrs. Lacey get settled with a nice girl. I like to know everyone's happy around here."

His frankness left Millie at a loss.

"Yeah, that's my job," said Fred, straightening his broad shoulders. "And if you come I'd like to know you're happy, too."

"I may come," Millie admitted, tossing her head offhandedly. But she knew now that she would. No power on earth would stop her. Those brown eyes of his, so honest, and yet with that gleam. . . .

"If I do, you'll be able to help me in and out with the baby's pram," she said.

"It will be a pleasure, miss."

After Millie had gone, Fred went off duty for an hour. This was when he had the supper his mother had prepared down in the basemennt flat, which would have been cozy enough had his mother not filled it with her bizarre collection of wigs and faceless heads.

But Fred was used to his mother's background, and also to her gray, spider appearance. In fact he scarcely noticed it. It suited him well enough her being here. She cooked and made his bed for him, and didn't get in the way. Now and again, of course, when she suspected he might be getting into trouble, she was a bit of a bore, the way her imploring eyes were fixed on him. But you could understand it, really. He had been a worry to the poor old girl, and, although that was all in the past now she seemed to expect him to break out again.

But he wouldn't. At least, he didn't think so. It was the straight and narrow for him now, and perhaps, before long, a wife. Not those easy-come, easy-go types, but someone soft and fresh and attractive. Young. . . .

"What are you thinking about, Fred?" he heard his mother asking.

She had set his place at one end of the table, and was sitting at the other end, combing a switch of long, dark silken hair. Her sensitive fingers moved gently over it, her lined old face was absorbed. But he knew how watchful her eyes were beneath the downbent lids. In a moment they would fly open to stare fully at him.

But her appearance was deceptive. She was an artist. It was almost a state secret, the people she had made wigs for.

He grinned suddenly, and because he wanted to shock her, said in answer to her question, "Girls."

The heavy lids lifted and the faded eyes, like a lizard's flew open.

"Fred!"

"What's wrong with that, Ma? I met a nice one tonight. She's coming to work for Mrs. Lacey in number 14. She'll manage young Jamie a lot better than the old one did."

"Jamie only needs love," Mrs. Helps said, folding the strands of black hair over her fingers.

"Well, let's hope the new girl doesn't give all hers to the kid. I might want a bit of it."

"I know you and your wanting. When are you going to take a girl seriously?"

"I might be doing just that."

"Humph! Well, let the girl give some attention to her job first. Don't addle her brains with your attentions. She'll need all her wits to cope with Jamie. I'm so afraid that child will get into trouble."

"A five-year-old!"

"I don't mean your sort of trouble," Mrs. Helps said contemptuously. "There are other things that can happen to a child."

A mile away, in a flat in one of the poorer Bayswater streets, Jones the immaculate man-servant, stood beside his wife's bed.

"Aw, love, look now at what you've gone and done!" he was exclaiming in despair.

He had put a carefully prepared tray of toast, biscuits, and hot milk on his wife's bed, only to have her move clumsily and upset the milk. It spilled over the edge of the tray onto the sheets and the floor. One wouldn't have thought one tumbler could hold so much.

"I didn't do it!" Nell declared petulantly. "You put it down crooked. Of course it spilled. Oh, get a cloth, quick. I'm wet and sticky."

Jones went swiftly to the kitchen of the small flat and came back with a cloth. His long, patient face was tired. His momentary anger had gone and he was all concern.

"Did it burn you, love? I'm sorry. We'll have to change your nightgown, I'm afraid. Not that it didn't need changing. I noticed it's the same one you had on yesterday. That Miss Lane doesn't look after you very well."

"Of course she doesn't. What can you expect? she isn't interested in me, a poor sick woman. She goes out for hours and leaves me. And she isn't kind. I don't like her. I don't like her at all."

The fretful voice went on in its monotone that was now a so-familiar sound. Jones looked down at his wife. He saw that her hair, once so curled and neat, had gone straggly, as if it hadn't been brushed for several days, that there was a faint distasteful smear of food on her chin. And that the nightgown was spotted not only with spilled milk, but with the vague spillings of other meals, which Nell's hands were too unsteady to manage skillfully.

A hot anger rose in him. Really, this was too much. He paid the woman to be here all day and to look after his wife properly. It was intolerable that she should be neglected. It was humiliating. She might have been tied to her bed for the last ten years, growing all the time a little weaker, a little less certain both mentally and physically, so that she forgot what day of the week it was or whether the next meal was tea or supper, or even where he now worked. But none of this was her fault. She hadn't deserved the very long dreary illness, an obscure form of paralysis which very slowly encroached on her body like the sea eating away at a chalk cliff. Once she had been so sweet and lively and gay. He had adored her. Strangely enough, her illness had made him adore her more than ever, but in a different way. Now she was his very precious possession, wholly dependent on him, to be petted and pampered, humored and teased and amused.

He was not cross that she had clumsily and, he suspected, deliberately spilled the milk, like a naughty child. But he was furiously angry that Miss Lane should neglect her the moment his back was turned.

"Don't worry about the milk." Nell's fingers, dry and fragile, plucked at his arm. "Talk to me. Tell me a story."

He knew her wandering attention would not follow the story through; she would fall asleep before he finished. But he sat down obediently and began.

"Shall I tell you about Jamie?"

"The bad boy!" she cried with pleasure, her face suddenly as empty as a child's.

Jamie, Harriet Lacey's ugly, attractive, stubborn five-year-old, was not really as bad as all that. But it pleased Nell to exaggerate his pranks into something enormously wicked. It amused her, so Jones enlarged on the subject.

"Yes, indeed, we all say we don't know what will become of him. He came down to Mr. Palmer again this evening. Strictly forbidden, you know, but he never obeys. There had been a ruckus upstairs before that. I'd heard. Of course, his mother is away at the theater and doesn't know half of what goes on. Zoe was with Mr. Palmer, and she doesn't like the boy. If it were up to her she wouldn't let him in, and then he'd probably go and wander in the streets and get lost. As he will one day. . . ."

The light breathing of his wife and her tousled head fallen sideways told Jones that she was already asleep. She wouldn't wake again that night. Gently he smoothed the sheets across the double bed into which, later, he would climb. Because there was not space in the one-roomed flat for two beds, and anyway he had never minded lying beside Nell's sick inert body. Though more often than not he lay awake worrying, or got up to walk about.

That Miss Lane! Nell was being neglected. Her

hair needed a shampoo and a good brushing. Her face had been dirty. She was being humiliated.

If only he could afford—but one managed, somehow. One crossed from one shaky bridge to the next. . . .

The fire had burned low. Flynn knew that because the heat had gone, and there was no longer a healthy crackle, but only the slight hiss of dying flames and the falling of ash. He could hear Zoe moving about in the kitchen. There was a clink of glass, and the jingle of her arm bracelet.

Zoe had not always been domesticated like this. He remembered the days when he had used to call for her, to find her flat always in a muddle, clothes lying about, dishes littering the kitchen. There was no time to stop for dull chores, she had said. Her Mrs. Mopp would do them in the morning. Where were they dining? Whose party were they going to?

But now all her spare time was spent here in his flat because he still could not face going out to eat or to dance, or to meet the people they had used to know. She had learned to cook, and she was even, Jones reported, reasonably tidy in the kitchen. She was loving and kind and thoughtful and she suffocated him.

The fire was almost out, and abruptly he shivered, although the room was still warm.

He wanted to be alone, to fumble his own way to bed, and there to lie silent, no kind or helpful or too possessive voices intruding into his darkness.

A dish clattered in the kitchen. The sharp sound stung him beyond endurance.

"What on earth are you doing out there?" He called, with the quick unpredictable irritation that he could not control. "Crashing about like an elephant."

"Oh, darling! That was only a teeny sound. I was just tidying up for Jones in the morning. He's such a sweetie. I hate him to find a mess. But I'll come and sit down now."

"No, you won't. You'll go home."

"At ten o'clock! Flynn, darling!"

Flynn moved irritably.

"I'm tired, I'm going to bed."

"But how can you be tired? I mean, you haven't had a strenuous day. Not like me, standing hours for fittings. Oh, darling, I'm sorry, I didn't mean—"

Flynn was standing, gripping his stick. But somehow he controlled his voice.

"If you've had a strenuous day, you shouldn't come here at night."

"And leave you to the tender mercies of Jones, and that actress upstairs?"

"Actress? Oh, you mean Harriet." Suddenly he was remembering Harriet's voice, low, warm, charming, stirred with some deep emotion as she had read his great-grandfather's letter.

"Who else would I mean?" Zoe was acid. "I didn't imagine you cultivated that child for his irresistible company."

Flynn's anger blazed. "Don't be completely idiotic!"

"You are in a bloody mood, aren't you? I'd better leave you to it."

"That's what I've been telling you to do."

"You'll feel better in the morning." The acrimony had gone out of her voice. She patted his cheek. "I shouldn't let myself get annoyed with you. Poor sweet!"

He was rigid, the blackness sweeping through him.

"Don't do that," he whispered. "I'm not completely decrepit."

"No, but you're damned touchy." She was cheerful again, her bracelet jingling, her perfume trailing behind her as she went to get her coat. "And don't take any notice of what I said about Harriet. I'm not jealous of her. She may be an actress, but her looks wouldn't set the Thames on fire."

"I've never seen her," Flynn said in a curiously low voice.

"You haven't missed a great deal. Oh, she's attractive enough. But people wouldn't turn to look at her. Darling, don't you remember how we used to be stared at?"

She had come to kiss him lightly.

"You're just as good-looking with your dark glasses. More, actually. Mysterious. People will stare at us when we go out."

"*And suddenly you were anonymous,*" the words were running through Flynn's head, "*you were any small anonymous woman hastening to what?*"

He was aware that Zoe had gone, and he was still standing there in the chilling room in the dark. . . .

The house was old and tumbledown and very tiny, a mere slit between its larger, stronger neighbors. It was also damp, and permeated with a smell of river mist and mud. But she would soon get it in order, Eve thought optimistically. A bit of paint and some new floor coverings, the damp-stained paper stripped off and some bright new design put up. Oh, yes, she would show him she could make an attractive home out of the most unlikely material. And loneliness was what they wanted, wasn't it? No prying landladies, no rules and regulations about late visitors. And there was the telephone. That was the important thing.

Although one got into the habit of waiting all evening for it to ring.

She had been wandering restlessly about, waiting for the preliminary ping of its bell, for the last hour. Now it was after ten o'clock. He didn't often ring much later than that.

But one never knew. That was the absorbing thing.

All at once, as she walked up and down, her arms folded tightly across her thin breast, the bell pinged and began to shrill. Eve hurried to the telephone, her face alight. . . .

Harriet couldn't sleep. That was not unusual nowadays. The nights were times of longing, and, blurred and distorted by half-sleep, a sad despair.

Usually during these restless nights a glass of hot milk soothed her, and she was able to go back to bed to sleep. But tonight her wakefulness was stubborn. She kept thinking of the new girl coming tomorrow, and wondering how she would get on. And there was that other disturbing thing, the way she had broken down over Flynn's letter. Of all people, he was the last one in front of whom she wanted to break down.

Harriet walked about the flat sipping her hot milk, then put down the empty glass, switched off the light and went to draw back the curtains.

The night was quiet now. The distant swish and roar of traffic down High Street was intermittent, and far off. The square was almost deserted. A few parked cars, an occasional stroller. . . . The air with its smell of winter and fog was refreshing on her face. She leaned a little out of the open window.

Someone had moved beneath a tree across the

street. Someone loitering there, not a couple locked in an embrace so close that it might have been their despairing last one, but a single figure in a long coat. It was too dark to see whether it was a woman or a man. Whoever it was seemed, in an uneasy way, to be staring directly at her flat.

But that surely must be her imagination. . . .

IV

By the morning Harriet had forgotten that slight incident. It wasn't that she had dismissed it as not worth thinking about, but she had genuinely forgotten it. It was not until a week later that she had an uneasy memory of it, but that, too, was fleeting at the time, and didn't seem worth worrying about.

Millie had settled down nicely. She was not perfect, perhaps. She had untidy, lazy ways and her voice and her giggle jarred. But she was young and lively, and good-tempered, and already Arabella adored her. Jamie was more cautious. He obviously in his secret mind had several tests yet to make. He had tried being disobedient and obstinate and very, very noisy. But finding this could not produce helpless, red-faced anger or tears, as with Nannie Brown, it palled, and he alternated by showing a heavenly innocence and basking in Millie's approval. This, too, however, was beginning to pall. So he was planning shortly to do something very naughty, something much worse than running off to Flynn or Mrs. Helps. He didn't know yet what his great naughtiness would be, but an opportunity to invent something would occur.

Mrs. Blunt, too, so far approved of Millie, as her cryptic notes showed. "Shall I wash bathroom walls tomorrow? Millie will help," or "Refilled cake tins.

"Don't let Millie eat all the chocolate cake," or "Don't sit on kitchen stools. We've just painted them." She could give her full mind to her part in the new play, and she began to enjoy it thoroughly. It was the gay lighthearted part of a frivolous young woman who adored hats that suited her own butterfly nature. Each time she had a sorrow or a celebration she bought a new frippery. With her improved domestic situation the part began to take hold of Harriet so completely that that day, on her way home from rehearsals, she suddenly stopped in Knightsbridge and went into her favorite milliners and bought a small, cherry-colored hat that Joe would have called admiringly another piece of nonsense. When the assistant serving her said, "Your husband's going to like that, madam," her impulse almost failed.

But if Joe had known that for almost two years she had not had a normal woman's desire to buy a pretty hat, it would have been much worse. So in the end her common sense prevailed, and she went out of the shop wearing the hat.

She must, she thought, wryly, have been letting herself grow frumpy, as for the first time Fred, the porter, gave her an admiring glance. It was there plainly in his face, the message from a man to a woman that he finds her attractive. Ridiculously, Harriet felt her spirits lift. Fred, with the bold roving eye, who would find a great many women attractive, from Zoe to the buxom Millie, was no great criterion, but Harriet was too feminine not to respond to that unspoken flattery. Her step was lighter as she went towards the lift. Then, halfway up she heard a scream, followed by the sound of running footsteps down the stairs.

Abruptly she stopped the lift at the third floor and

got out to see Millie come panting down the flight of stairs from the top floor.

"Millie, what's happening?" Harriet demanded.

"Oh, Mrs. Lacey, someone rang the doorbell, and when I answered it I was just in time to see such a strange woman put her head around the corner, by the lift, and then run away. Listen, you can hear her still!"

Distinctly Harriet could hear the hurrying, stumbling footsteps as of someone in very high heels, going down the stone stairs.

"She had long, sort of stringy blonde hair," Millie gasped. "I didn't really see her face because she ran the moment I came."

"Where's Jamie?" Harriet asked cryptically.

"I don't know. With Mr. Palmer, I think. I was just coming down to see."

The door of Flynn Palmer's flat at the end of the passage was open and Jones was standing there. His long face was full of interest.

"Jamie isn't here, Mrs. Lacey."

"Then one can make two guesses where he is," Harriet said grimly. "Down in the basement, by this time, with Mrs. Helps, taking off the wig he borrowed."

"Oh, the little beast!" Millie exclaimed. Then she clapped her hand over her mouth. "Oh, I'm sorry, Mrs. Lacey—"

"Its all right, Millie. He is a little beast, at times, as Jones will agree."

Jones nodded, with his wry humor.

"But actually, in this case, I don't think it was Jamie, Mrs. Lacey. When Millie screamed I came to the door and just caught a glimpse of the woman sneaking past. She had long untidy hair, like Millie said, and I could swear she was too tall for Jamie."

"Goodness! Do you think she was someone who had sneaked in to sell things, and Fred had caught a glimpse of her?"

"That's probably what it was. These hawkers pretend not to see the notices."

"But it couldn't have been Fred who startled her," Harriet remembered, "because he was at the front door. Millie, I've no doubt Jamie is down with Mrs. Helps, all the same."

"But of course!" exclaimed Jones, snapping his fingers softly. "Mr. Palmer will be expecting young women to call about the secretary job he advertised. Perhaps one of them went to the wrong door."

"And then ran off in panic?" Harriet said, turning to go.

"What's all this?" came Flynn's voice from the doorway. "Where's this nervous young woman? I'd like to meet her. It would be a new experience."

"Millie, go and get Jamie," Harriet said, turning to go.

"Wait a moment, Harriet." Flynn's arrogance was as unassumed as Jones's formality. "I wish you'd glance at some letters I've had from would-be secretaries. I'm bothered if I can tell from their neat statistics which one would be good at love letters."

"Including the one who's just got away?"

"Oh, she's jumped the gun. I haven't made an appointment with any of them yet. That's wishful thinking on Jones's part. He's got a sick wife, you know."

If that statement seemed unnecessarily acid, as many of Flynn's remarks were, Jones did not appear to mind. He gave his deferential smile and said, "Not the blondes, sir. Definitely not."

"Well, good for you, Jones. Do come in, Harriet."

He led the way back into his living room, walked

surely in the familiar surroundings. Flecks of gray showed plentifully in his untidy, dark hair. When he turned to wave Harriet to a chair the strain on his face and the underlying irritation were all too evident.

Her habitual feeling of guilt and uneasiness came back. Really, this was an impossible situation. She would have to say so, once and for all.

"Read this!" Flynn said, flourishing a letter. "I believe it's the one offering to send a photograph. To me! Harriet, can't you sit down? Jones, where are you? Bring some drinks. Oh, yes, I know it's after six, but your wife won't really expire if you're five minutes late."

"How is your wife, Jones?" Harriet asked, as Jones came in with the tray of drinks.

"Much the same, Mrs. Lacey, thank you. I'm not very happy about the new woman who looks after her, but I'm hoping she'll improve when she gets fond of Nell."

He spoke with such assurance that Harriet said, "Does everyone get fond of her?"

"You really couldn't help it," Jones answered simply. He was tall, thin, and probably in his late thirties. He must have been a very ordinary person until this air of dedication had lifted him out of the ordinary. It also gave him his patience with Flynn's irascible tempers and idiosyncrasies. He was really a treasure. Harriet wasn't quite sure that Flynn deserved him. She hoped that Nell, the delicate, pampered wife, did.

"Gin, Harriet?" said Flynn. "All right, Jones, dammit, man, get your coat and go."

When Jones had gone Flynn went on in caustic voice.

"The little woman! The dear little hypochondriac. Whew!"

"How do you know she's a hypochondriac?"

"Of course she is. Has Jones, who'd be a decent fellow otherwise, on a string. Slightest deviation from routine, tug goes the string. What are you drinking, my love? Do make up your mind."

"Do you mind," said Harriet slowly, "not calling me your love?"

He raised his head, interested. The quick, habitual irritation went out of his face and one thick black brow was raised amusedly.

"But I talk to all pretty girls like that, even to my late abysmally stupid secretary. And Zoe, of course, Zoe adores it. Don't you, Harriet?"

"The situation is impossible," Harriet burst out. "It would be much better if we didn't see each other at all, or at least no more than is absolutely necessary."

"If you mean I'm impossible—" Flynn began, fingering his dark glasses.

There it was, the constant pain, that she had to observe helplessly.

"It's impossible," she explained clearly, "because we both feel so hatefully guilty. You have to keep an eye on me in case I'm lonely. I have to do what I can for you because you are blind. And all the time Joe is between us."

Harriet's voice had risen a little and grown breathless. She was almost in tears again. It was humiliating. Suddenly she hated the dark, caustic young man who faced her with his self-contained irony.

But there was no irony in his voice when he answered.

"No one is to blame for what happened. It was destiny. That's the way to look at it. On the 24th February, 1955, Joe's and my guiding stars collided.

Mine got dimmed and Joe's went out. It had been due to happen, obviously, since the beginning of time. It couldn't have been altered."

"For heaven's sake," Harriet said, "don't be whimsical. It doesn't suit you."

"True. It doesn't. Have a pink gin, darling. It will do you more good than my fatalism."

"Joe's star, as you put it, went out, and you not only lost a career—"

"Oh, that. I'm going to write instead. Harriet, don't be morbid."

"There's another thing—Zoe. You'd marry her if you hadn't this—this protection thing or whatever it is, about me."

"Well," said Flynn thoughtfully, "you might almost have something there. Zoe's a poppet. I adore her."

"And so does she you, heaven knows why. But the thing is, Flynn, we're bad for each other. There's this—shadow—between us."

Flynn turned to pour the drinks. He knocked over a glass, swore, shouted for Jones, then said, "Oh, Lord, the fellow's gone running home to his sick wife! What a world! No, I'll pick it up. Leave it, can't you? I'm not completely decrepit. That's what gets me, you women waiting on me. Zoe's the same. One day I'll wring her pretty white neck."

He had groped for another glass and finally succeeded in pouring a generous drink. Handing it to Harriet he said in a milder tone, "Actually, I don't have what you call a protection thing about you, whatever you have about me. But I like to know you and the children are upstairs. I like having Jamie down when he feels like it. I like knowing you've got this luscious Millie who's young and bright for the children. I like to know your affairs are in order, Harriet."

"Thank you," said Harriet, rather stiffly.

"So perhaps I have got a protection thing. But for God's sake, don't talk about it. Here, read these letters. Tell me whom I'm to see. The whole lot of them bore me."

Harriet began to read the first letter, then was interrupted by Flynn, with one of his abrupt changes of mood, saying inquisitively, "Why were you walking so gaily when you came out of the lift? I heard you."

"I don't know. Because I had a new hat, perhaps."

"Haven't you had a new hat for a long time?"

"Actually, no."

"Let's celebrate, shall we? I'll ring for oysters and champagne."

"Flynn, don't be absurd! I have to go to the children. Anyway, Zoe's sure to be in."

"Can't I order enough for three?"

"Triangles and new hats. All incompatible. I must go, truly."

Upstairs in her own flat Harriet found Jamie, with the angelic expression that hinted at undiscovered naughtiness on his face, and Millie in a state of controlled excitement.

"Jamie was with Mrs. Helps, all right," she said breathlessly. "But he came home when he was told. Gosh, that old woman's room! Gives you the creeps, like a morgue."

"What's a morgue?" asked Jamie.

"All those heads of hair!" went on Millie irrepressibly. And then the reason of her excitement came out. "Oh, Mrs. Lacey, I wonder if I could have the night off tonight. Fred's asked me to go to a dance."

"Fred?"

"Fred Helps. The porter." Millie's voice was slightly astonished, that Harriet should be in doubt as to which Fred was meant. To Millie there obviously was only one Fred, and he was the tall, bold-eyed young man who, to her, looked so glamorous in his uniform.

"Oh, him. You want to watch your step with him, Millie. He has an eye for pretty girls."

"I can take care of that," Millie said confidently, and for a moment her eyes were as bold as Fred's.

"It's a place where they keep dead bodies," Jamie said suddenly and startingly.

"Jamie, pick up your toys tidily," Harriet said. "Yes, Millie, I think you can go to the dance. It's rather short notice."

"I know, but he only just asked me," Millie said excitedly.

"Well. All right, but I do warn you not to take Fred too seriously," Harriet suddenly felt old and sedate, and thought of Flynn's offer of oysters and champagne, and was both angry and sad. "Have you got something nice to wear, Millie?"

"Only my blue net." Millie pouted, then brightened. She had the kind of vacuous face that never stayed gloomy for long. "I'll be able to get a new dress when I've earned some money."

"So you will. It's much more fun buying clothes with money one has earned oneself." Good heavens, she was growing staid and prosy. "You can borrow my white wool stole, if you like. It's in my closet."

"Oh, Mrs. Lacey! Can I really? Oh, you are kind."

"Not at all. Put the children to bed first. And I think you ought to be home by midnight. I shall still be up."

"Yes, Mrs. Lacey. And thanks ever so!"

An hour later Millie, flushed and plump in the blue net, and with the white stole swathed dramatically over her young, smooth shoulders, was on her way to enjoy the first dividends that the new job was producing for her. Harriet called good-bye to her cheerfully, and did not know that on the landing outside the closed door Millie stopped to put on the earrings she had daringly borrowed from Harriet's jewel box which she had thoroughly investigated on her first day at work. They were slim, dangling ones, not quite large enough for Millie's taste, but with a sparkle that she liked. They made her feel even more chic and expensive than the soft white stole did. She was very excited and very pleased with herself indeed. She could scarcely wait to get to the ground floor and have Fred's bold, bright, admiring gaze on her.

Left alone, Harriet firmly resolved not to brood. Today she had known, when she had enjoyed buying a new hat and walking in the sunshine, that sitting at home in the evening with sleeping children was not her role forever. She would be content with it meanwhile. She was very lucky. She had a comfortable flat, a good part in a new play, two charming children. She did not have oysters and champagne for dinner, but she had her eyesight . . . .

She had scarcely time to think of anything, however, before the doorbell rang. When she went to the door she saw the strange spiderish figure of Mrs. Helps, Fred's mother.

Suddenly, for no reason at all, an unnamable feeling of dread swept through her.

"Can I do something for you, Mrs. Helps?"

The old lady spoke in her habitually anxious voice.

"It's your Jamie, Mrs. Lacey. He's very welcome to visit me and he likes watching me work, but I can't have him running off with my wigs."

"You mean he's taken one!" Harriet exclaimed.

"I think he was playing a trick on the new girl," the old lady said apologetically.

"Mrs. Helps, did he wear one of your wigs this afternoon? And high-heeled shoes, by any chance?"

"It was the new one for the lady in Eaton Square. Must be ash blonde, she said. Jamie must return it, you know. I can't have him down if he does things like that."

"Then it was he who Millie saw," Harriet murmured. "No hawker, after all."

"What did you say?" Mrs. Helps asked in her thin, impatient voice that was like a thread of gray cotton, growing thinner and thinner until it snapped.

"Only that both Millie and Mr. Palmer's servant thought they saw a strange woman, but it would have been Jamie, as I said. Of course he must return the wig, Mrs. Helps. I don't think he's asleep. Come in while I go and ask him about it."

Jamie lay on his back, his wide eyes staring innocently at the ceiling. His little pug face, sprinkled with freckles, endearing when it was lit by his sudden smile, formidable in a stubborn mood, gave nothing away.

"I should be asleep," he said reproachfully. "Now you've woked me up."

"So I have," said Harriet calmly. "And you'll stay awake until you tell us the truth about this afternoon. It was you who frightened Millie, wasn't it? You dressed up in one of Mrs. Helps's wigs and a long coat and high-heeled shoes."

"No, I didn't," said Jamie, with his wide-eyed innocence. "But I met a woman who looked just like that. She was running down the stairs. One of her shoes came off."

Harriet stiffened her lips to prevent a smile at the thought of her scartlet-faced harum-scarum son tumbling down the stairs, shoeless, clutching at a blond wig. Really, what next would he do, this bad child of hers and Joe's?

"Jamie, darling, whoever the woman was, she took off her wig and put it somewhere. I expect you saw where she put it just as you saw her pick up her shoe. Now where was it?"

"In the coal bin at Mrs. Helps's door," said Jamie glibly. "Now can I go to sleep?"

"Coal! On the ash blonde. Oh, my dear heaven!" Mrs. Helps, who had been listening at the door, gave a strangled moan.

And she was gone, scuttering away in a panic.

"Jamie," said Harriet inexorably, "why did you play such a silly joke? Apart from damaging Mrs. Helps's property, which is valuable, you gave Millie a bad fright."

Jamie began to giggle. And now his little pug face, alight, was irresistible. Although his naughtiness drove her to distraction Harriet loved his originality, his stubborn determination never to be beaten. But it made life very complicated.

"Don't you like Millie?" she persisted.

"She's all right. But she's silly and I like hearing her scream."

"Jamie! That really is the naughtiest thing. If you behave like this Millie will leave and we'll get another Nannie Brown. You won't like that."

"I'm not always naughty," Jamie pronounced philosophically. "And I guess Millie will stay because she likes Arabella and Fred. Do go away now, Mummy. You're keeping me awake."

His eyes were resolutely shut, his face relaxed and innocent. Harriet's smile, unobserved now, was no longer hidden. He was an actor, this child. He was incorrigible and adorable. Perhaps she wouldn't tell Millie of this prank, in the hope that it would not be repeated. Because one didn't want to drive her away.

When Millie came home, however, Harriet wasn't sure what there was to tell her. For the girl came in breathlessly, her face first flushed from running up the stairs, then suddenly white from whatever had frightened her.

"Oh, Mrs. Lacey! That woman was out there again! The one with the blonde hair."

"Out where?" Harriet demanded sharply.

"Not inside the flats. Just lurking across the street. Watching me. When I turned around she went the other way, in a hurry."

"Now, listen," said Harriet, "where was Fred when this happened? Didn't he bring you home?"

"Yes, of course he did. I left him at the lift. He put me in it, and then went down to the basement."

"Then how did you happen to be outside watching a strange woman?"

Millie's quick color came and went. Her eyes were protuberant, full of fear.

"I was hot. I suddenly thought I was going to faint. I rushed out to get a breath of fresh air before coming up. And there was this woman, standing staring at me. I tell you, I nearly screamed."

Millie stuffed her fingers in her mouth, as if she were again suppressing a scream. There was no doubting that she had had a fright.

Suddenly Harriet was thinking of the still figure she had thought was watching her flat the other night, at about this time, from beneath a tree across the road. At that distance she had not been able to tell whether it was a man or a woman.

"If you felt faint you should have come straight up."

"Yes, I know, but I didn't stop to think, somehow." Millie went across to the window and rather gingerly holding the curtain back peered down into the square. "There's no one there now," she said. "But, lor', it did give me a turn, I can tell you."

Harriet, at her side, looked down on the dark, silent square. Nothing moved. The tree trunks sheltered no lurking figures.

"Did you and Fred have something to drink tonight Millie?"

"Only a glass of beer. At least, Fred had more, but I only had one. I'm not drunk, Mrs. Lacey, if that's what you mean."

"No, I didn't think you were. But you see it can't have been the same woman as this afternoon, because that was Jamie, as I suspected. Mrs. Helps came up to tell me. Wait a minute. I want to ask Mrs. Helps something."

She rang through to the basement, and Fred's voice answered.

"Fred, this is Mrs. Lacey here. No, no, Millie's all right. I just want to ask your mother if she found the wig she had lost. Ask her, will you?"

A moment later Mrs. Help's voice, frail and lost as the cry of the wind in the chimney on a stormy night, came.

"Covered in soot, Mrs. Lacey! But don't upset yourself. It will wash. And don't scold the child."

"Where is it now?" Harriet asked faintly.

"In the shampoo, soaking. I'll leave it till morning. It was kind of you to ring, Mrs. Lacey."

"It wasn't the same woman, Millie. She probably wasn't watching you at all. She was probably on her way home, or—"

"Well, she might have been one of those," said Millie frankly, "but she was watching me, all right. Because she hurried off, guilty like."

It was disturbing, yet what was there to worry about? A vague figure in the night, by chance having similar pale hair to that of Mrs. Helps's wig. If it really had been Jamie whom Millie and Jones had seen that afternoon. . . .

"Let's go to bed," said Harriet wearily. "There's really nothing to worry about."

Half an hour later the telephone rang. It was one o'clock in the morning. No one in his senses would ring at that hour unless it were an emergency. It was evidently no emergency, for when Harriet, half asleep and for no reason trembling with apprehension, answered, there was no sound at all. Unless there was a faint sound of breathing. That, she could not be sure about. But she was sure of the click that indicated someone had gently laid the receiver down. . . .

V

ANOTHER TELEPHONE had rung late that night. By that time Eve, in the house by the river, had given up hoping he would ring. The long evening had worn away drearily. Last night when he had been there the house had seemed cozy and full of possibilities. He had talked of the important well-paid job he was shortly going to get for her, and she had begun to plan, in a housewifely manner, how to decorate the small chilly living room, and the bedroom above. She would even do the basement, she had said optimistically, making a little dining room down there the way smart people did.

She hadn't added that perhaps, when the house was dolled up and cozy, he might come and live there permanently. One had to feel one's way about those things. His moods were apt to change so suddenly, and sometimes frighteningly.

Although he had mentioned a job, she had not expected him to do anything about it so quickly. She had certainly not expected to be told of one at midnight, just when she had given up hope of hearing from him, and was putting her hair in curlers preparatory to going to bed.

She said eagerly. "A job? Do tell me, darling."

His voice was lowered, little more than a whisper, but remarkably clear. "Sinister, your voice on the phone is," she had said once, laughingly, and he had given his one-sided smile, as if the adjective had pleased him.

"Have you a spare bed, or bedding?"

"What, am I to take in lodgers?" Her voice was facetious. Instantly she knew it had been wrong to be flippant. She could hear him breathing.

Then he said shortly, "Not lodgers. Guests. At least, one guest. A baby."

"A baby!"

"Haven't you heard of such a thing before?" Now it was his turn to speak with heavy irony, irony for her sort of woman who took care to involve no responsibilities with her pleasures.

"Of course I have," Eve rejoined tartly. "But how old is it? How'm I to look after it? How long for?"

He answered the last question first. "A day. Maybe two. It might be as well to drop the word around, to the milkman and so on, that you're expecting your sister's child to stay. You'll have to get in a few supplies that might cause notice, although I suggest you get as much as you can in another shopping district. I'd go to Woolworth's, for preference."

"What sort of supplies?" Eve asked, a little faintly.

"Good heavens, don't you know what a baby needs?" Again the irony was heavy in his low voice. "Diapers, and so on."

"But won't the—the baby bring its own?"

"No."

The denial was curt, final. All at once, as if a window had been open and a waft of damp, cold river breeze had come in, Eve shivered.

"Are you listening?" There was no love in his voice tonight, none of that caressing wheedling that made her go weak with pleasure. It was cold and objective.

"Yes. Yes, my love."

"Good. There's also the point that you may be seen arriving with the baby. Which makes it all the more important that you should drop the word that you're expecting it. Understand?"

"No!" cried Eve, suddenly breathless. "No, I don't. I mean, why do I have to arrive with it?"

"Because you have to go and get it, of course."

"Just—just snatch it out of a pram?" She was trying hard again to be facetious. She wasn't letting herself think what this extraordinary request of his might really be.

"Not quite." He laughed. "It's all very simple. So long, of course, as you know which way up to hold a baby."

The joke, and the wheedling note creeping into his voice, made her think she was being absurd to have had that deadly cold feeling about a bad crime about to be committed. He was dramatizing the thing, of course. Presently he was going to tell her that the kid was his sister's child, and that she was being asked to help out in a cozy domestic arrangement. That would have flattered her tremendously, because so far he hadn't even mentioned having a family, much less that she should meet any member of it.

"Okay," he said briskly, "are you ready for your instructions, or do I have to come and give them to you?"

He had meant to come all the time, of course. He had only been teasing her, frightening her a little. It was his unexpectedness that was part of his fascination for her.

"Oh, come! Come, please!" she begged. "I'll make coffee."

"Something out of a bottle would suit me better," he said. But now his voice was genial, the way she loved it. Abruptly she was happy again, and the cold breeze creeping in from the river had died.

How much, if anything, had that watching woman, the strange person with the untidy long blonde hair, seen? After the telephone call, when Mrs. Lacey called blithely and too cheerfully that apparently someone had got the wrong number and wouldn't speak, Millie was thrown into a panic of fear. She lay curled up in the comfortable bed in the pretty room that she was so pleased with, and tried vainly to sleep.

She and Fred had had such a smashing evening, too. Fred had proved, not unexpectedly, to be a most ingenious and fancy dancer, and everybody had watched them when they had tried out new steps. Also, he had had a nice line in flattering conversation. He told her she was the prettiest thing he had seen around Manchester Court, and hoped she would stay a long, long time.

Millie had said, "Oh, go on with you. What about Mrs. Lacey?"

"Her? Oh, she's nice enough. Not really pretty, though. And she's an old married woman with two kids."

"Then what about Mr. Palmer's girlfriend? The fashion model, Zoe." Millie was growing much more confident, and could even be a little scathing about someone as attractive and sophisticated as Zoe.

"H'mm," said Fred, looking down his straight handsome nose. His brown eyes glinted, and were delightfully intimate. "If you go for that real slim type. Myself, I like something to put my arm around."

Millie giggled. "Oh, go on with you!" and half-heartedly tried to resist his embrace. They both knew and enjoyed this game. Millie debated whether she would play it in a long-drawn-out way, or whether her impatience would make her take a short-cut to the first serious kiss for which already she was longing. She was thinking of the dark, quiet square gardens to which, of course, Fred had a key. If it wasn't too cold a night . . .

"Smashing earrings," said Fred. "Real sparklers."

His eyes had narrowed a little, as if he were assessing their value. Millie fingered them in embarrassment.

"Mrs. Lacey lent them to me," she said.

"Did she, then? I hope you've got them fastened on properly. They might be valuable."

"They're not all that big," Millie said critically. "Bit small, actually, for my liking. Of course they're fastened properly. Anyway, Mrs. Lacey trusts me. She lent me this stole, too. She's ever so nice, really. I like the job awfully. Jamie's a bit of a handful, but the baby's cute. Hey, easy there, you're squeezing me."

"You're cute, too," said Fred's voice in her ear. "Let's go soon. Let's walk around the square."

So her thoughts had also been his. Millie smiled to herself. Oh, this was a thousand miles from the dreary house in Bethnal Green, with Mum yelling at her not to be late in, for she'd be awake listening. This was living.

It hadn't been all that warm in the square. Fred had opened the gate with his key, and they had found a seat beneath a spreading mulberry tree. Millie had looked forward as impatiently as he to this first kiss, but she hadn't intended to permit any further intimacies. Not, yet, anyway. She might want to make him marry her, mightn't she? In which case it was much wiser to play hard to get.

Fred obviously had looked beyond the kiss, but when, after a short struggle, she had made it quite clear that she allowed no liberties, he had accepted the rebuff good-naturedly enough.

"All right, kid, I'll behave, if that's how you want it."

"You're nice, Fred."

"You're not too bad yourself. I might even take you out again."

"Might you, darling. That'll be smashing. O—ooh, it's cold out here."

"Well, let's go, if I'm not enough to keep you warm."

Millie giggled. "Silly. But Mrs. Lacey told me not to be too late, and she was nice letting me have the evening off. Oh, Fred!"

"What's the matter?"

Millie was standing up, fingering one ear.

"I've lost an earring."

"Probably on the ground here. Let's have a look."

Although the moon was shining, it was veiled by mist, and not strong enough to show any small object, even a sparkling one, on the ground. Fred obligingly went down on his hands and knees, and struck matches, but there was no earring to be seen among the scattering of dead leaves and withered grass.

He stood up. "It's not all that important, is it, love? They weren't real, were they?"

"Real?"

"Diamonds, I mean." Fred was laughing, his white teeth gleaming. A nursemaid wearing diamonds. That was a queer joke.

Millie thought it was a joke, too. But she was still alarmed and upset. After all, Fred didn't know she had borrowed the earrings without permission, and she didn't intend to tell him that. But even if they weren't valuable, they were nice, and Mrs. Lacey would be sure to miss them.

"Of course they weren't diamonds, silly," she said vaguely. "But I liked them, rather."

"I'll come over and look in the morning. You couldn't see the Koh-i-noor by this light." Fred laughed again at his joke, and gently tugged the remaining earring that dangled from Millie's right ear. She grabbed it from him sharply.

"Hey, there!" Fred protested. "Did you think I was stealing it, or something?"

"No. But you probably made me lose the other one when you were messing around a little while ago."

"Well, if it's there I'll find it in the morning. I told you, didn't I? Come on home. We're catching our death in this wind."

Millie caught his arm.

"Fred, you haven't a spare key to the gardens, have you?"

"Sure."

"Then give me yours now. I might get up earlier than you."

"Gosh, I believe you think you have lost the rajah's fortune, or something. All right, have it your own way."

Millie didn't seriously believe that the earrings might be very valuable, but she was upset and nervous about having lost one. She liked her new job, and didn't want to lose it so quickly. Especially now there was Fred. . . .

The earring must be on the ground somewhere, if not near the seat where they sat, at least lying in the grass on the way from the gate. She didn't want

to make too much fuss to Fred in case he suspected there was something funny about it, but when he
had said goodnight to her she would slip back with
the key he had given her, and have another look. If
she couldn't find the one earring she would have to
lose the other, too, bury it, or something, so that
there would be absolutely no proof that she had ever
had them. Mrs. Lacey could think she had mislaid
them herself, or that there had been a burglar.

All the same it was strange and eerie tiptoeing out
of the block of flats after Fred thought he had seen
her safely into the lift on her way up to the top
floor, going back into the deserted gardens and
searching in the short frost-damp grass for a tell-
tale gleam. She must have been there nearly half an
hour, crawling on her hands and knees around the
seat, staring until her eyes were popping out of her
head. It was very quiet, almost the only sound the
faint rustle of thin leafless twigs, and at intervals,
along High Street, the swish of a fast car. All at
once an owl called, and she started violently. The
call was so unexpected, and so lonely and forlorn.
An owl in the heart of London. How queer. Mum
wouldn't believe it. In Bethnal Green there was nothing so countrified as an owl. Oh, darn this old earring! Well, good luck to it, she'd have to bury the
other one, pushing it deep into the soft winter earth
and then stamping vigorously on it.

It was a pity. They'd been nice and Fred had admired them. But now Mrs. Lacey would never find
them, and perhaps Fred, knowing how upset Millie
had been, might buy her some more.

Millie smiled with happy anticipation, and standing upright looked right at the strange woman with
the long silvery fair hair.

She had to clap her hands to her mouth to repress

a scream. *Where* had the woman come from? How
long had she been standing there? But, most important,
what had she seen?

She was not actually in the square gardens. She
was a little distance away, looking over the railings,
standing completely in shadow except for her queer,
distinctive, witchlike locks. You couldn't see her
face at all, or her body, though vaguely it seemed
bundled up and tall. She stood so still, like a ghost . . . .

Then all at once, as if she realized Millie was
staring at her, petrified, she glided away. Millie
saw her form moving, vaguely beyond the bushes
and tree shadows, down the narrow lane that led to
High Street. When at last Millie was able to persuade
her own quaking limbs to carry her to the gate, to
fumble with the key and turn it in the heavy lock
and get herself out onto the street, the woman had
disappeared.

She could, of course, have dashed along to High
Street and tried to see where she had gone, but at
that moment, Millie told herself, wild horses would
not have dragged her. She wanted only to get safely into Manchester Court and up to Mrs. Lacey's
flat.

She was deeply thankful that there was no sign
of Fred to observe her guilty return. She could not
hide her fright from Mrs. Lacey, and indeed did not
want to, as she had to tell someone or die, but at
least she had the presence of mind to pretend the
woman had been lurking at the door of the flat, and
not over in the gardens. Then at last she had got
to bed, and had curled up with the covers around her
ears, telling herself reassuringly that the strange,
staring woman could not possibly have any personal
interest in her. It was just chance that she had
been there in the gardens to be stared at. And it

had been much too dark for the woman to see what she had been doing. So really everything must be all right.

But then the telephone ringing had started her quaking all over again. Who would ring at one o'clock in the morning? Who, in spite of Mrs. Lacey's cheerful assurance that it must have been a wrong number, would not have had the courtesy to apologize if that had been so?

From weariness and fright Millie's fancies grew into enormous realities. She knew who the mysterious caller had been. As plainly as if she had watched her in broad daylight with her own eyes Millie could see her striding up High Street, going two blocks, three blocks, until she found a telephone box, glowing red and warm in the cold night, then entering and dropping her money into the slot, dialing with long, thin fingers, smiling a little as she listened to Mrs. Lacey's questioning voice at the other end of the wire, saying nothing, just smiling, her long stringy pale hair falling into her eyes. . . .

VI

"WELL, JONES, and how is the little woman this morning?"

Flynn was walking about the flat in his dressing gown, flicking impatiently at things with his stick. It was a sunny day. He could feel the warmth on his face when he went to the windows. He was like a cat, groping with his senses for the most comfortable spot.

But it was winter sun, he thought, that pale, champagne-colored, heatless stuff, only vaguely warm when concentrated in one windless spot. The sky would be a washed-out blue, slightly veiled with mist, like an old woman's faded eyes; the trees would be fresh and keen and full of life. It was the kind of day in which to let down the top of the car, and drive very fast, until one's cheeks stung and every separate root of one's hair tingles.

Should he ring Zoe and ask her to come for a drive? But Zoe was nervous in a fast car. Anyway, the impulse had already died in him. Zoe had stayed too late last night. He had begun to grow bored with her. She had hinted obliquely at marriage, and he had been suddenly aghast at the thought of three hundred and sixty-five days a year in her company. A steady diet of champagne, he had thought.

Yet there it was. When the champagne stopped one hankered for it. Or for something to fill in the hours, some gay sound, some semblance of light.

"She seemed a little more cheerful, sir. Thank you for inquiring, sir."

Flynn realized belatedly that Jones was answering his question.

"What's she got to be cheerless about, anyway. She has a faithful husband."

"She is tied to her bed, sir." Jones's voice was deferential, but firm.

"Oh, so she is, of course. But I predict one of these days you'll arrive home and find her getting your supper for you. Wouldn't that be a surprise!"

"It would indeed, sir."

The man's voice was so heartfelt that Flynn was suddenly ashamed of himself. Perhaps one day he would marry Zoe, and people would talk to her exactly in the same way. "Oh, I'm sure he could see if he tried. . . ."

He gripped his stick with sudden fury.

"Jones, I've got to work. I've loafed for three months. Bring me those applications and read them to me again. We must sort out these young women. If I interview one or two I can cope with the mental ability. Can you deal with the physical? How are you on appreciating girls?"

"I beg your pardon, sir."

"Jones, don't be such a hypocrite. I know I can't see, but that doesn't necessarily make me want to have a rabbit-toothed or wall-eyed female about the place. Besides, a pleasant face is a pleasant face. It indicates the kind of nature its owner has."

"Yes, sir, I understand."

"Well, let's go through those letters again."

"Yes, sir. This was one you'd thought of phoning. Actually I thought you had called her when that woman went to the wrong door yesterday."

"Oh, yes. And Millie screamed. Odd, that. You

say you actually saw this woman?"

"Just a glimpse of her, sir. She seemed to be hurrying. She had blond hair."

"So have most girls nowadays," Flynn said in a bored voice.

"Mrs. Lacey hasn't, sir."

"Hasn't she?"

"No, she's a dark brown, almost chestnut. She's not exactly pretty, the way you think of a woman being pretty, but she has an alive sort of look."

"You've been staring at her, Jones." The flippant note was back in Flynn's voice.

"Not really, sir. It's only that Nell—my wife—likes to hear about the people I see each day and I sort of describe them to her. Passes the time for her."

"Well, it doesn't pass the time for me," Flynn snapped, with one of his unpredictable changes of mood. "Let's get on with this job. What's the name of that girl I was going to see?"

"Wendy Browne. Browne spelled with an 'e'."

"Oh, God! And she'll have a genteel accent. She'll read those exquisite letters as if the people in them live in her own sordid little surburban villa with lace curtains and pot plants. Jones, ring up Harriet."

"Mrs. Lacey, sir?"

"Yes. I've got an idea. Tell her to come down at once."

"I'll try, sir, but she might be out, or busy."

"Well, try, man, try."

Jones had, however, no sooner got Harriet on the telephone before Flynn snatched the receiver from him and spoke.

"Harriet, I want you to come down."

"Now?"

"At once. There's something I want you to do for me."

"I might be making a cake."

"Let Mrs. Blunt finish it."

"Or washing my hair."

"You're doing nothing of the kind," Flynn said impatiently. "I want to see you."

He put the receiver down and sat back. Joe's shadow was between them, she had said. That was a woman's way of looking at things. Anyway, he couldn't see shadows. He could see nothing, not even Harriet's face, to decide whether or not she was pretty. She was a good actress, they told him. She was also a good mother who cared about the welfare of her children. To him she was impersonal and kind, and she walked with gaiety when she wore a new hat . . . . She was also the widow of the man who had died in the car that he, Flynn, had been driving. It was true that he had a conscience about her, and was glad to have been able to help her. Would he have wanted to go on helping her if he hadn't liked her light step, and her low, charming voice? He didn't know. Perhaps that shadow was there, after all.

Harriet was ringing the doorbell almost at once. When she came in, Flynn with his acute hearing, heard Jones's whisper, "He's in one of his instantaneous noods again, Mrs. Lacey."

"Instantaneous? Oh, you mean things are to be done on the instant."

"Yes, on the instant," Flynn called imperiously. "Harriet, I want you to be my secretary. I'll pay you a good wage, and you can fix your working hours. Fair enough?"

He knew that she was looking at him in amazement. Her voice was low with astonishment.

"But, Flynn, what an extraordinary request! I'm really much too busy. I have the children, and rehearsals every day, and when the play opens—"

"You will have two matinees and six evening shows a week, leaving you all the rest of the day. You have a good girl to look after the children, you told me so yourself, and judging by the bumps overhead Mrs. Blunt must scour your flat three times a day. So how else do you plan to fill in time?"

"But I have outside appointments, hairdressers, lunches. I may be doing some television work later. And I like to see something of my children. Anyway, what about that sheaf of applications you had for the job?"

"Useless. They bore me. They all spell their names with an 'e' on the end. Harriet, you are the only person who can read those letters. You read them beautifully."

He knew, by the sudden softness in her voice, that she was remembering the letter she had read, "you might be any small anonymous woman. . . ." And so she might, standing there, with her low voice, and deep brown hair Jones had described, and the not pretty face, and her controlled sympathy for him that did not jar. . . .

She was the person he could work with over those precious letters. He was not used to being denied things, and he did not mean to be denied this. It was a brilliant inspiration.

"Harriet, please do this for me," he said, not wheedlingly, but with simple sincerity.

She was hesitating, he knew. He could hear her move uncertainly.

"Even if you can't see," she said, "you've got to stop being such an autocrat. Do this, do that, as if everybody exists to look after you."

"Even when you're scathing, my sweet, your voice is charming."

"Oh, yes, you can say nice things when you want your own way. If I do this for you, it will be in my own time. A couple of hours in the morning, or the evening. And only until the book is done."

"We don't need to hurry over the book. Harriet, you are unbelievably good to me."

"Don't be a hypocrite. And what will Zoe say?"

"It's none of Zoe's business. If she could read like you do, I'd have offered the job to her."

"Have you always gone through life getting what you want?"

Automatically he touched the dark glasses that hid his injured eyes. His voice was at its most flippant.

"Trying to. But even I can't always succeed."

His flippancy, alternating with his moods of anger and impatience and arrogance, were all one ever saw of him, Harriet thought, as she left the flat. What sort of a young man had Joe seen at that Boston party two years ago? Joe had been quick to make friends. It would not have worried him had the visiting Englishman had more than his share of arrogance so long as he was amusing. And Joe must have found him amusing to have gone driving with him. But what had he been like before he had had to build up this prickly and at times maddening façade to hide the hurt of his blindness? She would never see his face as Joe had seen it, lit with the intelligence of observing eyes.

But then neither would he ever see her. Ever at all. She was as anonymous to him as that woman in his great-grandfather's letters. . . .

She opened the door of her flat to see Millie springing away from the telephone, her face pink and guilty.

"What is it, Millie? Another wrong number?"

"No, Mrs. Lacey. Just Fred."

"Oh!"

"He hopes I'll have more free evenings," Millie blurted out.

"Within reason, Millie. We'll have to go into that. I will be working at nights myself occasionally, even before the play opens."

Millie's eyes were all curiosity. Her mouth hung open slightly. She looked stupid and gullible. Harriet wondered momentarily why Fred found her so attractive.

"But we'll arrange things to suit us both," she added, and as Millie's face cleared she suddenly felt happy herself, happy and lighthearted, as she had when she had the impulse to buy a new hat yesterday.

It must be the spring morning. . . .

Just after Harriet left the flat that afternoon the telephone rang again.

Fred's call that morning had had the effect of making Millie recover from her temporary nervousness of the telephone. After all, that wrong number last night need have had nothing at all to do with the strange blonde woman. She had been tired and frightened, and had begun imagining things. If it came to that, the woman hadn't necessarily been staring at Millie at all as she had scrabbled on the ground in the gardens for the lost earring. She was probably someone who was odd, anyway, and wandered about the streets like a lost soul. If she had been watching Millie, she would have seen her come out of Manchester Court, and guess that she lived there, but how could she possibly know which flat she lived in, or the name of the owner of the flat?

Even though it might have been she who had rung
the doorbell yesterday afternoon, and then so strangely ran away. (But it was Jamie who had done that.
She had got the truth out of him this morning, by
a little judicious cajoling and pinching.)

No, that beer Fred had bought for her must have
been too strong. It had made her see ghosts!

Millie giggled to herself as she went blithely to
answer the telephone. This might be Fred again, she
told herself. He would have seen Mrs. Lacey leave,
and guess that it was an opportunity to have a long
talk. She would tell him she was about to take the
children for their daily walk. Perhaps he could get
an hour off and come along. . . .

"Hello," she said, in what she hoped was a deep
provocative voice. She waited a moment, and when
no answer came, she said sharply in her natural
tones, "Hello! Who's there?"

It was then that she heard the breathing. It seemed alarmingly close, almost as if the breather were
at her shoulder, fanning his hot breath against her
cheek.

"Are you alone in the flat?"

Surely she hadn't really heard those sinister half-
whispered words. It was as if she was in the cinema
and the husky voice came from the villain, dramatically only half visible in a dark room, his face a pale
threatening blur.

She could hear Jamie in the living room, pound-
ing about in one of his noisy games, while Arabella,
watching from her rug on the floor, gave a succession of her throaty gurgles. With one ear all was
normal. With the other . . .

"Are you alone, I said?"

"Y-yes. No, the children—I mean, Mrs. Lacey,
too—"

Too late she had floundered. She knew she should have said firmly that Mrs. Lacey and Mrs. Blunt were both there. But Harriet had left fifteen minutes ago, and Mrs. Blunt, her shapeless brown felt hat pulled securely on her head, her sturdy figure wrapped in her working coat that had seen many a winter's day, had gone just before noon.

"So you're alone except for the children."

"Who are you? What is it you want?"

Millie tried desperately to maker her voice firm and abrupt, but it ended in a woeful squeak. The worst thing now was that she couldn't be sure whether it were a man or a woman speaking. At first she had thought it was a man, but now the husky whisper could have beeen that of a woman, deepening her voice deliberately. The blonde woman, with the strange nocturnal habits.

"The first question you ask is none of your business. The second is. Now listen carefully. You are to do something for me. Quite a small thing, quite easy."

"W—what is it? And how do you know I will do it?"

There was a faint, throaty chuckle, indescribably sinister.

"You will do it, my dear. Because if you don't I will make it my business to let your mistress know that last night you stole her diamond earrings, one of which you lost, and the other you buried in the square gardens. I can take her exactly to the spot where you buried it."

So it *was* that awful woman! Millie felt her scalp prickling. She could scarcely speak.

"Di—diamond!" she heard herself repeating foolishly.

"Yes, real diamonds, my dear. Quite valuable. Mrs.

Lacey wouldn't like to lose them nor to hear that you had stolen them."

"But I didn't!" Millie screamed. "I only borrowed them. You can't prove I stole them."

"I can prove you lost them, because I have both of them now, here in my hand."

"O-ooh!" Helplessly Millie began to sob.

"Don't cry, my dear." The hateful voice was almost kind. It was unbearable. "Mrs. Lacey shall hear nothing about this if you do as I say. Now listen. You are planning to take the children for a walk in a few minutes."

"How do you know?"

"I have ways. Are you listening?"

Millie wanted to shout. "No, no, no! Go away!" and put down the receiver. But some awful compulsion made her hang onto it with her perspiring hands, and whisper helplessly, "Yes."

"You won't take the little boy with you this afternoon."

"B-but—"

"I'm telling you you won't take the boy. You'll leave him with one of the neighbors. You'll just take the baby."

"But Mrs. Lacey—"

"You will take the baby alone."

There was no denying that implacable order. Fragments of thought went through Millie's frantic head. Jamie was always naughty. She could say he had refused to come, run away to Mr. Palmer when she was ready to go, anything. . . .

"Yes," she whispered again.

"Good. You will wheel her in her pram to Woolworth's in High Street. There you will leave her for a few minutes while you go in to buy something, nylons, hair clips, anything—When you come out—

But that's all. It's very simple."

Millie had her free hand pressed to her face.

"NO!" she screamed.

The faint ghosty chuckle came.

"It's only for twenty-four hours, my dear. Nothing will happen to the baby. Nothing at all."

"No! You can't!"

"Better than six months in prison for stealing." The telephone clicked. The woman, the man, whoever it was with the blonde witchlocks, had hung up. Had deliberately gone, leaving her on this precipice. There was no way to turn because on one side was prison, Fred, whom she had fallen in love with, lost, and on the other side an empty pram, Arabella, plump little smiling Arabella gone.

But the voice had promised it would be only for twenty-four hours. It had promised the baby would be all right. And babies of fifteen months didn't remember. Not like Fred would remember, if she went to jail. She couldn't go to jail. That was absolutely out of the question. Think of Mum's shock, apart from Fred.

If only she hadn't lost that wretched earring. If only she hadn't panicked. It was Fred's fault for messing about with her in the gardens. He had knocked it off her ear, so that that awful woman had found it.

But she had told him the earrings were lent to her. He had particularly noticed them. Perhaps he had known they were diamonds. In that case, he'd never believe she hadn't stolen them. If he found out. . . . He mustn't find out. That was all there was to it.

So really there was no alternative. . . .

VII

JAMIE WASN'T particularly interested in going for
long walks with Millie, holding on to Arabella's
pram all the time, as she insisted on his doing. It was
very dull, especially since Millie liked staring in
shop windows at silly blouses and things, and when
she got to the park kept on calling to him to be
careful, not to fall in the water, not to go too far
away. She was as bad as Nannie Brown. Although
she was nice sometimes and played games. But this
morning she had pinched him hard and made him
tell about yesterday's prank, borrowing the wig and
pretending to be a lady. Yet she didn't seem to
believe him when he did tell her, and said he was
making it up. He didn't care, silly old Millie.

Then all at once, when he was ready for a walk,
and only waiting for her to stop talking on the telephone, she came in and said he wasn't to come.

He didn't care about the walk, but it wasn't fair
being suddenly told that he wasn't wanted.

"Why can't I come? It isn't raining."

"I know it isn't raining. You just can't come. I'm
in a hurry and want to walk fast."

"I can walk fast," Jamie said in a hurt voice.

"Not fast enough. Oh, for goodness' sake, don't
argue. As if I haven't enough on my mind. Here,
put Arabella's gloves on while I get the pram ready."

Millie's face was red and she looked as if she were going to cry. Jamie stared at her in hurt bewilderment.

"Why can't I come? Mummy said I had to have walks."

"Look, I told you not to argue, didn't I?" Millie's hand was raised ready to strike him. Then she refrained, and instead bundled Arabella onto her lap and began pulling on her gloves. "I'll only be gone fifteen minutes. You can go down and see your precious Mrs. Helps, the way you're always sneaking off when you're told not to. Well, go on then. Don't just stand there."

Jamie's lower lip was thrust out mutinously. Arabella, he thought, was going to be bought ice cream and he wasn't. That was what it was. Mean old Millie didn't want him to see.

Well, he would just see. He'd show her.

"Go along," said Millie more kindly. "Arabella and I will come and get you on our—I mean, I'll get you later. I don't know what it is you see down in that old woman's room, but you're welcome to it."

Jamie knew why he liked Mrs. Helps's dim basement room. It had the quality of a fairy story. This was enhanced by the old lady's gift as a teller of tales. As she combed and curled silver, golden or black hair, turning it around her skillful fingers, shaping it into a realistic head, she would tell long involved stories about people who had come to her, heads she had made hair for. Half of it did not make sense to a fascinated five-year-old, but biscuits and chocolate fingers and kindness did. Escaping from Nannie Brown's crossness and hysteria, Jamie had found the dim room and the talkative old woman a refuge.

But today he was ashamed to go down because of what he had done to the pale golden wig yesterday. He hadn't meant to throw it in the coal bin, but he had thought Millie was chasing him. It had been such a splendid joke, until then, and he had collapsed, giggling wildly, at the foot of the basement stairs, waiting for Millie wrathfully to appear.

But no one had come. No one had seemed to miss him. So he need not have thrown that lovely wig into the dirty coal after all. And now it was awkward visiting Mrs. Helps because she would be cross with him. Which made him all the more determined not to obey Millie this afternoon.

Though he would pretend to, of course. Millie really thought she had seen him safely down to he basement. She waved to him in the hall, then tucked Arabella more warmly into her pram and went off.

Jamie waited until she was outside, then sneaking on tiptoe, he followed. He was only going to see whether or not Arabella got an ice cream. If she did he would pounce suddenly on her and Millie, demanding his share.

Outside, the air was sharp and frosty. Millie walked quickly, as if she didn't like the cold and wanted to be indoors again. She turned the pram into busy High Street, and made her way brisky. Because of the numbers of people in the street, Jamie was able to keep close to her. Her red beret was always in view. She didn't stop at all until she got to Woolworth's, and then she pushed the pram close up to the window and said something to Arabella.

Arabella bounced and smiled, holding up her arms.

Jamie heard Millie say quite clearly, "No, you can't come in. You'll be all right. Really you will." And then she turned and went into the shop as if she were suddenly in a great hurry.

Arabella began to whimper. Jamie couldn't resist suddenly bobbing up in front of her to make her gurgle with delight.

"I came," he said triumphantly. "I'm going to have half your ice cream."

And at the same moment a completely strange woman dressed in black leaned calmly into the pram and picked up Arabella.

Arabella was obviously too startled to cry. It was Jamie who did that.

"Hey!" he yelled, grabbing Arabella's foot. "That's my sister." He remembered a television program, and added toughly, "What do you think you're doing?"

The woman, who wore dark glasses, as well as a black hat and coat, whispered fiercely, "Let her go, you little fool."

"She's my sister! Where are you taking her? If you're taking her somewhere, I'm coming, too."

One or two people had turned to look.

"Then come," Jamie heard the strange woman say urgently, and the next thing he knew, she had his hand firmly in hers and was whisking him past the shop windows and around the corner.

He had to run to keep up with her. Arabella was beginning to whimper. Jamie, too, would like to have opened his mouth and bawled. Because he was frightened now. Something strange was happening. He didn't want any longer to go with this woman, although she had Arabella, but she held his fingers so tightly that he couldn't extricate them.

A taxi was going slowly past, and somehow the woman managed to signal it. It stopped and the driver leaned out to open the door.

"Bit of a handful you've got, lady."

"You're telling me!"

The woman was breathing quickly, as if she had been running. She gave Jamie a sharp push towards the open door. "In with you."

She half lifted, half pushed him in, then scrambled in with Arabella, and sat back panting. After a moment she leaned forward to give the driver an address, then she pulled the dividing window shut, and looked at Jamie.

"If you make one sound," she said in a low angry voice, "I'll throttle you!"

VIII

As HARRIET was hurrying out that afternoon to catch a bus to the theater she encountered Zoe just leaving Flynn's flat.

"Hello," she said. "How's Flynn?"

"Wouldn't you know?" Zoe asked, her narrow green eyes fixed coldly on Harriet.

"Not necessarily."

"But I hear you have a new job." Zoe's smile was pure malice.

"Helping Flynn with his great-grandfather's letters? I've promised to give him what time I can."

"I would think," said Zoe, "that if I were a mother I would want to spend more time with my children."

Harriet thought fleetingly of the children she had just left, Jamie, busy with his own pursuits, lifting an unwilling face to be kissed. Arabella, soft and plump on the hearthrug, bestowing her friendly smiles on anyone who approached. Was she neglecting them, she wondered guiltily? But they were happy and well cared for and loved, and anyway, what right had this slim, smart young woman to criticize?

Suddenly Harriet was angry. "When you are a mother, Zoe, I'll listen to you. And is it any of your business that Flynn has asked me to do some secretarial work?"

"Yes, it is!" Zoe exclaimed, suddenly losing her sophisticated mask and speaking heatedly. "I knew him long before you did. I've stood by him ever since his accident, and it hasn't been easy at times. But I've done it, and now, when I expect my reward, you walk in."

"I don't understand, Zoe. Your reward?"

"Why, because we've always meant to be married. You know that very well. We were only waiting until Flynn was better adjusted, and he was doing fine until you arrived."

"I think he's doing fine now," said Harriet.

"That's what you think! You don't know him as I do. He's gone right back to being difficult and bad-tempered and unpredictable. It's only because of you and your children. Jamie always in and out, and then you coming for him and there always being interruptions. It's utterly changed everything."

"Well, I'm sorry about that, Zoe," Harriet said more kindly. "But Flynn got me that flat and would have been very hurt if I hadn't accepted it. Besides, I was very grateful for it. But I assure you there was nothing personal."

"Then why can't you stop living on his doorstep?" Zoe flashed. Her face seemed to have narrowed. It was sharp and vixenish. Harriet thought abruptly that it was lucky Flynn could not see Zoe's face. If he was fond of her, or even in love with her, it would be a pity for him to see her looking like this.

"I'm not living on his doorstep. That's utterly untrue."

"You encourage Jamie to come down, for an excuse to come yourself. I've watched. You can't fool me."

"I've no desire to fool you." Harriet's voice was

ice. "I'm sorry we can't continue with this illuminating conversation, but I have a bus to catch."

"You have plenty," Zoe's shrill voice followed her as she walked away. "Children, a nice flat, servants, money from America. So look after them. Or something might happen to them."

Ridiculously, Harriet found herself trembling as she got onto the bus. That had been very unpleasant and also unfair. She had always known Zoe did not like her, but she had not realized her jealousy was as bitter as that. She would be sorry for her if the girl were not so obviously mercenary. She may indeed have been in love with Flynn, but it would be interesting to see what happened were he stripped of his possessions. Take away his luxury flat, his man-servant, his car, his ability to ring any shop or hotel in London, and have what he fancied at the moment delivered, whether it be orchids or caviar. Even though he was blind he could open to her a world she would not otherwise have known. Being blind made him, to her mind, much easier prey.

That was crude and horrible of her, Harriet thought, but with her memory of Zoe's sharpened face she was afraid it was true.

How was she now to face Zoe in front of Flynn? His acute perception would soon detect the enmity. It might amuse him. One never knew what would amuse him. But it would be deeply distasteful to Harriet, and that, she realized, was what Zoe was probably counting on. Anything, to prevent Harriet doing the proposed secretarial work and keep her out of the flat.

And was her accusation about Harriet's neglecting her children untrue? Should she give up her theatrical career and meekly allow herself to be kept by Joe's mother, who disliked her?

No, her way was right. She knew that Joe would wholeheartedly approve. He had wanted her to keep her career, no matter what happened. "You can't cut off a woman's right arm," he had said, with his rare understanding. "Your left one is big enough to go around Jamie and me." He had known that an intellectual interest was necessary to a woman of her type, and he had also understood, when there had been the unfair hostility from his family over his marriage, that Harriet's pride was a matter of great importance to her. Those things still existed, although Joe was no longer there. But it was the way on which he had started her, and she knew he would not wish her to turn back. Particularly not because of a venomous attack by a silly, shallow, jealous woman.

In the face of what happened, however, Harriet found it almost impossible to give her mind to rehearsals that afternoon, and had the most impelling urgency to rush home and see that all was well with the little world that was left to her, the "plenty" that Zoe had talked about. Len Brinker, the producer, finally lost his temper with her, and asked her to stay to run through her part again after the rest of the cast had been dismissed.

"Look, Harriet," he said wearily, "you were good yesterday. What's gone wrong today?"

"I'm sorry, Len. I was worried about my children."

"Are they sick?"

"No, they're perfectly well, but it just happens it's a day I have them on my mind."

"Well, my dear, I'll tell you frankly, either you get them or the theater off your mind. You can't cope with both."

"Can't I?" She looked so tense and worried that he

ran his hand through his untidy hair and sighed.

"Not with that intensity. When you're with them, you're a mother and all the silly things you should be. When you're here you're Mrs. Whosit in a silly hat, and not a care in the world."

"Yesterday I was," Harriet said defensively.

"And tomorrow you will be. And the next day. And also on opening night. Or else—"

"That's fair enough, Len. I'm sorry. I have a thing today."

"Who hasn't, sometimes? Go home and wallow in your nursery world. Tomorrow you'll hanker for this grind."

When she reached Manchester Court she wanted to slip in quickly without anyone seeing her. She would find Millie upstairs, with the children bathed and waiting for her, Arabella to be kissed goodnight, Jamie to have his bedtime story. The flat would be cosy and inviting, with its shaded lights, its deep chairs, and pleasant pictures. She did not think she could go down to Flynn that evening. This thing about Zoe's jealousy would have to be thought over.

It was not possible to go in unobserved, however, for Fred was suddenly at the lift, holding the doors open as if he had been waiting for her. She remembered his bold smile of admiration the previous evening, and thought that it must be something he turned on and off at will, for tonight he was frowning and serious.

"Good evening, Mrs. Lacey."

"Good evening, Fred. Are you taking me up?"

Fred got in the lift beside her, but made no move to press the button.

"Mrs. Lacey—there's been a bit of trouble."

"Trouble." It was as if she had known all afternoon that something disastrous had been about to happen. It had begun with Zoe—but that had only been a beginning. Somehow she had known that.

"Someone seems to have been having a sort of joke on Millie," Fred said. "With the children."

"Fred! What is it?"

"Millie had to tell Ma and me because you see she thought she'd left Jamie with Ma. But she hadn't, really. At least, Ma swears he never arrived."

"Fred!" Harriet was gripping his arm. "Are you telling me Jamie has disappeared?"

Fred pressed the lift button at last and they began to ascend. He nodded. Beneath his important seriousness was excitement.

"You'd better talk to Millie. She's pretty upset. She thought it was just the baby and Jamie would be all right. But then she got home and found he'd gone, too!"

It was a nightmare. Harriet stared blankly, unable to take in Fred's roundabout story.

"We didn't call the police, ma'am, because of the note. It said so strong not to. Anyway, we thought we'd better wait till you got home. I rang the theater, but you'd left, they said. So we just had to wait. Ma's in a state, too. But no one knows except us. Not a soul."

It couldn't be true, of course. It was another of Millie's fantasies, such as the blonde, staring woman had been. When she got into the flat she would find Fred had been having a grim, humorless joke with her.

But it was no joke. Millie's swollen, tear-stained face told her that. She opened the door for Harriet, and immediately began to sob. By the sound of her hiccuping, exhausted sobs she had been doing that most of the afternoon.

"Oh, Mrs. Lacey—" she got out, then wordlessly

thrust a crumpled and rather dirty piece of paper at Harriet.

Fred called it the "note." The sort of thing that one nation politely sent to another when it was deeply aggrieved about some lawlessness, spying or encroaching on someone else's territory. Absurdly, Harriet now imagined herself the recipient of one of these impersonal, coldly warning epistles.

She had to take it to the light because, absolutely in the style of fiction thrillers, it was composed of words cut painstakingly out of a newspaper and stuck onto a plain piece of paper. These words, stuck at slightly higgledy piggledy angles, seemed to dance in front of her eyes. But they made sense. Awful cold threatening sense.

I HAVE GOT YOUR BABY. SHE WILL BE RETURNED SAFE AND WELL IF YOU DO THE FOLLOWING—TOMORROW GET FIVE HUNDRED POUNDS IN SINGLE NOTES. AT 8 P.M. LEAVE THEM IN A PARCEL ON THE SEAT UNDER THE BIG ELM ABOUT A HUNDRED YARDS FROM THE ROUND POND KENSINGTON GARDENS. YOU CAN'T MISS IT. IT IS THE ONLY SEAT IN THAT AREA. DON'T BE LATE. DON'T INFORM POLICE. GO ALONE. IF YOU OBEY THESE INSTRUCTIONS YOU WILL BE ADVISED BY TELEPHONE WHERE TO FIND YOUR BABY. IF YOU INFORM THE POLICE IT WILL BE TOO BAD FOR YOUR BABY. I WILL PLAY FAIR IF YOU PLAY FAIR. THIS IS HONEST.

Harriet looked up bleakly. This couldn't be true. These things happened in the United States, but not in London. This was London.

But her children were half American. Had that

anything to do with it? Did the kidnapper know this? Did he know she received a more than generous allowance for them from their Boston grandmother? Or had he just guessed that, living in a block of luxury flats and having a servant to take care of the children, she would find no difficulty in laying her hands on five hundred pounds in cash?

"I'll have to do this," she heard herself saying in a tense whisper. "I'll have to do it *exactly* as he says."

Millie gave a convulsive sob, and Fred, who had been standing uninvited just inside the door, nodded approvingly.

"That's just what I said, ma'am. You can't take risks with those people. They kill quick as think. I mean, what's a bit of a kid to them, if it's to save their own skins."

"I can't believe it!" Harriet looked around frantically. It was a diabolical prank of Jamie's. He had hidden himself and Arabella. In a moment he would come bouncing forth, laughing hilariously.

When would she see his gleeful, mischievous, so like Joe's face again. . . .

"Millie!" she said sharply. "For heaven's sake, stop crying and tell me exactly what happened. Come now. Control yourself."

"Oh, it wasn't my fault, ma'am!" Millie wailed. "I'd just slipped into Woolworth's to buy myself a home perm, just two minutes, no more. And then there was the empty pram and the note sort of pushed under the pillow."

Harriet looked at Fred. "Ask your mother to come up, will you, Fred. You say no one else knows of this?"

"No one, ma'am. I told Millie not to say a word. You can't fool about with this. I know these—I mean,

I've read enough in newspapers and so on, to—"

"Fred! Just bring your mother."

But the old lady, when she came, was no more help than Millie. She had been curling a raven-dark wig and she absentmindedly still had it in her hands, like a grisly trophy from the guillotine. Her own hair was wild and unkempt.

"Fred and me didn't see anything!" she said in her distressed voice. "Not even Jamie, though Millie said she told him to come down. But he didn't come. It might be because he was afraid I'd be scolding him for what he did with the ash blonde yesterday, but the shampoo brought that right, so I wouldn't have scolded the lad. Only he just didn't turn up."

Harriet, in a desperate desire to get some calm sensible picture of the afternoon's events, turned to Millie.

"Millie, why did you tell Jamie to go down to Mrs. Helps instead of taking him with you and Arabella?"

"Because I didn't want to be long, Mrs. Lacey. My feet were tired after dancing last night, and I wanted to put them up."

Harriet thought tiredly that she might have known when she engaged Millie that a girl with that sort of amiable, vacuous face would not be trustworthy. She would be lazy and untruthful. At the time, however—was it only a week ago?—her good qualities had seemed to exceed her possible bad ones.

"So you told Jamie to go down to Mrs. Helps for half an hour and you went out with Arabella alone?"

Millie nodded. "But he must have followed me, the ba—I mean, that's what Fred said must have happened."

"You didn't actually see him at all, Fred?"

Fred shook his head vigorously.

"No, ma'am. It was my two hours off. I was having forty winks. Wasn't I, Ma?"

The old lady nodded. "Yes, Fred was on his bed until four o'clock." Her voice was unusually firm and vehement.

Abruptly Millie plunged into a fresh bout of sobbing.

"Oh, Mrs. Lacey, that empty pram! I ran all the way home with it, really I did."

Harriet tried not to see the picture of the distraught girl pushing home the pram, the mattress still warm from Arabella's soft, plump little body. One must not let the awful worry overwhelm one. One had to think clearly and logically.

"Didn't you scream or anything when you came out of Woolworth's and saw that Arabella had gone?"

Millie gulped and shook her head. "At first I was sort of thunderstruck. I thought some old lady must have picked Arabella up. You know the way old women hang over babies in prams. I was just going to look around when I saw the note, half stuck under the pillow, and I read that, and then I just came home as fast as I could. I thought Jamie would be here, at least, but when he wasn't—oh, it was awful."

"I still can't think," said Harriet slowly, "why you didn't scream and call a policeman." That, she would have thought, would have been the inevitable reaction of a girl like Millie.

"I did look, but there wasn't one about," said Millie. "All I wanted to do was to get home. To Fred," she added, and a rather dreadful travesty of coyness came into her blotched and swollen face.

"And I told her to keep clear of the police, in view of what the note said, and do nothing until you got home," Fred said importantly.

"You going to call the police and risk your baby being murdered?" The abrupt question in Mrs. Helps's high, thin voice was somehow the ultimate in horror.

Harriet lost her desperate logical grip of the situation and sat down, burying her face in her hands. Jamie and Arabella had gone. They had been snatched away as ruthlessly as young spring leaves off a tree in a sudden storm. They would come back. Of course they would come back. Didn't that dreadful note say so? "This is honest," it had ended, ironically. But in the meantime there was the long night, all the next day, and another long night to be lived through. All the time wondering where they were, whether they were cold and frightened, hungry, bewildered, sick perhaps, or cruelly treated. Thirty-six hours. . . . In one's whole lifetime one would not expect to have to endure more than a few hours of such agony.

"Excuse me, ma'am," came Fred's voice. "I took the liberty to pour this for you."

He held out a glass of brandy. His handsome ruddy face was kind, but all the time there was a lurking glow of excitement in his eyes, as if this were the kind of situation that stimulated and pleased him.

Mechanically Harriet took the glass and drank. Thirty-six hours. . . . They had to be endured somehow.

"You weren't planning to get the police, were you, ma'am."

"Fred, how can I, how can I?"

"That's what I say. What's five hundred pounds compared with the kids' lives?"

Harriet swallowed the rest of the brandy and shuddered uncontrollably. Arabella and Jamie. Jamie and Arabella. Jamie who had adored, and been adored by his father. Arabella whom Joe had known nothing about. The little anonymous Arabella, with her round laughing face, her beautiful red-gold curls .... Her babies, of whom she was not allowed to think when she was at the theater, whom Zoe said she neglected. Zoe! With her pretty face turned thin and malicious, her wild threats. . . . Was this some ghastly trick of hers?

But it couldn't be. Even Zoe would be capable of no more than jealous words. . . .

She forced herself to behave politely.

"Thank you, Mrs. Helps, and Fred. Will you go now? I want to think. And please say nothing to anyone."

Fred nodded solemnly. Mrs. Helps, looking suddenly small and shriveled, with the black wig incongruously in her hand, also nodded. There was a look of defeat on her face. She seemed beyond words. Her tall son had to take her arm and lead her away.

When they had gone the flat seemed so empty that it was frightening. Harriet shivered, lifting her haggard eyes to Millie.

Millie sniffed, her reddening eyes threatening once more to overflow.

"You don't blame me, Mrs. Lacey, do you? I couldn't help it. I mean everyone leaves babies outside shops."

"I don't know yet whom I blame, Millie. I have to think. It might even be myself." She forced herself to look impersonally at the wretched girl, a travesty of the pert, confident creature who had gone out dancing with Fred last night. "You'd better go to bed, Millie. You look worn out. I'll bring some hot milk."

This kindness was too much for Millie who promptly burst out into fresh sobs.

"Oh, ma'am. I know who done this, although I didn't see. It was that woman with the witchy blonde hair. I know it was. She's been haunting me!"

IX

AT EIGHT O'CLOCK the telephone rang. The sound was unbearably violent in the quiet flat. It made Millie, in her bedroom, give a muffled scream. She said something that sounded like, "It's her again!" but when Harriet called out "Who?" she said "Nothing," and lay trembling while Harriet answered the telephone.

The caller was only Flynn.

"Is that you, Harriet? I thought you were coming down tonight."

"Is anything wrong?"

She couldn't tell Flynn. She knew instinctively that he would insist on ringing the police immediately. She had already spent two agonized hours wondering if she were wrong not to ring them, but knowing all the time that she would not. Wasn't there that case in the States where by too eager and unimaginative police action, the kidnapper panicked and strangled the baby not a mile from its home? She couldn't risk anything going wrong. Five hundred pounds was a cheap price to pay to get her babies back safely.

Fred, with his distrust of the police and anything to do with the law, she could trust, but Flynn would not be like Fred. She had to keep this catastrophe from him somehow, in case he put his well-meaning foot in it, and by morning Jamie and Arabella would be found dead in Epping Forest, or some lonely place like that.

"I said, is anything wrong?"

"No. I'm just rather tired."

"Are you telling me the truth, Harriet?"

"Why should you think I'm not?"

"Nothing. I just wondered if Zoe had been getting at you. She was in a foul mood today. A woman scorned. What the devil is it to do with her if I employ you in a perfectly respectable way?"

Zoe had said something might happen to the children. But it was fantastic to think she would do such a desperate thing, purely from spite.

The blonde woman Millie had said was haunting her. . . . Zoe was blonde. She could have deliberately ruffled her hair and looked strange. But Millie would surely have recognized her. Unless it were too dark. . . .

That vague person had seemed to be watching the flat the other night—it could have been either a woman or a man . . . The telephone call, when no one spoke. . . .

"Harriet, are you there?"

The sharp impatience in Flynn's voice dispersed her exaggerated fancies.

"Yes, I'm here."

"And asleep, apparently. Do pull yourself together and come down for an hour."

Again her impulse was to refuse. But the night stretched long and bleak and sleepless ahead of her. If she could assume some kind of concentration it would at least pass a little of it.

"All right," she agreed. "Though I warn you I'll be very stupid."

Millie huddled in her bed, not wanting to be left.

"Supposing the phone rings," she whimpered.

"If anyone wants me you will come down at once and get me. Don't be such a scared rabbit. No one can eat you over the telephone."

Which was true, but to both of them the innocent white instrument in the hall had become sinister, a sleeping snake that could on an instant vibrate with noise and menace. Harriet washed her face and straightened her hair. Everything in her bedroom was the same as it had been that morning—the neatly made bed, the toilet articles on the dressing table, the photograph of Joe, serenely smiling, the bowl of winter roses, still as fresh as they had been when she arranged them that morning. Only her face looking back from the mirror was different. It was white and strained, her eyes enormous, a vertical line etched into her forehead. Tonight she reflected wryly, even Zoe would not have been jealous. Tonight she was almost grateful that Flynn was blind and could not see her hideous anxiety. But how could she conceal it in her manner?

Flynn was seated before the fire in his luxurious living room. He had rather touchingly placed a reading lamp on the small table where she was to work. He was obviously pleased with his arrangements, for he called cheerily, "Come in and we'll start at once. Am I a slave driver? But you did promise, you know."

"What shall I do first?"

It was useless to try not to think of the empty beds upstairs, and Millie a sodden heap of misery and funk. Harriet endeavored to put some life in her voice.

"Sit down and have a drink. I told Jones to leave everything ready. He was in a hurry, as usual, to rush home to his pampered wife."

"I won't have a drink, thank you."

"Nonsense. It's just what you need if you're tired. What's wrong? Jamie been getting the best of the new girl? At least she's keeping him occupied. I haven't seen him all day."

"No, it wasn't Jamie. Rehearsals went badly. I was threatened with losing my job."

"Oh, too bad. What was your mind on?"

Lounging back in his chair, his face in shadow, he might have been watching her intently. His face, at that moment, was relaxed and placid, but that could be deceptive. At any moment his quick temper might come flaming forth. He looked so large and strong, it seemed almost absurd that he was tied virtually to these four walls. Even in his blindness he was tremendously vital, and a little uncomfortably full of intelligence. Harriet had the sensation that her mind was being accurately read and analyzed.

"Oh, the children," she said vaguely, answering his question.

"They're not sick, are they?"

Len Brinker had asked the same question. She prayed that they were not sick, that they had been fed and put in a warm bed, and soothed to sleep. Even a kidnapper, if he promised to return one's children safe and well, must make some plans for their temporary welfare. Perhaps he would have an innocent and gullible old mother or aunt. That was if he were a man. He could, of course, be a woman who knew how to care for children. One hoped this was so. A woman would not kill. . . .

"Harriet, you shivered!"

"Did I? I told you I was tired."

"And full of nerves about something."

"You're too observant. Were you like this before you lost your eyesight?"

"Never noticed a thing," he said cheerfully. "Let's begin on the letters following that one you read the other night. I think they're all there on my desk. I dared Jones on pain of banishment to Clapham, not to touch them."

"Yes," said Harriet, touching the yellowed paper covered with its thin faded writing, and long-ago inscription of someone else's hopes and agonies. "This one begins, 'My dear Mary.' He calls her Mary now. She's no longer anonymous. Who was she?"

"Mary Weston. She was nineteen and lived in Chester, but sometimes visited an aunt in London. That's all I know about her."

"Didn't your great-grandfather marry her?"

"No. He went abroad. When he came back her family had forced her into some sort of marriage of convenience. It's all in her letters. Harriet, are you listening?"

"Of course."

"I heard you fidgeting. If you don't want to work, come and sit by the fire."

"I came down to work."

"It doesn't matter. I really only wanted company."

It was the first time he had made an admission of any kind of weakness to her. She knew that she should have been moved by it and at another time would have been.

"You should begin to go out more, Flynn. You could go to theaters. Zoe would take you."

"Zoe! The greedy little hound only wants to guzzle champagne."

"Flynn, where does Zoe live?"

"Oh, Lord. I can't tell you at the moment. In Chelsea somewhere. She's always moving to another flat. Says she does it to economize. I can never quite work that out."

"And she's moved just recently?"

"Only last week. She isn't even on the telephone."

"I wish you would find out where she lives."

"Why do you want to know?"

"Oh—something private. And rather important."

"All right. If you want to be so mysterious, I'll ask her tomorrow. Tell me, Harriet, does she seem to you to be short of money?"

"Her clothes are good," Harriet said briefly.

"Sometimes I wonder about her. But if I offer her a loan she refuses."

Playing for higher stakes, Harriet thought sardonically. Was the fact that she had changed her address and now had not even a telephone, or said she had not, significant?

"I shouldn't like her to be in want. That's an expression my great-grandfather would have used, isn't it? I must be reverting to type. But I don't think Zoe's the kind to be in want. She'd do something about it. Why did you start just then?"

"I thought I heard a telephone."

"Are you expecting a call?"

"No, not particularly."

"Then for heaven's sake relax. You're on wires. By the way, Jones tells me Millie and Fred are getting along nicely. Quite a romance, he says, being the eternal romantic himself."

"Jones is a gossip."

"He has to live vicariously, poor devil. Come and sit here, Harriet. Here." He patted the chair beside him impatiently as she did not move, then gave his wry grin.

"What's the matter? Can you see Joe's shadow

there? I'm not planning anything. Only sometimes one feels damned lonely."

"Yes," said Harriet involuntarily.

"Oh, I know I can import stuff, get on the telephone, have music, wine, dancing girls. Sometimes it helps. Sometimes it doesn't. Tonight it doesn't. You understand that, don't you?"

"Yesterday, when you walked in, in that new hat, I knew you were an attractive woman. Only a woman who knows she is attractive walks with that lightness and confidence. I wanted to see your face. And instead you chose to talk about Joe's shadow!" He sighed deeply. "Well, it would be a nice shadow, wouldn't it?"

"Of course."

"What's your face like, Harriet?"

"Oh—ordinary."

"Can I look at it? Do you mind?"

He had never touched her before. He had never behaved like this, so gently, almost sentimentally, all his familiar arrogance gone. But why must it be tonight, when she was so tense that she could scarcely speak, when he would think her tension was due to his unexpected behavior, and perhaps misinterpret it as emotion for him.

Was that the telephone ringing in her flat? But Millie would call her if she were wanted.

His hands, like his body, were large and strong, but full of sensitivity. His fingers on her forehead, her nose, her cheekbones, were a feather touch.

"The nurses in the hospital taught me this," he said lightly. "But it's a poor substitute for eyes. Harriet, you're crying! Your cheeks are wet."

She moved away sharply from his touch. Her hands were pressed to her hot cheeks.

"I'm sorry, Flynn. I'm not feeling well tonight.

Will you forgive me? I—I think I must go."

"Harriet, have I offended you?"

"No, you haven't offended me. It's just—I can't tell you now, Flynn. It's really nothing to do with you."

"It's as if Joe had touched you," he said abruptly.

"No, not that. Not that at all." (Although for a moment his touch had been unbearably poignant.) "Please forgive me, Flynn. I must go."

She had literally run away. Ten minutes later her doorbell had rung, and when she went to answer it Flynn was there. He had found his way up the stairs, with the aid of his stick.

"Is that you, Harriet?"

"Yes."

"I've brought you these tablets. They'll make you sleep. In the morning it will be all right."

"What will be all right?"

"Whatever you're worrying about."

He still thought it was Joe. His concern, added to her deadly secret worry, was almost intolerable.

"Flynn, that is kind."

"Think nothing of it." He waved an airy hand. "Sometimes I can be almost human."

X

IT WAS a long night, the first twelve of those thirty-six hours.

In the dark, rather stuffy, basement flat Mrs. Helps sat at her table, working mechanically at the long silken locks of hair. She was shaping them onto a papier mâché head which had no face. From the back view it was an elegant woman with curled glossy hair, from the front it was as featureless as an egg, a faceless woman, an enigma.

Every now and then the old lady stopped work and turned the head around to look at that smooth somehow sinister expanse, as if she were trying to imprint eyes, a nose, a mouth, on it, turning it into the imaginary face of the person who had so wickedly taken away Mrs. Lacey's children.

It was a stranger's face, of course. She could imagine the narrow, cunning, furtive eyes, the hard mouth. Someone who had watched from the street for days, observing the times Mrs. Lacey was away, seeing Millie coming and going with the children, laying his evil plans.

But all the time the features that seemed to drift across the blank model were those of Fred. Fred, her own son, who had always been far too imaginative about ways of making easy money, and whom she could no longer trust.

She dropped the hair brush with a clatter, and Fred called impatiently from his bedroom.

"Ma, aren't you ever coming to bed?"

"Soon, love, soon. I feel like working."

"You're not working, you're worrying about those kids."

Fred came to the door in his pajamas. He looked big and strong and impudent, his brown eyes full of mockery.

"You don't trust me, Ma, do you?"

Mrs. Helps looked appealingly.

"Fred, you didn't do it, did you? Swear to me you didn't."

"Nice thing, when your own mother thinks you're a kidnapper. Not that it doesn't sound like an easy job, if only I'd thought of it first. But I didn't, see."

He wouldn't tell her if he had done it, she thought tiredly, and could not get out of her mind Fred's empty bed that afternoon, and the tea she had made for him cooling in the pot.

"Then where were you this afternoon?"

"Out," he said laconically.

"I said you were having your two hours' rest, as usual."

"Good old Ma. Lying for her worthless son."

"Fred, where were you?"

"Out. I had some urgent business. As far as you're concerned, I was on my bed. Don't want to lose my job, do I, being missing when I should be on call."

"That's why I told a lie for you," his mother muttered.

"And you stick to it, Ma. It's not that I'm afraid of the police. Gosh, I wouldn't harm the kids. I call that kidnapping a real dirty trick. But I don't want the boss to know I was missing, see?"

"Fred, I'm worried."

"Oh, come off it, old lady." Fred laid his hand heavily on his mother's shoulder. "I was only doing a little deal. Quite harmless and above board. I didn't even see Millie take the kids out. Do you think she's telling the truth about leaving Jamie here?"

"Fred, I don't like that Millie. She's too careless altogether."

Fred grinned. "I don't like her so much myself, if it comes to that. She didn't look so old when she'd been blubbering all afternoon, did she? Now, Ma, don't look like that. I've done her no harm, and I'm not interested in doing her any. That's how it is. And now, for Pete's sake, come to bed."

Mrs. Helps searched her son's big handsome face. But it told her nothing. It never had. That smiling, innocent exterior had hidden so much always, whether it be devious plans for making money, or the latest girl who had taken his fancy. Fred cheerfully grinned his way through life, trusting to his luck to get him through. He would seem to be kind, but his kindness would turn to callousness in a moment. She couldn't trust him. What had she done in all her hardworking life to deserve this?

Although Jones had no news of the kidnapping to tell his wife and excite her out of boredom and apathy, yet for some reason she, too, could not sleep that night.

She had felt much better that day, she told Jones when he arrived home, and had even done a little of her embroidery. She had also combed her hair herself, and put on lipstick.

Jones was delighted. He sat on the side of the bed, and admired the faded gold hair, still a little wild in spite of its combing, and the lipstick, too bright and slightly askew, but nevertheless giving a transient animation to Nell's wan face.

"Was Miss Lane kinder today?" he asked.

"Not really, but I spoke up and told her what I wanted, and she had to do it. She just had to." Nell giggled with pleasure, like a petted child, and Jones said approvingly.

"That's the way. Soon you'll be telling her where she gets off, eh?"

The animation died in his wife's eyes. "But then I'd have no one. Would I?"

"Nonsense! There are hundreds of nicer women in the world than Miss Lane."

"But would they look after me? A poor little creature like me?" Nell's pitiful eyes searched his face. Jones felt the habitual anger and indignation burning in him.

"Of course they would!" he said emphatically. "I'd make them. You'd see."

Nell giggled again, with her swift change from pathos to pleasure.

"Mr. Palmer's lucky to have someone like you to look after him. But you do tell him not to keep you late at nights, don't you? Sometimes it seems so long before you come home."

"I'm no later than usual, love. Actually, I was just leaving when he called to me to fix drinks. You have to leave things exactly where he can find them, you see. And he was expecting Harriet down to do some work. Zoe doesn't half like that, I might tell you. She's waiting for wedding bells, and she thinks Harriet's cooking her goose."

Nell listened, absorbed. She adored her husband's mixed metaphors. She loved him to speak familiarly of the people he saw by their first names. Harriet, Zoe. . . . Once there had been a Linda, and a Margot. But Zoe had lasted the longest. She was the one Nell expected to win. Though why should an attractive girl want to marry a blind man? Just the same as why should her own devoted husband remain so devoted to a sick, useless woman?

She frowned, with her transient sorrow, then listened again to the fascinating story of events in that, to her, fabulous flat.

"What about Jamie? Was he in today?"

"No, we didn't see him. Millie, the new girl, seems to keep him quieter. She's young and energetic, of course. Though I wouldn't trust her, I might say. She's flirting with Fred, and before long I can see her mind won't be on her job. I'm wondering how I can drop a word to Harriet if she doesn't see for herself."

"Oh!" said Nell pleasurably, "you can't interfere."

"Perhaps I could drop the word to Mr. Palmer," Jones reflected. "That's if he doesn't see for himself. Mind you, he doesn't see, not with his eyes, but he doesn't miss much, I can tell you. Now, love, I'm to make your hot drink and tuck you up."

"Tell some more," Nell pleaded.

"Not tonight, love. You'll get over-excited and then you won't sleep, and no more will I. And I'm a bit tired tonight."

At six o'clock, in the narrow house by the river, while she was waiting for the telephone to ring, the doorbell rang instead.

Eve was in a panic. Was it him? He had never come without ringing first, and then being at least three quarters of an hour on his way. It couldn't be him, but if not who was it? Was it safe to open the door? Would there be a policeman standing there?

She tried frantically to peep out of the window first, but without throwing it open and sticking her head out she couldn't see a thing. The caller was out of sight.

As she hesitated Jamie called impertinently. "there's someone at your door. Aren't you going to open it? Shall I?"

"No, you stay where you are," she said sharply, and pulled the living room door firmly shut. Then she patted her short dark hair tidy and went, with exaggerated composure, to the door.

On the doorstep, in the damp foggy half-light, stood a completely strange woman, plump and rather blowsy.

"You're Miss Smith, aren't you?" she said in a friendly voice.

Eve nodded. (That was another thing, he had suggested she didn't use her real name when she took this house. It was always useful to have a nom de plume.)

"I saw you coming in with the children this afternoon. Didn't know you were having guests, even such small ones." The woman gave a loud hearty laugh. "Wondered if I could do anything for you, lend you extra milk or anything? I always like to see young ones about. I said as much to my husband. I'm going over to make myself known, I said. Never know when a neighbor can lend a helping hand, especially to newcomers in the district. Oh, I live next door," she explained belatedly.

Wouldn't you know! thought Eve, panic-stricken. It had been such a reckless plan. She had told him so, but he had just said that the most reckless schemes were the successful ones if you just carried them off with aplomb. Aplomb. That had been his word.

"That's kind of you," she said hurriedly, to the too-friendly and obviously too-inquisitive caller. "But right now we're doing fine. They're my sister's children, only here for a couple of days while their mother is in the hospital."

Aplomb—that was it.

"Ah, dear, poor thing. Not serious, I hope."

Visions of desperate struggles for life glazed the woman's eyes. She reveled in other people's troubles, that was obvious. The only thing to do, Eve realized, was to have no troubles.

"Not at all serious, thank you. And thank you for calling."

Her voice was final. The large foot reluctantly withdrew from the doorstep.

"Just a neighborly thing to do, Miss Smith. I think of you here all by yourself. Bit damp for a young lady, I says."

"I am not alone at present," Eve said pointedly.

"No, that's true. Well, if I can do anything for the little ones just give me a shout. My name's Mrs. Briggs. Goodnight then, Miss Smith."

Nosey Parker, Eve muttered, as she shut the door. Now what? Certainly he had had the forethought to tell her to drop the word around judicially that she was having a baby for a day or two. But even he had known that there were going to be two children, one a very shrewd five-year-old who could use his tongue far too much. Supposing these inquisitive neighbors hung around and got into conversation with the boy.

There was only one answer to that. He had to be kept out of sight. Down in the basement, out of sight and sound.

The baby began to cry again as she went back into the living room. She had been fretful all the time, whimpering when Eve appeared and screaming when she was picked up. The boy had not cried. He had merely stared. Everything Eve had done had met with this disconcerting stare from large gray eyes beneath a lowering forehead.

Eve had to confess to herself that she was a little scared of the boy. When he found his tongue and began to act he would be quite unmanageable. And then what? Another neighborly visit from the inquisitive Mrs. Briggs?

But if only the baby would stop crying. She had changed her as well as possible for someone completely inexperienced, and tried to make her drink some milk. She had put her on the floor and given her sundry objects to play with. All these overtures the child had met with her high-pitched scream, while the boy had stood squarely watching and giving his disdainful stare.

Eve was on the verge of screaming herself. Never again, no matter how much money there was in it. He had said it would be child's play. Child's play, indeed!

"Look now, stop crying, do!" she begged the scarlet-faced baby. She turned to the watching boy. "Does she always cry like this?"

"No."

"Then why is she now?"

"I expect she wants to go home, the same as I do."

"Well, you can't go home tonight. I've told you that. And you needn't hang your lip. It's your own fault you're here. If you hadn't interferred you wouldn't have had to come."

"You were taking Arabella away. I had to look after her. Mummy always said I had to."

"All right, then. So you looked after her. What's your name?"

"Jamie. And it's none of your business. We don't like you. That's why Arabella cries."

Eve regarded the belligerent freckled face with

dislike and alarm. The thing was, what *he* would say when he knew the boy was here. But what else could she have done, just all in a minute like that?

"I'll get you some supper," she said shortly, "and then you'll both go to bed."

"I want to go home," said Jamie, with his air of delivering an ultimatum.

"You can stop that sort of talk because I've told you you're not going home tonight."

"My mother will be pretty cross with you."

Eve gave a crooked smile.

"Well, until they come you can eat your supper without a fuss."

The thing was to get through the time. About thirty-six hours. He had said that was all it would be. But what about now that the boy was here, too? If only he would ring so she could tell him.

Yet when he did ring she hadn't the courage to say anything. He sounded so tense and grim. He would hurl angry words at her, making her shrivel up with hurt and fear if she told him now. She would have to wait until he came, and then give him a drink and make love to him, getting him into a good mood first.

"Was it all right?" came his tense whisper.

"Yes. Yes, it was all right."

"No one spoke to you?"

"No one except the taxi driver. Oh, and Mrs. Briggs."

"Who the devil is Mrs. Briggs?"

"The next door neighbor. She saw me come home although I walked from the corner as you told me to."

"What did you tell her?"

She smiled with satisfaction at her quick wittedness.

"That they"—hastily she corrected herself, "that the baby was my sister's child, who was in the hospital."

He grunted, neither approving nor disapproving.

"The baby's been crying like mad. Darling, you're coming, aren't you?"

"I don't think——"

"But you must, you must! I can't do all this time alone. Not thirty-six hours. It all seems easy and simple when you're here. But I'm scared when I'm alone. Honest!"

"Crazy girl!" he had relaxed, for his voice had the caressing note in it.

Suddenly, with her ability to live entirely in the present, she saw nothing more than the evening ahead, the room cozy in the firelight, the couch drawn up to the hearth, only the light of the flames to show her his face, shadowed and exciting, his hands reaching out for her. . . .

Putting down the telephone she hugged her arms around her thin body in momentary ecstatic anticipation.

Then the belligerent voice of the small boy behind her said, "I don't like bread and milk. I'm not going to eat it."

She spun around, tense and anger.

"Then go to bed without it. And in the basement where no one will hear you if you start yelling. In fact, I'll show you what will happen to you if you do yell."

She pushed the child ahead of her to the small window at the end of the passage. It gave a dim view of sliding yellowish gray water and mist.

"There's the river, see. I could open this window and let you fall right into it, and no one would even hear the splash."

The boy's eyes were widened in disbelief.
"You wouldn't do that."

She permitted herself a thin smile.

"Not if you keep quiet and behave yourself. Anyway, I'm going to make sure you'll be quiet."

She thought she'd always liked kids, she reflected, with ironic amusement. So she had, too, but not when they were forced on you in this guilty way. And now she was so pleased and excited about his coming, and everything being nice for him, that she couldn't bear to tell him about Jamie. Not at the beginning, anyway. Just before he left, so that it wouldn't have spoiled the evening.

She had the brilliant idea of putting some brandy in the milk and persuading the children to drink it. It wouldn't hurt them, but just make them a little tipsy so that they'd sleep soundly. The trouble was to get them to drink it. But the baby was hungry enough now, and Jamie, after some more hints about the silent yellow river outside, finally drank his, his small squarish face wrinkled in disgust, his eyes still defiantly tearless.

After that it was easy enough to get them to bed in the basement room, the baby in the packing case she had made into a dry cosy bed, and Jamie on an old mattress on the floor. Jamie's bed was not what it should be, but she hadn't known he was coming so could not be expected to have prepared for him. The room smelled damp and airless, but the children couldn't hurt for one night, surely. And now she was free to go upstairs and wait for the doorbell to ring.

At the beginning, the evening was all she had hoped for. He was pleased with her.

"I told you it would be easy, didn't I? Nothing to it. Money picked up in the street."

"There's still tomorrow," she said cautiously.

"Oh, that'll be no trouble. I've studied psychology, you see. I pick on people who'll react the way I want them to."

Like me? she asked provocatively.

He grinned. His teeth were white in the dim light, his eyes gleaming. Already his hand was running over her with the familiarity of possession.

"You haven't done too badly so far."

"Oh, I was scared at first."

"Course you were. Only natural. But you just have to keep your head and reason things out, see. Know your opponent, know what she'll do."

"Mighty clever, aren't you? You like yourself, don't you?" She was laughing a little, rubbing her cheek against his. "Don't be in such a hurry! Aren't we going to have a drink first?"

"Might do. Might like your dress off, first."

They were both pleased with themselves, enjoying the reaction from tension, but the tension was still there, like a coiled snake, waiting for the slightest disturbance to make it strike.

The disturbance came when the door into the dim, firelit room opened and a hard yellow beam of light from the passageway shone in.

Eve leaped up with a stifled scream. The man instinctively sank lower in the couch, out of sight.

"I was sick," came Jamie's flat voice. "That milk you gave me made me sick."

Psychology! thought Eve contemptuously afterwards. He might have understood the mother's psychology, and knew that she would inevitably pay the money without going to the police, knowing that the method would be the most likely to ensure her children's safety. But what about the psychology of the unexpected? That little tricky thing, human na-

ture. How was she to have known that the boy would
be there in the street, grabbing his sister and threatening to yell blue murder?

He wouldn't see it that way. He was coldly, furiously angry. After she had cleaned up Jamie and
got him back into bed, shivering and miserable but
still dourly refusing to cry, she had to face that
scene in the living room.

All the charm had gone now. He was muffled into
his coat ready to go, to leave her once more alone,
with the long hours till morning ahead of her, and
all the next difficult day. She was utterly exhausted,
too, shivering as Jamie had been, but he didn't care
about that.

He lashed her with his tongue, his eyes blazing.
He wouldn't admit that she had done the only possible thing. He said she had come near to wrecking
the whole scheme, and it would be only a miracle
if it now succeeded. A boy of five who could talk and
remember! It was suicidal! The one thing that could
possibly save them was that so far the boy knew
very little, only that he was in a strange house by
the river to which he had been brought in a taxi.
He could not know what part of London it was, nor
was it likely he would be able to identify the house
again. But if he found out too much. . . .

Eve felt a strange little shiver running down her
back as she looked into the intense eyes.

"If you let that pokey-nose neighbor come prying,
or let the boy overhear anything, or mention me—"
his eyes bored into her, "there's only one thing to do.
And you know what that is, don't you?"

Instinctively Eve glanced around to the small window at the end of the passage. She couldn't hear
the river, nor could she see it in the darkness. But

she could imagine the cold hiss of the water and the
wreathing fog. . . .

It had been one thing to threaten the boy herself,
but this was different, this was cold and diabolical.

"No, no!" she whispered. "No!"

"You've got us into this mess."

"It wasn't my fault. I tell you!" Her face puckered
up pathetically. "Oh, I never knew it was going to
be like this or I'd never have said I'd do it. You
said it would be easy. Child's play, you said."

He gave a brief, humorless smile.

"So it is, if you play it the right way. Chin up,
love, and mind what I said. Now I'm off."

"Oh, stay—"

But that plea was no use, she knew. Already, he
had opened the door and was looking stealthily out to
see that the footpath was deserted, and all the
houses, apparently, asleep.

A chilly breath of river fog swirled into the house.
Eve listened to his light, quick footsteps, growing
faint in the distance. Now he was only a dark shape,
now he was gone, swallowed in the dank mist. Closing the door, she began to tremble violently. She had
never felt so alone in her life.

XI

IT WAS MORNING. Mrs. Blunt had arrived and was proceeding to deposit her things about the kitchen, the old shapeless coat that wilted into shabby insignificance when not adorning Mrs. Blunt's plump figure, the equally shapeless hat, the string bag that no matter the time of day was filled with bulging packages which occasionally spilled out such articles as brussels sprouts or cracker biscuits.

"Good morning," she called cheerfully. "Everyone slept in this morning?"

The night had been like a lifetime. But it was over. Everything was over in time. Even today and the coming night would pass. Harriet tried to rub the tiredness out of her eyes.

"You don't need to stay long today, Mrs. Blunt. The children are away and there isn't much to do."

"But Millie and me were going to wash down the bathroom walls." Mrs. Blunt stopped to stare. "You didn't tell me the children were going away!"

"No, I didn't. I decided rather suddenly I wasn't feeling well and I thought a couple of days with one of my aunts in the country would be a good idea for them."

"That'll be a nice change for them," Mrs. Blunt said cheerily. "What part of the country, madam?"

"Oh—Sussex."

"I didn't know you had an aunt so close, madam. I thought all your family was down west."

"Did you?" Harriet let that pass. She could not make endless explanations to her daily woman.

"Bless me, the place will be quiet today. Never mind, that means Millie and me can do a good job. Will you be going to he theater, madam?"

"Oh—oh, yes. And I have to go out this morning, too."

Mrs. Blunt shook her head disapprovingly.

"Tch, tch! And you looking so poorly. Be sure to wrap up well. It's real pneumonia weather. I'll leave a note, as usual, if there's anything I want to tell you. Perhaps we could give the children's room a good turn-out while they're away. I hope Millie's feeling energetic."

Later, when Harriet was dressing, she heard Mrs. Blunt's raucous voice, "Gawd! You look like something the cat brought home. What's wrong with you?"

And Millie's exhausted whine. "Overslept."

"Well, some hard work will just set you up nicely. I must say you got yourself a good job. Not a week, and the children go on holiday. Now isn't that funny. Mrs. Lacey never mentioned that she had an aunt in Sussex. There's the telephone. Are you going to answer it? Good gracious, girl, you're all of a dither. Are you expecting your boyfriend? Or the police?"

"I'll answer that," Harriet called crisply.

"Just as well," she heard Mrs. Blunt muttering. "Looks as if Millie has lost her wits today."

The caller was merely Flynn. He wanted to know how Harriet was.

"Quite well, thank you," she said politely.

"Good. Those tablets knock one out, don't they?"

"They do, indeed," Harriet agreed, thinking of the

tablets lying untouched on her bedside table. Because much as she had longed to sink into oblivion last night, she had not dared to. She had kept thinking some message might come. Millie's tension about the telephone had been infectious. They had both found themselves listening, ready to start at the first ping of the bell.

"Is the sun shining?"

"No. It's very gray. It looks like snow."

"Oh, hell! What can one do?"

She realized then, with compassion, that each day began as an enemy to him. Later in the morning it would improve. Jones would come, as likely as not Zoe would drop in, the telephone would ring, the mail would arrive, there would be things to do, and slowly the day's hostility would be overcome.

But the beginning was bleak.

He ought not to be alone, she thought. He ought to marry Zoe? No, not after yesterday's revelation. One of the other lighthearted and pretty girls from his former life who periodically called on him? Any one of them, if she dispelled his loneliness.

Where did Zoe live? Was it she who had played this macabre trick? From jealousy, hate, need of money?

"Harriet, come down and work this morning."

"I'm sorry, Flynn. I can't. I have some business to do in town."

"Can't it wait?"

"No, it's urgent, I'm afraid."

"A fine secretary you are!"

"I know. I'm sorry."

"Harriet, are you sure you're not worried about something?"

"You asked me that last night and I said no." She was so tense, so unreasonably irritated by his persistence that it was difficult to reply politely. "Even if I were, really, it would be no concern of yours."

"On the contrary." His voice was light, but she knew she shouldn't have said that. Now, with his too acute perception, he would be convinced that something was wrong. "But I won't pry if you don't want me to."

"Oh, Flynn, there's nothing to pry about." How long could she keep her voice casual and light? "By the way, if Zoe, comes in, do remember to get her address. It's important."

She hung up before he could inevitably begin to ask questions. She was sorry about the blank morning in front of him, but she could not have him to worry about, too. That was too much to endure.

The thing was to get through the hours until tomorrow morning. Ten o'clock now. The banks would be open. She could get the money and arrange it into an inconspicuous and innocent parcel. Was she doing right or wrong? Should she have rung the police? What sort of a night had Jamie and Arabella had? Had they cried? Had they thought she had deserted them? *Oh, Joe, what should I have done?*

The winter roses were still blooming in her bedroom, fresh and unfaded. That was how little time had gone by. The colored photograph of Arabella on the dressing table, taken to send a copy to her grandmother in Boston, showed her fine, red-gold curls, like Harriet's, the hair Joe had admired. Had anyone brushed Arabella'a hair this morning?

Joe's picture beside it was an adult picture of Jamie, ugly, good-humored and lovable. Would Joe blame her for this frightening thing that had happened?

She shivered as she put on her fur coat, one of Joe's last presents. The only other valuable thing he had been able to give her were her diamond earrings. They were in her jewel box at the back of the glove drawer. No, they weren't. That was funny. Well, never mind, she would remember later where she had put them. It was immaterial now. She occasionally changed their hiding place, for no apparent reason, as a burglar had only to find them once.

She had to go now to get that money from the bank. It was lucky she had had a remittance from Joe's mother in Boston only last month, and that it was in the bank, untouched as yet.

Looking at her strained white face in the mirror, still wan in spite of makeup, she wondered fleetingly if Joe would know her, supposing she met him in the elevator on the way out. Two strangers meeting, a woman with a white anxious face, a man with Jamie's adorable grin.

"Please take down exactly any telephone message that might come," she instructed Mrs. Blunt.

Mrs. Blunt looked aggrieved.

"I always do that, madame, to the last letter."

Remembering Mrs. Blunt's multitudinous notes scattered about the flat in the places appropriate to their contents, Harriet agreed. Mrs. Blunt would make a good landlady. "Do not bath after 11 P.M. Do not bang the front door. Them as has no consideration for others can't expect it themselves. . . ."

Was she a little lightheaded? Or was her brain desperately chasing foolish thoughts to escape the real ones?

She saw no one except Fred as she left the flats. In his working overalls, but still looking handsome and virile, he came over to her and whispered, "Any news?"

She shook her head silently. Fred's eyes were sympathetic, and she couldn't face them and keep her composure. She hurried on, and catching a bus in High Street, made her journey to the bank through the leafless dark morning. She had thought it might be difficult to get five hundred pounds in single notes. The cashier certainly looked at her oddly, and no doubt thought she was planning some surreptitious under-the-counter deal. But after verifying her check he counted out the money and suggested that she should have a bag to put it in. She hadn't thought of that, she was so wooley-headed. She had to cram the bundles of notes into her handbag until it bulged.

But she did have the sense to do one other thing before she returned home. She got off the bus at the Albert Hall and walked across to the Round Pond, carefully noticing the isolated and lonely seat which she must visit that evening.

It had begun to rain, and from overhanging twigs large drops fell with a flat, plopping sound. A faint wind had begun to whine through the bare branches. The mist hanging about the avenues of tree trunks was smoke gray, the water of the Round Pond glassy. Flynn had asked if the sun was shining. Suddenly Harriet felt that it would never shine again.

Mrs. Blunt was beaming all over her round face when Harriet arrived home.

"No messages," she said, "but look in here!"

For one wild joyful moment Harriet thought it must be the children safely home and unharmed.

But it was not. It was flowers, a bower of flowers, tulips, white lilac, daffodils, anemones. The colors burst like a rainbow on her tired eyes. And the room smelled like a funeral.

Even Millie had brightened, obviously deeply impressed by someone who could spend so much money on flowers.

"They must have cost him a fortune," she said.
"Him? Who?"

"Mr. Palmer. There's a note there somewhere. Jones brought all these up. He says Mr. Palmer's gone quite mad. He's got new phonograph records and books, and there's a grouse coming up, and champagne."

The note simply said, "Now is the sun shining?"

But mine is not your sort of darkness, Flynn dear, she whispered to herself.

And neither kind can be cured by this sort of foolish, charming lavishness.

And of course you didn't know that today flowers made me think of funerals. . . .

"You have to ring him as soon as you come in," Millie went on, "because there's something else."

Zoe's address? But she hadn't wanted Flynn to guess the urgency of that requirement.

"He wanted Jamie, you see," Millie whispered hurriedly, her eyes dilated again with the terror that had come there yesterday. "I said, like you told me, that he was in the country."

"I'm off now," Mrs. Blunt called from the kitchen.

"And he didn't believe you?" Harriet said in a low voice.

Millie shook her head. "I don't think so. I haven't been out and I haven't talked to anyone, the way you told me not to, but I didn't know what to do about this."

"Good-bye," called Mrs. Blunt. "I've left you a note in the bathroom, madam. It's about soap. And have a good rest while the children are away. It will do you good."

The door slammed shut. Harriet said tensely,
"Millie, you didn't tell him?"

"No, I didn't. At least, not completely. But he

guessed something was wrong. Oh, Mrs. Lacey, what are we going to do?"

Millie's gulping, hopeless sobs were too much. The cold mist from the park had come into the flower-filled room.

"I'll have to phone him," Harriet said, speaking to herself. But how now was she to banish his suspicions?

It was inevitable that he should be on the telephone before she had had time to think of a plan.

"Hello, my love," he said cheerily. "Zoe can't come to lunch, so you are invited instead. Grouse and champagne. Jones is cooking the sprouts. How are they, Jones? Oh, he says they're fine. So at one o'clock, please."

"Second best?" queried Harriet, with a faint and uncharacteristic attempt at coyness.

"Because Zoe can't come? Not actually, but I had expected her. The greedy little hound enjoys a free meal."

· "She has a job that's going to take most of the day."

"Did you find out where she lives?"

"Harriet, you have an obsession about this."

"I tell you, I need to know."

"Well, it's down by the river in some Godforsaken spot. Some lane. I wrote it down. You can see when you come down. Now what's this about the children being away? Why have I been kept in the dark? I particularly wanted Jamie today. I've got a puppy we're going to share. Jamie's to be responsible for the exercising. Jones will have to do the house-training. He's a golden cocker, blueblooded or golden-blooded or whatever one would say."

Harriet could hear the boyish enthusiasm in his voice. She had never heard it before. She should have been pleased for both his and Jamie's pleasure. Her lips were dry.

"That's wonderful Flynn. Jamie will be enchanted. But the children are in the country at present. Millie told you. Flynn, thank you a thousand times for the flowers. You've been wickedly extravagant."

"Harriet, the children are not in the country."

His unexpected accusation had her off her guard.

"How—do you know?" she asked, and then was lost.

"For one thing, you'd have told me last night. For another, Jamie would have come down to say good-bye to me. We're good friends, Jamie and I, so naturally he wouldn't go off without telling me. What is this enormous secret? Have they been kidnapped?"

"S-sh!" The frightened exclamation forced itself out of her, and then she stood gripping the telephone with damp palms, while Millie peered around the doorway, goggle-eyed and dumb.

"Harriet, come down here at once." His voice was calm, matter-of-fact, somehow immensely reassuring. "Then you can tell me everything that is worrying you."

He was waiting at the door when she went down.

"What is this, Harriet? Are you romancing?"

"I wish I were."

"Come and sit down. Jones will get us a drink." He took her arm and led her across to the fire. The puppy, golden-yellow and fat, slept in a basket. Jamie was going to adore him.

Jones appeared with a tray of drinks. His long face was lugubrious.

"What can I offer you, madam?"

"Give her a double whisky, Jones. Now, Harriet, what is this all about? You say the children have disappeared. But that's preposterous. Don't go away,

Jones. You must hear this, too. Do you mind, Harriet? He may have seen something that will be of help. Let's have the story."

He was so calm and quiet that her own panic died and she was able to tell the story quietly, almost as if she were talking of someone else's children and someone else's heartbreak.

It was Jones who gave the exclamation of shock and incredulity. Flynn merely said, "Where's the letter? I hope you haven't covered it with fingerprints. The police will want it."

Harriet sat up sharply.

"No, Flynn! That's just what I don't mean to do. That's why I've told nobody about this except Fred and Mrs. Helps. Because I won't risk having the police brought in. Don't you see, I *can't?*"

"Frankly, I don't see that at all. In my opinion you have been quite mad not to have got hold of them at once."

"No, Flynn, I refuse. I want my children safely back. I told you what was in the note."

"Bluff."

"It may be bluff. It may be deadly earnest. Don't you see that I can't risk it."

"And so you'll let this villain escape."

"What do I care what happens to him so long as I get my children back?"

"Harriet, my dear, do you really think you can trust the word of someone who will do such a thing as kidnap babies?"

She pressed her fingers to her temples.

"I don't know. I don't know, but I've got to try. It's a better chance this way. I know it is."

The puppy in the basket yawned and turned around, with laborious care. The fire sparked. The moon was warm and bright. Fear seemed a stupid and an ill-mannered thing to have in here.

"Jones," said Flynn sharply, "you're listening to this. What do you think?"

Jones stepped forward, his long face thoughtfully serious.

"I agree with you, sir. I think the police should be called. But on the other hand they're Mrs. Lacey's children, and I expect it's her job to make this decision."

"We're all in it now," Flynn said. "We should have been in it from the beginning. Where's that letter, Harriet? Oh, God, I can't *see!*"

Jones took the letter from Harriet. His actions were always neat and unobtrusive, the perfectly trained servant.

"It's the way Mrs. Lacey described it, sir. Words cut out of a newspaper."

"Read it again."

Jones did so, but in his flat voice the words sounded theatrical and unreal. One wondered why one could be so terrified by them.

"He refers to only one child," Flynn said. "Obviously he wouldn't mean to take Jamie, a child who can talk and remember and identify."

"Yes, we realized that." Harriet agreed. "But yesterday he would have seen Millie leave with only Arabella. He had probably been waiting for that opportunity for days. That's if it is a man."

"You think it might be a woman?"

"Millie has been talking about this strange blonde woman, the one Jones caught a glimpse of the other day. I thought she was imagining things, but now one doesn't know what to think.

"Jones, you were about at that time yesterday. Did you happen to notice anything at all?"

"I'm afraid not, sir. I didn't even see when Millie took the children out."

"Do you think Millie's telling the entire truth, Harriet?"

Harriet sighed wearily. "How does one know? She simply bursts into tears when one says anything at all. But one thing is certain, she's had a nasty shock. She's absolutely terrified."

"The police would question everybody. Someone in the flats must have seen something."

"It didn't happen at the flats; it happened outside Woolworth's at the busiest time of the day, when no one would notice a child cry, much less who took it away."

"Harriet, my sweet numbskull, this a most urgent police job."

"All right," said Harriet bitterly, "fill the place with police. And have my babies dredged out of the river or suffocated in a cupboard."

"Oh, Mrs. Lacey!" exclaimed Jones in a shocked voice.

"Well, can't that happen? Don't you agree?"

"In America, perhaps—"

"This may be an American kidnapper, someone who knows of Joe's family in Boston. How does one know who it is? But one thing I do know. I have the money. I drew it out of the bank this morning. The kidnapper gets his chance to return the children safely."

"You really think he'll ring you and tell you where they are?"

"I have to take that chance."

"There I agree with Mrs. Lacey, sir," Jones put in. "He'd prefer to do that rather than have two kids to feed. Or shall I say two corpses on his hands? You have to be realistic, sir. They're flesh and blood and can't disappear into thin air when they've served their purposes, so to speak."

"Unless he becomes greedy and asks for more money."

"Flynn, stop it!" Harriet cried. "I can't stand this. Just stay out of it, will you? And you, too, Jones, with your horrible suggestions."

"Jones is thinking of the smashing story he'll have to tell his wife tonight." Flynn's voice was full of its old bitter sarcasm.

"That isn't quite fair, sir," Jones said in a hurt voice.

"All right, all right, I'm sorry." Flynn got up and began walking about the room, slashing at things with his stick. "Nothing's fair on this beautiful planet. You won't have the police. I'm as much use to you as that fat spaniel in the basket—"

"Flynn! Flynn!" His sudden impotent rage had the effect of calming Harriet, and she went to take his arm. "If this fails tonight, I promise you tomorrow I will get the police."

"Heaven's above, that may be too late!"

"On the other hand, there is something you can do for me. Take me out to Zoe's."

"Zoe's?"

"Yes, I don't suppose I'm right, but she may have been playing a trick on me."

"A trick like this!"

"I know it seems improbable. I suppose it is. But she was very upset yesterday, and a jealous woman can lose her sense of proportion. She may have decided it would be amusing to give me a fright. And you must admit she has been mysterious about her address."

"Damned mysterious. I only pried it out of her when I asked her where to address a case of champagne! It's a forlorn hope, but we can try it. Jones will drive us. Go and get the car out, Jones."

"Before lunch, sir?" Jones turned an anguished glance towards the kitchen, from which appetizing aromas were coming.

"Instantly."

XII

MILLIE HATED to be left alone now. She wanted to protest when Mrs. Lacey went down to Mr. Palmer's, but even more so when Mrs. Lacey rushed up to get her coat and said she would be out for an hour or so. It wasn't fair to be the one who was told to stay in in case the telephone rang. Mrs. Lacey wouldn't like to be there alone herself, with that sinister voice likely to speak in her ear at any time the telephone rang. But then Mrs. Lacey didn't know about the sinister voice. Only Millie knew that. The secret was so frightening that she didn't think she could keep it much longer. She would almost rather go to prison.

The flat was so empty! It made her feel queer to see the children's toys. Mrs. Blunt had tidied them up, with some puzzled remarks about it being strange that Arabella hadn't wanted to take her rabbit or Jamie his very prized set of trucks. But tidied up was almost worse than having them scattered about. It looked as if they were neatly put away forever.

Oh, dear, how her head ached. For two pins she'd go home, except for all the questions Mum would ask. And, of course, giving up Fred. Why didn't Fred ring? It was funny that he didn't. He would have seen Mrs. Lacey leave in Mr. Palmer's Bentley, and know that she was alone. It was really

mean of him not to when he knew how upset she
must be.

Supposing she rang him. That was the idea. That
also would save her the awful cold feeling of dread
she got every time the telephone rang.

She dialed the number of the basement flat and
waited eagerly. Oh blow! It was Fred's mother who
answered.

"Hello, Mrs. Helps. This is Millie here."

"Who?"

"Millie. From Mrs. Lacey's flat. Can I speak to
Fred?"

"Oh, Millie." The old lady's tone was faintly acid.
"Fred's on duty. He can't speak to you now."

"I wish you'd tell him I want to see him, Mrs.
Helps."

"What do you want to see him about?" Yes, the
old lady's voice was definitely suspicious. Silly old—
geezer.

"Oh, just things, I'm all alone up here and Mrs.
Lacey said I mustn't go out. I'm that lonely."

But that last pathetic plea had no effect on Fred's
mother.

"You wouldn't be if you'd taken better care of
those children." Her voice was sharp, yet it seemed
to have something desperate and frightened in it, as
if they were her children, for goodness' sake!

"You will tell Fred, won't you, Mrs. Helps?"

"I'll tell him you were ringing."

The phone clicked implacably, Millie sniffed and
sighed. Silly old fool! What would she have done if
she had been threatened the way Millie had been?
After all, the children would be back later tonight,
wouldn't they, and no one the worse for it except for
Mrs. Lacey losing five hundred pounds. But she could
afford that. Look at the lovely flat. Some people

didn't know how lucky they were.

But supposing, after the children were back, that blackmailer threatened her again about the earrings! She hadn't thought of that.

Oh, Fred, it was all your fault! she thought despairingly. You made me lose them.

The telephone gave a preliminary ping which nearly made her jump out of her skin, and then began to ring steadily.

Millie looked at it in frozen horror.

Oh, but it would be Fred, she suddenly remembered joyfully. His mother had given him her message and he'd ring instantly, the darling.

She picked up the receiver and sang gaily, "Hello!"

"Is that you, Millie?"

There was no mistaking the husky whispering voice, anonymous, sexless. Millie wanted to drop the receiver as if it were red hot, as if it would bite a piece out of her plump young cheek. But like a magnet it hugged to her ear.

"H-how do you know my name?" she asked quaveringly.

There was a hoarse chuckling, low and dreadful.

"I know a lot. I made it my business to. Tell me, has Mrs. Lacey called the police?"

"No-no."

"Good. That's what I wanted to know. See that she doesn't. That's a good girl. Au revoir, now. If you don't know what that means, it means you will be hearing from me again."

To the accompaniment of the hoarse chuckling the receiver clicked and went dead.

Millie stood rigid. She couldn't stay here alone! She just couldn't. She'd run down and find Fred. But no, she couldn't. Because he knew nothing about these telephone threats, and if she told him she would have to admit her guilt. She would go home, pack her things and run away. But Mum would want to know why. Mum always ferreted things out, and she was a stickler for honesty. She would think it her duty to tell the police. And that way Millie would lose Fred forever. . . .

There was nothing she could do. There was no one to help her. She had to stay. But she felt so terribly alone, as if there were no one else in the world. . . .

Harriet, who had been nervous in fast cars ever since Joe's death, was urging Jones to break speed limits. She was not happy about leaving Millie in the flat alone. The girl seemed to have become quite stupid, scarcely taking in what was said to her, and obviously in a state of constant terror. It was doubtful whether she would be able to take a telephone message correctly, or whether she would behave sensibly if anything at all happened. Besides, one had to be a little sorry for her, when she was suffering from such acute shock and remorse. Perhaps Fred would go up and talk to her. One could only hope she would not be foolish enough to leave the flat and talk indiscriminately outside.

She scarcely noticed the direction in which they were going. If Zoe were perfectly innocent what was she going to say about their bursting in like this? But it was all so strange and suspicious. She had been so mysterious about her address; she had refused to lunch with Flynn when hitherto her day had revolved on Flynn's wishes. If she were engaged on a macabre practical joke such as this she was giving the whole day to it, perhaps hoping Harriet would discover the children earlier, perhaps seriously planning to collect the money this evening for her own use. . . .

No, these were fantastic thoughts. The kidnapper

would be some anonymous person off the street, who had watched assiduously and laid his plans, some thin, desperate, wandering straw in the wind, leaving no clues because of his anonymity.

The back of Jones's head was long and narrow, like his face. He drove with the same unobtrusive ability with which he prepared meals and valeted Flynn's clothes.

"Where are we now?" asked Flynn, with that edge of impatience in his voice?

Jones half-turned his head.

"Just crossing Battersea Bridge, sir."

"Lord, what sort of a place does Zoe live in? Why doesn't she tell me if she's short of money? She's the last person I would have thought to have false pride. What did you say, Harriet?"

"I said nothing."

"You sniffed. Or you did whatever is the modern equivalent of the expressive Victorian sniff. Open the window, would you mind?"

"It's very cold."

"At least I can smell the water, can't I?"

His touchy rejoinder shamed her. She opened a window, and the ice cold wind came sweeping in.

"Just for a minute," he apologized. "I used to row on this stretch of river. Are there any swans?"

"I can't see any. Only barges and a tug and a few seagulls. And, of course, the power station. The water is the color of dirty mud."

Flynn patted her hand. "My love, if I'm to hire the use of your eyes, they'll occasionally have to see more charming things. No swans? Only dirty mud. Jones does better than that. What can you see, Jones?"

"We're just turning off the bridge, sir. The houses here aren't what you'd call palatial, sir."

Harriet, to her extreme surprise, found herself laughing.

Then she knew that was what Flynn had meant to happen with his apparently idle chatter. Perhaps he had been trying to make himself laugh, too. Passing remembered spots, with no eyes to see, would not be amusing.

"Where do you live, Jones?" she asked.

Jones didn't turn his head this time. "Well, we're sort of temporary, see," he said, as if Harriet were planning to go snooping. "Our place is too small and it's on the ground floor, and damp. I'm looking for something all the time. I want just the right place, so Nell won't have to shift again." He turned his head slightly. "We're coming to the street now, sir."

Flynn sat forward. "What's it like?"

"Facing the river, sir. Bit run-down looking."

Harriet looked at the row of narrow shabby houses, tightly packed, as if one supported the other. They all had the dreary look of second-rate rooming houses. Their paint was faded, and at high tide there was no doubt that water sometimes lapped into their basements.

Zoe, the smart and immaculate, with her pert air of self-sufficiency, lived here. But only recently, and probably only temporarily.

Harriet leaned forward tensely.

"Jones, it might be better if the car isn't seen. Park it around the corner. I'll go to the house."

"I, also," said Flynn.

"No, you wait here." Harriet laid her hand on his arm, restraining him. "Because if we're wrong how will you explain what we're doing?"

"How will you?" he retorted. "I, at least, have come to take her home to lunch. Anyway, if she spoke the truth she won't be there. If she didn't, I guess there's a reason."

"If only the children are here!" Harriet scarcely dared put that hope into words. Could it be possible? Could this nightmare end so simply?

The woman who opened the door was gaunt-faced and tired. She said shortly, "Miss Mansell ain't home."

"Oh, dear, how unfortunate!" said Flynn in his most beguiling voice. "And we'd come to take her out to lunch. Now, Harriet, isn't that too bad!"

Flynn has his arm tucked in Harriet's. They looked, Harriet reflected, like a respectably married couple, with none but the most friendly intentions towards Zoe. This was obviously what the woman was thinking, for her curtness relaxed a little, and she volunteered, "I can give her a message, if you like."

That was Harriet's opportunity, and she quickly seized it.

"I wonder if we could leave one ourselves in her room."

"I don't know as I should let you do that," the woman said doubtfully. "She locks her door, anyway."

"But you would have a key, wouldn't you? Actually we've walked quite a long way, and my husband gets tired. He hasn't been long out of the hospital."

Harriet felt Flynn's fingers tighten on her arm. She also noticed the woman's quickened interest as she looked at Flynns' dark glasses.

"Oh, dear, poor soul! Tch, tch, tch! Then you'd better come in. After all, if you're old friends of Miss Mansell's I expect it's all right. There's a step down into the hall. Mind that, sir. And some stairs to climb."

"Miss Mansell does live here alone, doesn't she?" Harriet asked casually.

"Oh, yes, madam."

Her thin figure had flitted away up the stairs ahead of them. In the clean, dingy hall, with its polished brown linoleum and brown and cream banisters, Harriet was overcome with disappointment and despair. It was no use. Her children were not here. One could see that.

"It's all a mistake," she whispered to Flynn. "I apologize to Zoe."

Tears filled her eyes. She was grateful, suddenly, that Flynn could not see them.

"It's all my fault. It was a foolish thing to think. Let's go home."

"No, let's go up and see the room now we are here," Flynn insisted. "One might as well know where the crazy kid lives."

His voice held concern and affection. It irritated Harriet who now could think of nothing but that they had followed a hopeless trail. Unreasonably, she expected him to be thinking of nothing but her children, also.

"But why bother? You can't see it when you do get there."

He didn't seem to mind her cruelly factual words. He said lightly, "On the contrary, your eyes are mine. What does this hall look like?"

"The rolling stock of the Great Western Railway."

"This way, sir," called the woman, out of sight along a passage at the top of the stairs. "There's a nasty turn halfway up."

"That's all right. My wife is used to helping me."

Harriet stiffened. He whispered, "You started this particular game."

"It seemed easier with a woman like her. More respectable."

"Oh, indeed. Respectability is the thing."

"Can't you manage the stairs, sir?" Harriet might not have been there any longer. All the woman's morbid attention was fixed on Flynn.

Flynn, curbing his sudden explosive anger, proceeded up the stairs as quickly as possible. A door was opened halfway down a narrow passage. The woman stood aside as Harriet, followed by Flynn, went into the simple shabby room. There was a window that looked over the river. Beneath it was a divan with a shabby cover. There were chairs, a threadbare carpet. Zoe's clothes hanging half-concealed behind a cretonne curtain that comprised the closet, and a clutter of cosmetics on the tiny dressing table.

But it was the center of the room that took Harriet's attention. On a circular table stood a hand sewing machine, and spread out beside it, covering the rest of the table, was a gleaming piece of cream-colored satin, cut out and pinned into the shape of a dress. A wedding dress.

The woman, with unexpected tact, had gone away. Flynn stood within the door, his head up in its arrogant manner, all his senses concentrated on forming an impression.

Why? Did he care so much where Zoe lived? Was his casual and sometimes impertinent attitude towards her a disguise covering his real feelings, which because of the intolerable fact of his blindness he would not show?

"Well," he said impatiently, "What's it like? Has the girl a bed to sleep in?"

Of course it was a wedding dress. Zoe was making it herself. Probably she made all her clothes. If she were a clever enough dressmaker, as she seemed to be, that would explain why she could look so smart, and yet have so little money.

But the wedding dress was for her wedding to Flynn. She must have counted on achieving that very soon indeed. Since Flynn had not so far made the anticipated proposal she was furiously blaming Harriet. That could well explain her attack yesterday. For if the girl were almost penniless she had to bring off this gamble successfully as soon as possible.

"Harriet, is it that bad?"

"Bad?"

"The room."

"Oh, no. There's a perfectly adequate bed, and comfortable chairs. No, it isn't that bad. Not Manchester Court, I grant you." She looked again at the gleaming satin of the half-finished dress. No, that must remain Zoe's secret, for the next few weeks, or forever, as fate decided. It was no business of Harriet's. Although, in that moment when, in her best actress manner, she had told the woman that Flynn was her husband, and his fingers had pressed her arm, her heart had given a strange leap, as if it had just awakened after a long sleep.

"Flynn, do let's go."

"The house smells," said Flynn, sniffing fastidiously. "Floor polish, mold, dusty carpet. Intriguing, but not to live with. Why didn't Zoe tell me she lives like this?"

"You'd better ask her. At the moment I'm afraid I'm more interested in finding my children."

"Oh, poor Harriet, of course."

"Poor Zoe, poor Harriet! You must be getting a little tired of your forlorn female friends."

"Don't be absurd."

"It was absurd of me to think Zoe might have taken the children . . . . You'll have to thank the woman for letting us in. But please hurry. I must get home to Millie. And I haven't rung Len telling him I won't be at rehearsals. He'll be livid."

"And we have to explain, of course, to Zoe what we have been doing here. That poor blind man and his wife."

"Oh, God," said Harriet. "Shall we leave a note, after all?"

Flynn put out his hand, feeling for her arm.

"One thing at a time, my love. No, we won't leave a note. I'll explain to Zoe when I see her."

Jones was waiting around the corner. He had been walking up and down, his coat flapping open from his tall spare figure. Seeing them alone, he forebore to make obvious remarks, but with his usual discretion opened the door of the car and said soothingly, "Nasty bleak place this. I wouldn't care to live so close to the river."

"Well, we drew a blank, Jones."

"I'm sorry to hear that, sir."

"It was a long chance. But one has to explore every avenue."

"Indeed, sir. Human nature being what it is."

He means the unexpected things, Harriet thought, the little quirks that come in and make plans go awry, make one revise one's opinions. The unanticipated moment of joy when Flynn's fingers had pressed her arm. The wedding dress that was to culminate Zoe's carefully laid and unscrupulous but somehow pathetic plans. . . .

The kidnapper had correctly anticipated hers and Millie's reactions and behavior. But he was a human being, too. Could he be so sure that somewhere along his dangerous way some little thing, some unexpected behavior on someone's part, would not let him down. . . .

XIII

HARRIET WENT into the flat wearily. It was the same as it had been when she had left it, filled with the scent of lilac, deadly quiet.

Millie said nothing had happened. There had been no callers and no telephone messages.

"Not even a word from Fred," she said, and her lip quivered. "It's all so awful, I could die."

Harriet looked at the time and realized she could just catch Len on the telephone before rehearsals started. She explained that she had flu, and then had to endure five minutes of indignation and threats of dismissal before he calmed down and told her to take four aspirins every four hours, and if incipient flu was the reason for her bad performance yesterday he would forgive her.

She went into the bathroom and found Mrs. Blunt's note. "You need more bath soap. If you get that new French kind, don't waste it on the children."

Mrs. Blunt, she said to herself, when my children come home they may use my expensive soap or anything they please. Just, please God, let them come home.

It semed years ago since she had gaily bought a new hat and enjoyed wearing it.

The time was two o'clock. Another six hours to

wait. The gloom of the gray day had deepened. The wind had strengthened and whined, like a muffled puppy, in the chimney. It looked as if it were going to snow.

Flynn had asked if she minded him talking to Fred and his mother, and also to Millie. She had assented wearily, knowing that this would achieve nothing. Which was exactly what happened. They all reiterated what they had already told Harriet, and Millie once more became a sodden heap of misery. There was only one thing Harriet could do, and that was to live through the six hours until eight o'clock. To live without thinking, if possible, of what the children were doing, whether they had eaten, whether Arabella was having her afternoon nap, whether Jamie was escaping trouble. . . .

Or thinking of Zoe's half-made wedding dress, all her hopes spread on a table in a shabby, depressing, anonymous room. . . .

Of what Grandmother Lacey in Boston would think of her care of Joe's children. . . . Or of what Joe himself would think. . . .

Or of what one would do if Jamie and Arabella had disappeared as completely and finally as Joe had. . . .

The telephone did not ring again, Flynn came up once to ask her to have tea with him, because he insisted that food was vitally important in a crisis. But Millie, at the prospect of being left alone again, threw her such a stricken look that Harriet suggested Flynn having tea with them. This he agreed to do, and sat opposite her, his face turned to her as if he were watching. He had dropped his earlier efforts to make idle conversation in order to distract her and was almost completely silent. But it was comforting, somehow, having him there. The flat did not seem quite so empty.

When he left it was six o'clock. Unbelievably as it seemed, time was passing. Those hours would never have to be lived again. They were gone forever.

"You do look tired, Mrs. Lacey," Millie said timidly.

"I'm all right. Are there plenty of eggs and milk? We may have to get a meal for the children later."

Millie gasped. "Oh, ma'am, do you think they'll come back tonight?"

Harriet turned on her, angry at the girl's disbelief.

"Of course they will. I refuse to think anything else."

Millie was at the window, looking out into the darkness.

"It's awful cold and dark for a baby," she muttered.

"Where do you suppose they'll be left, Mrs. Lacey?" Millie asked.

That was a question Flynn had kept flinging at her, too. In his argument that the police should be called immediately, he had kept demanding how the kidnapper could safely return two live children to any given spot without being detected himself—or herself.

But that, Harriet had insisted, could be done as unobtrusively as the kidnapping had been done. What was wrong with them being left in a doorway, or at a quiet bus stop? The kidnapper could then keep his promise to telephone her and instruct her as to where the children waited.

The only flaw in this argument was that it would be night time.

It may well be that she would not get any information until morning, that there would be another long night to live through.

But she clung to her perhaps naïve belief that whoever had watched the flats so closely as to be accurate about her and Millie's movements would also know at exactly what times Fred went off duty. What was to stop the children being slipped inside the front doors at an unguarded moment?

This hope she now told Millie, but Millie's reaction was disappointing.

"Coo! Wouldn't she know Fred would be watching, after all this?"

"She has no reason to know that Fred is in this horrible secret. Millie, why do you keep saying 'she'?"

Millie pressed her nose against the window, staring down into the dark square. Nothing moved among the bushes and tree trunks. There was no lurking woman with a white face and tattered blonde locks. But how did one know there wasn't?

She shuddered uncontrollably.

"Because of that awful woman who watched me."

"But you only saw her once. There could be nothing significant about that."

"Millie, that was Jamie. He told me so. And Mrs. Helps found the wig he had used, the little scamp."

"It wasn't Jamie that night," Millie said hysterically. "Not after midnight. Besides she was *tall!*"

"Just a passer-by. You can't be so scared about someone who seemed to stare at you only once."

"It was the same scraggly hair," Millie insisted. "And then the phone ringing and no one speaking. That was to scare us more."

Harriet looked with distaste at the girl with her tear-blotched face and stupid, staring eyes. How could she once have thought that Millie was pleasant and kind and pliable?

"Come now," she said sternly, "Mr. Palmer doesn't place any more importance on those things than I do. We think you've imagined half of it and the other half is pure coincidence. Now what about seeing if you can make a nice omelette for supper, because shortly I have to go."

Millie opened her mouth to speak, then thought better of it. But a strange knowing look, which was vaguely disturbing, had flickered in her eyes.

"What were you going to say, Millie?"

"Nothing, ma'am. Only that I'm not very good at omelettes."

"Never mind. It will give you something to do, and we really ought to eat. As you say, it's cold and dark outside."

In the basement flat Mrs. Helps was watching her son Fred. He had finished his supper and changed into a tweed jacket and slacks. Now he was peering into the mirror over the mantelpiece, slicking down his hair and carefully studying his appearance.

She had to be careful how she asked questions. If she made them too obvious she got no answer.

"It's an awful cold wet night," she said, feeling her way to the final question—as to whether he was going out.

"It's going to snow," he answered briefly.

"That Millie rang up again."

"What's wrong with her now?"

"She said she was lonely."

"Serves her right, letting those kids get stolen."

He sounded so indignant that the old lady's heart lifted with relief. He couldn't be indignant like that if he were guilty, could he? He wasn't as good an actor as that.

"Fred, you're not going out in this cold without a scarf?"

"Now, Ma, don't fuss. You know I can't stand fussing."

Helplessly, her eyes went to the clock. It was just on eight o'clock. The time that had been specified in the note.

And Fred was going out. It was useless to ask him where because he would not tell her.

Supposing he had been in league with that silly, giggling Millie, and somehow between them they had planned something diabolical.

It was no use, she could no longer carefully feel her way, she had to burst out in her high worried voice, "Fred, you're not going to the park?"

He turned, his handsome face full of outraged innocence.

"You mean, follow Mrs. Lacey! Don't be daft, Ma! You might as well call the police and be done with it. I'm not going to put a hitch in the works that way. If those kids are to come back safe and sound no one must interfere. There's a desperate man in this, and I know what a desperate man's like, because I've had experience of them, see? Mrs. Lacey's got to play this game the way he says, or else. Me going to the park! Certainly I'm not!"

"Then where—"

His big hands rested momentarily on her shoulders. But he did not become angry this time with her inquisitiveness.

"It's none of your business, old lady. You want to know too much."

"I'm not going far, and I'm not going with a girl. If Millie rings up you can tell her that." He grinned. "Cheerio, Ma. Be seeing you."

It had begun to snow in scattered flakes. Never-

theless, Harriet decided to walk on her errand. It
was horrid, but she felt furtive and suspicious. People on the bus, she thought, would stare at her. A
taxi driver would query her strange desire to
be dropped at the park gates on a dark and blustery
night.

She would walk. She would time herself to take
exactly twenty minutes from Manchester Court to
the lonely seat half way across the park. In another
twenty minutes she would be home.

And then she could allow herself the luxury of beginning to hope.

"Don't be away long, ma'am," Millie begged pite-
ously, as the door of the flat closed behind her.

Harriet saw no one as she went out. She thought
that Fred might be lurking about to wish her good
luck, but the red-carpeted foyer was empty, the double glass doors unattended.

The wind struck her as she rounded the corner.
High Street, well-lit and populated with hurrying top-
coated forms, stretched ahead. No time to look in
shop windows, no time to linger by Woolworth's and
note again the spot of the children's disappearance.

It seemed the kidnapper had not expected to take
Jamie, too. But if that had made any difference to
his plans he would have let her know. That was
what she had kept telling Flynn, who had been in-
furiating skeptical.

Flynn was more deeply worried than he let her see.
He was angry about her stubborn refusal to get the
police until after tonight, and the disability of his
blindness in an emergency like this was intolerable
for him. Strangely enough, the whole thing had made
her forget the way she had imagined Joe's shadow
came between her and Flynn. Now they were just a
man and a woman, both in trouble.

It was ten minutes to eight. She had passed the last big department store and reached the row of small shops and restaurants that dwindled away to the edge of the park grounds.

A snowflake struck her eyelid, and, melting, ran down her cheek in a cold tear. The leafless trees, swaying and cracking in the wind, were tall before her. Beyond them stretched the long broad pathway and the grassy acres that led to the Round Pond. Lights swayed, casting moving reflections over the wet pavements. Cars swished past and the few hurrying pedestrians went on their way. She was the only person to enter the dark and deserted gardens.

She walked quickly, looking straight ahead. If someone lurked behind a tree to watch her she did not care to see him. Or her. Millie was so certain the culprit was a woman, but, apart from playing a nasty joke such as Zoe might have done, what woman would perpetrate such a dastardly scheme?

The Round Pond was a gleaming circle, empty of swans and ducks and of the lighthearted boats of juvenile sailors. Here, there was no one about except herself.

The kidnapper had chosen his time well, a dark snowy night and a deserted park.

Was that a movement behind that broad tree trunk? Harriet suddenly wanted to break into a run. She stumbled on a protruding root and almost fell. The seat was twenty yards away. It was even sheltered from the sparsely drifting snowflakes. When she carefully put the package on it, pressing it slightly between the slats, she could count on it remaining comparatively dry for at least half an hour.

But it would not be left there half an hour. As soon as she was out of sight someone, like a timid and suspicious wild animal, would pounce on it.

Now all she had to do was hurry home. Hurry, hurry, stamping to warm her feet, thrusting her hands deep into her empty pockets.

The lights along Kensington Gore seemed almost dazzling. She blinked and would not have seen the Bentley drawn up there if Flynn had not put his head out.

"Harriet! Quickly, get in!"

He waited, listening to her footsteps which Jones must have told him were approaching long before they were audible. Jones himself sat silently at the wheel.

Harriet was overcome with fury.

"Why did you come?" she demanded. "Why did you interfere?"

Flynn's long arm groped for her, and finding her dragged her into the car.

"You clot! Did you think we would let you do this on your own? You wouldn't have police protection, so you have ours instead. Isn't that so, Jones?"

"That's correct, sir."

"But you might have spoiled it!" Harriet cried. "How do you know he hasn't been watching you? How do you know he doesn't think you're police in plain clothes?"

"That was a risk we had to take, rather than have you knocked unconscious under a dark bush. Jones watched you as far as he could see. If you hadn't come back immediately he was going to investigate."

"But you might have spoiled it!" Harriet reiterated angrily.

"I don't think so. We're not near the gates, and there are cars parked all the way. Jones was discreet about that."

Harriet pressed her hands to her eyes. The swaying lights down the broad road seemed to be exploding in her brain.

"For God's sake, let's go! Don't linger here. Whoever is waiting to get that money will be ringing up shortly, if everything hasn't been spoiled."

"Everything hasn't been spoiled," Flynn said quietly. His hand had found hers and was curved around it protectingly. But she could feel a not quite controlled twitch in his fingers. She did not know whether that was caused by his anxiety for her, or by the desperate frustration of his blindness that excluded him from a more active part in this nightmare.

Fred was not in sight when Jones swung the Bentley in at the gates of Manchester Court. Harriet shook the flakes of snow out of her hair as she got out of the car. She heard Jones saying in his correct voice, "Will you be wanting anything more tonight, sir?" But she could scarcely wait to hear Flynn's answer, so impatient was she to get upstairs and wait for the telephone to ring.

"No, you may go now. But take the car, and let's have your telephone number in case I want you back quickly."

"You have the number, sir. It's written in the desk pad."

"All right. Harriet will look it up if we need you."

"You mean if you want me to help pick up the children, sir? I'll be more than happy to do that."

Harriet turned and smiled wanly.

"It was good of you to stay late, Jones. Now get home to your wife."

"Yes, madam. And I think you've done the right thing tonight, if I may say so."

Flynn felt for the steps with his stick, and put out his hand to take Harriet's arm.

"We wait till midnight. That's the deadline. If nothing has happened by then we call the police."

Jones sprang ahead to hold the door open.

"You're sure you wouldn't like me to stay, sir?"

Harriet could see the agonized indecision in his face. A fleeting thought passed through her mind as to what Jones was like when he discarded his skin of the perfect valet and became a human being.

But then he was the long-suffering, patient husband, hurrying home to regale his wife with tidbits of gossip. The human that was left beneath these two skins must be sadly undernourished and either undeveloped or well-disciplined.

Before Flynn could answer his question, she asked quickly, "Jones, are you going to tell your wife why you were so late tonight?"

"Oh, no, madam!" he exclaimed in a shocked voice. "I rang earlier and explained I was being kept to supervise a special dinner for Mr. Palmer. Purely fictitious, madam, as you realize. But I couldn't devulge this sort of thing, both because of its secret nature, and because my wife, in her delicate state, would never sleep until she knew the children were safe." He moved back a step, nodding worriedly. "As I won't myself, madam."

"Oh, get on with you, Jones!" Flynn exclaimed impatiently. "Don't be so astonishingly cheerful, or we'll all die laughing!"

Flynn did not wait to be asked to go up to Harriet's flat. He simply said he was bringing some work with which they could occupy themselves to pass the waiting time, and assumed that she would be able to concentrate on it.

She was grateful for his company. Millie, sodden with tears, would be a dreary companion, and the other companion, the telephone, was too nerve-racking. Although completely silent now, at what minute would it become vociferously alive, screaming to have its message delivered?

The time was eight-thirty. Surely by now the money would have been collected and the possessor of it making his way stealthily to a telephone box. At any moment the shrill bell in the hall would begin to ring.

Harriet took off her damp coat and told Millie to build up the fire.

"Then go to bed," she said. "There's no need for us all to sit up."

"I couldn't sleep a wink, Mrs. Lacey!" Millie protested.

"Nonsense, Millie, of course you will. You're young, and you must be exhausted. But close your door, so the telephone won't wake you."

Millie cast a quick, furtive look into the hall at the telephone, silent and innocent, in its cradle.

"I'd hear that thing from behind six doors," she muttered.

But she seemed glad to go to her room. So there was just Flynn, standing easily in front of the fire with her. It seemed to be becoming a habit, spending the evening with him. She must apologize to Zoe about all sorts of things when she saw her. Zoe, who was suddenly not aggressive any more, but, with her secret dreams, rather pathetic. Perhaps, after all, she was the right wife for Flynn. . . .

"Harriet, sit down and let's begin work."

He seemed, as always, uncannily to be watching her. She surmised that he knew she had put her hand to her brow and grasped at the thought of fixing her mind on the happiness and unhappinesses of someone long dead. . . .

And in another hundred years these agonizing

hours, also, would be a matter of no concern to any-body.

"I won't be able to concentrate."

"Not completely, perhaps. But we may have several hours to fill in."

"I never knew hours could be so long."

"They won't be if whiled away by great-grand-father Adam. You haven't even begun to look at these letters yet. Which period shall we do, the romantic, the Grand Tour or the political?"

"Did he take the Grand Tour to recover from a broken heart?" Harriet forced herself to be interested.

"One assumes so."

"And did he recover?"

"Again one assumes so, because he married five years later. But tell me what you think. He doesn't mention Mary Weston again until he is quite old. Then he says, 'If I had married Mary—'"

But if he had, Harriet thought, her blood would have been in this young man's veins, she would no longer nave been that anonymous strangely haunt-ing figure, a gentle ghost. . . . Why was it right this way?

"Look at these letters," said Flynn. "You'll find the one I mean. I had them sorted into periods when my last secretary was with me. These are the last ones."

"The handwriting changes."

"Of course. He was growing old. Read them aloud."

Incredibly, the time went by. Although she was still alert for the first ping of the telephone bell, the minutes were not quite so leaden. It was ten o'clock, then ten-thirty. . . .

Harriet suddenly flung down the letters she had been mechanically reading.

"Why doesn't he ring? It couldn't take this long!"

"We agreed to wait till midnight," said Flynn calmly. "Or do you change your mind about calling the police immediately?"

Harriet's mouth was dry.

"No! Not just yet! There may be a hitch. He may be taking the children somewhere. But it's so late for them. How can he manage them at this hour?"

"If your children are safe, Harriet, you can depend there's a woman in this."

"The blonde woman—"

"Blonde or not, let's imagine she knows how to take care of babies."

"Yes," Harriet agreed feverishly. "Yes."

"Now I should think that when this call comes, if it does—"

"It must!"

"Very well, it must. But when it does, it will be to say the rendezvous is for the morning. What's the time now?"

"Half past ten."

"And it's snowing. So naturally babies couldn't be left on doorsteps or anywhere else."

"I suppose not," Harriet whispered. "It's so long till morning."

She went to the window and drew back the curtains. The snowflakes were still scattered, making no more than a shivering of white on the roofs and pavements. The tall trees in the square garden bowed and cracked in the wind. Down the dark avenue of the roadway no one moved.

"Tomorrow I must apologize to Zoe," she said, half to herself.

"Zoe's a good kid."

"Yes."

"Was that room very awful?"

"Oh, not as bad as all that."

"I must do something for her. The little fool, why didn't she tell me she was in trouble?"

"She's in love with you, Flynn."

"You told me that once before."

Harriet remembered the wedding dress, incongruously pure and shining in that dreary room. Even though now he knew her background, Harriet guessed that Zoe would still refuse to take money from Flynn. She was playing for the higher stakes of matrimony. Supposing she succeeded, would her happiness last? Did any happiness last? Once Harriet would have thought her own completely secure. But Joe had gone, now the children had gone. . . .

She gave an uncertain laugh.

"Flynn, I wish you'd lose your temper. This isn't like you, being so unnaturally calm and gentle."

"You don't really know me, Harriet."

Again he seemed to be looking at her. She had a momentary illusion that his eyes were keen and aware.

"You haven't wanted to know me," he went on. "And, to be truthful, I haven't wanted to know you. All right, I suppose it was Joe's shadow."

"And now it's my children—Joe's children's—" Harriet pressed her hands to her face, feeling the hot tears trickling through her fingers. "Only trouble brings us together."

"Listen!" Flynn cried suddenly.

Her head shot up, she went tense.

There was no sound at all. Yes, there was, a very faint whimpering. . . .

"It's that damned puppy. I'm sorry. Did I frighten you?"

"I expect it's—lonely," Harriet got out.

"Yes, that's what it is. My poor darling—"

She went rigid as his arms came out protectingly.

Somehow she knew that to have him touch her now would destroy the last shreds of her desperate control.

"Bring the puppy up here. After all, you did say it was half Jamie's. I'll make some tea while you're gone. Can you manage?"

"Of course I can manage." The sudden curtness of his voice brought her to her senses. She would not have said that ordinarily. She would not have lost her tact. But his characteristic anger had brought her off that dangerous plane of emotion when even his hand on her arm would have been too much to bear.

Now she could go into the kitchen and make tea. When they had had that she would resolutely continue with the letters that had already helped to pass one more hour. . . .

Time was not interminable. This day, this night, this week would pass, just as the happy ones had also passed, bearing with them their varied emotions.

Joe had never seen Arabella's red-gold curls. And he had wanted a daughter with hair like Harriet's. Like sun through a fog, he had described it. The red sun of London through thinning fog.

Fog. . . . Did he know how it would overtake her and baffle and terrify her. . . .

Flynn came back, carrying the puppy in its basket.

"All the neighbors will be talking," he said cheerfully.

"Who's to see or hear you at this hour?"

"That's it. Visiting an attractive girl at eleven o'clock."

"Eleven!" cried Harriet in a stricken voice.

"Harriet, my love, the children will be sound asleep by now."

"Y-yes. Yes, I expect so. But I left the money where he could see it. I thought he would be waiting behind a tree."

"As I've no doubt he was, the swine. Now, we have one hour left. Did you say tea? And then a little more of great-grandfather?"

"Oh, Flynn!" she cried despairingly.

"You're astonishing wonderful, Harriet dear! Don't weaken."

And then the telephone rang....

XIV

EARLIER THAT EVENING, in the house by the river, Eve could not sit still. She did not care to remember the day that had gone before. It had been the longest in her life. She was not used to looking after small children. Even if she had been, she could not have managed those two. The baby had whimpered all day, screaming if one approached, going rigid with terror or temper if one picked her up. She had eaten almost nothing and been sick twice. But at least she was only a baby, acting from instinct. The boy was another thing. His naughtiness was deliberate. He asked for food, then tipped it on the floor. She told him to be quiet, and he promptly shouted and stamped like a wild Indian. He went into the bathroom and ran water into the basin until it overflowed, drenching the floor, and seeping through into the basement. When, in desperation, she threatened him with the river again, showing him its chilly, shining darkness through the little window, he refused to show fear. He looked at her with his clear, derisive eyes and jeered. "You wouldn't throw me in there. You'd be too scared!"

And every other minute he reiterated angrily, "You promised to take us home today! Why don't you take us home!"

"I told you some time this evening," she kept re-

peating. "But if you're such a bad boy no one might
ever take you home."

She had to lock the front door and hide the key,
and also bolt the windows that looked onto the street.
All the time she was afraid Nosey Parker Mrs.
Briggs would come back inquiring about the dear
little children, and Jamie, hearing her, would start
screaming for help. She should have gone out for
more bread, and for milk to compensate for what
Jamie had deliberately spilled or Arabella knocked
over with her flailing fist. But she didn't dare to
leave them, even for five minutes. One couldn't guess
what the boy would get up to. He had the most cunning brain she had ever encountered.

What with waiting for the telephone to ring, and
listening for real or imaginary footsteps, she was
limp with exhaustion and nervous strain. At six
o'clock to persuade Jamie to behave, she let him put
on his shoes and the jacket he had been wearing
the previous day. She also dressed Arabella in her
woolly coat and beret. They were ready, then. It
gave semblance to her story that this evening they
could go home. Even Jamie seemed convinced and
became quieter, treating her to one of his rare illuminating smiles.

"Will we go soon now?"

"In about an hour, perhaps."

"Tell us a story while we wait. Please!"

Eve was nonplussed. She had never told a story
to a child. She didn't even know any, except for
vague memories of the three bears and something
about a little girl and a wolf. Oh, and there was Cinderella, the girl who had to wait alone in the shabby
house until some wonderful thing happened. . . .

Well, there would be no harm done in making up
a story with a happy ending. A combination of Red

Riding Hood and Cinderella, she thought.

"Once there was a girl who lived all by herself, and she was always waiting for the doorbell or the telephone to ring, but when it did ring she was afraid to see who was there, because sometimes it was a wolf. . . ."

They were in the room at the back of the house where no light was visible to the street. With the heat from the fire and the closed windows and doors, the atmosphere was close and muggy. It had the effect, shortly, of sending Arabella, in her little woolly coat and beret, fast asleep, and Jamie's eyelids, also, began to droop.

He opened them wide, and gazed at Eve earnestly. Not only was he interested in the story—although she was not nearly such a good storyteller as Mrs. Helps, with her witches and giants, but Jamie passionately loved stories, and all was treasure to him—but he did not intend to fall asleep in case that would mean he was cheated out of going home.

He must have fallen asleep, however, for suddenly, he was awakened by the telephone ringing. As he struggled up he saw the thin dark woman run eagerly into the hall to answer the telephone.

The fire was almost out in the tiny room. Jamie began to shiver and he badly wanted to cry. He felt as he did when he woke from a nightmare, scared and forlorn and wanting his mother.

But his mother, he knew, was not here. He was in the strange house with the unkind dark woman who did not even know how to tell fairy tales properly, and at this moment was talking on the telephone in the hall.

He could hear her voice raised in protest.

"Not tonight! But you said—I've had the kids ready

for hours. Honestly, I can't! Not another night!"
There was a short pause. "But I'm scared. I don't
like it." Then another longer pause, and then the
helpless almost whispered voice, "I guess I'll have to,
if you put it like that."

She came back into the room very slowly, as if
she were too tired to walk.

"Come along, kids. Bedtime." Before Jamie could
speak her eyes gleamed fiercely and she said, "One
word out of you, my boy, and that'll be the end of
you. Splash! Into the river."

Jamie stiffened, his chin thrust out defiantly.

"But you said we were going home. You promised!"

She turned on him, her face white and narrow
with anger.

"My God, kid, do you think I haven't had enough
of you, too! Do you think I want to keep you? Does
anyone keep dynamite for fun? Now off to the cellar,
and don't argue."

Jamie, by now very frightened indeed, whispered,
"What about Arabella?"

"She stays here."

"W-what are you going to do with her?"

"Nothing, of course. She's asleep, and if I move her
there'll be more yelling. I've had enough for one
day."

The tears quivered on Jamie's lashes. He tried
hard to blink them away.

"I'm h-hungry."

"Of course you are You've despised everything
I've given you to eat. Oh, all right, I'll bring you
some milk."

Jamie made a last forlorn protest.

"It made me sick last night."

"It won't tonight because I won't put brandy in it.
I'm not wasting any more good brandy that way."

"B-but—"

Her tone was so fierce that Jamie was at last without words.

"Stop arguing! Go downstairs!"

Having awoke so abruptly he could not sleep again. The bed made up on the floor was cold and hard: the cellar, lit by one dim bulb, was full of shadows.

He was frightened.

He had been frightened all the time, but so far, by making a lot of noise and being as naughty as possible, he had managed to bluff both the horrid thin woman and the strange person who had hidden behind the couch last night.

Now he could no longer keep up the pretense. Sobs kept catching in his throat. He wanted to open his mouth and bawl loudly, but somehow he couldn't. He just crouched on the makeshift bed, trembling and sobbing quietly.

Presently the sound of the doorbell ringing, two short secret rings, made him hold his breath to listen. Had someone come for him and Arabella at last? Had, by any chance, his mother or Millie come?

He heard quick footsteps, and then a murmur of voices. Was it again that person who had hidden behind the couch?

His lively curiosity overcame his fear. He would go up and see. The woman might hit him on the ear, as she had done several times that day, and send him downstairs, but at least he would see first who had come.

Stealthily he climbed the stairs and crept along the narrow passage. If he was very quiet he could look in without anyone seeing him.

He could hear the woman talking in a rapid voice. Suddenly he heard her gasp.

"No! Oh, *no!*"

Someone gave a low laugh. There was a strange sharp noise, and Arabella whimpered.

Jamie summoned up all his courage and looked quickly around the half open door.

The only person visible was the now familiar figure of the thin dark woman. She was holding up something in her hand, and looking at it transfixed.

Jamie saw it, and also stared transfixed. He forgot to be careful. He suddenly heard, from behind the half-open door, a thick angry whisper, "There's that damned boy again!"

The woman dropped what she had been holding and flew to him. Without speaking at all she bundled him down to the basement, pushed him into the dimly-lit room, and pulling the door shut, locked it.

But she did not put the light out. At least she had not left him in the dark. Crawling forlornly into the tumbled bedclothes Jamie had a strange adult feeling that the woman was as frightened as he was.

XV

AT FIRST, when Harriet answered the telephone, there was no sound at all. But one knew someone was there because there had been a slight click indicating that the call had come from a public phone booth.

"Who is there?" Harriet demanded again, desperately controlling her impatience and fear.

Then the answer came in a low throaty voice that could have been a man's or a woman's. A man's, she thought, disguised in this throaty whisper.

"Is that Mrs. Lacey speaking?"

"Yes, it is."

"Have you called the police?"

Instinctively she answered, "No."

"That's a good girl. Now I can tell you your kids are well."

"Where are they?" Harriet demanded tensely.

"That would be telling, wouldn't it. Especially since I got to keep them another day. Too bad, isn't it?"

"You can't! You promised. I did exactly as you said—"

"Except for one important thing. You had me watched."

She was gripping the receiver hard. She knew Flynn was at her elbow, with his acute hearing probably able to distinguish the words coming through the receiver, but she could pay no attention to him. With all her strength she willed this nightmare to cease.

"No, you're wrong!" she exclaimed. "I didn't have you watched."

"I beg your pardon, dear." The voice was heavily ironic. "Oh, I know the blind man couldn't see, but his chauffeur could. Or did he have his eyes shut too?"

There was a grotesque chuckle that sent a shiver down Harriet's spine.

She cried angrily, "If you don't bring my children back by midnight, I intend to call the police."

"I wouldn't do that if I was you. I really wouldn't. Wait until you see what comes in the mail in the morning. It will be a parcel. Nice getting parcels, isn't it? And don't worry about your kids. I won't hurt a hair of their heads—" for some reason this statement brought forth another breathy chuckle, "so long as you don't go to the police. And there's a little matter of some more money. I'm sorry about that, but you brought it on yourself by employing watchdogs. You'll get your instructions in the morning, with the parcel. Now are you going to the police?"

"I—don't know."

"Course you won't, dear. Not if you're wise. See what's in the parcel first. It's just a beginning of what will happen if you have cops nosing about. Understand?"

"No!" Harriet cried vehemently. "No! If you don't bring my children back tonight—"

But she was talking into a dead telephone, for the speaker had hung up.

Flynn caught her as she swayed against him.

"Harriet! This is all my fault."

"I don't know. I don't know. He might be just making an excuse to ask for more money—as you said he would—"

Millie was at the door then, interrupting them. Newly awakened, she stood there in her nightgown, her cheeks flushed, her eyes staring.

"Oh, Mrs. Lacey, was it her?"

"It was a man," Harriet said carefully. "At least, I think so. It seemed to be too deep a voice for a woman. It was difficult to tell, because it was a sort of thick whisper."

Millie nodded in a mesmerized way.

"Harriet, I couldn't hear everything that was said," Flynn interrupted. "Something about a parcel, and not calling the police."

"The gist of it was that I mustn't call the police until I see what is in this parcel."

"He's bluffing!" Flynn said sharply.

"He or she? It's all the same. Whoever it was has my children, and I'm to get a parcel containing —heaven knows what."

"Dial the police at once," Flynn ordered. "I'll speak."

"No!" cried Millie. "Don't, don't!"

"You stay out of this!" Flynn said angrily. "You've done enough harm already."

Millie's fist went to her mouth, like a hurt and terrified child. But she had enough spirit to plead. "Don't get the police till you see what's in the parcel. Please, Mrs. Lacey! She won't stop at nothing if you don't do as she says!"

"Millie is utterly convinced this person is the blonde woman she saw hanging about here the other day," Harriet explained to Flynn. "But I still think that voice was a man's."

"If it should be a woman," Flynn said consideringly, "things may well be rather more hopeful."

"Because a woman would hesitate to harm a child?"

"Partly. And I don't think she would be quite so ruthless."

"You won't get the police, Mrs. Lacey?" Millie begged.

The sight of the girl in her crumpled cotton nightgown irritated Harriet unreasonably.

"Millie, go back to bed."

"I can't sleep. I'm too scared."

But the girl wandered off, nevertheless, and Harriet turned to Flynn.

"Millie's right though, isn't she? I can't get the police until I see what's in that parcel."

"What on earth has a mysterious parcel got to do with it?"

"How can I know? How can I know anything except that I've got to believe what he said. I don't dare believe anything else."

"What's the time?" Flynn asked heavily.

"It's nearly midnight."

"We said we'd wait until then."

"But that means it isn't so long till morning. The postman comes early."

"Get the police, Harriet. Dial that number."

"But he'll know, just as he knew—"

"That Jones and I were there?" His face was taut with pain. "A fine protector I have been."

"Flynn dear, don't worry. If he hadn't been able to blame you, he may have made another excuse to get more money."

"Can't you curse me, at least!" he demanded savagely.

She tried to smile. "I'm too tired. I'm not very

good at it, anyway. I think we ought to try to get some sleep."

"You really mean to go on waiting?"

"It's only a few hours till morning. Yes, I have to."

"You'll let this scoundrel walk away with your five hundred pounds and tomorrow demand another five hundred?"

"It's what may be in that parcel," Harriet said hypnotically.

"You're behaving with lunatic carelessness! If the police had been there tonight they'd probably have got him."

"They'd more probably have scared him off even more successfully than you and Jones did."

She saw him wince, and instantly cried, "Flynn dear! Children sleep well at night. The time will go more quickly for them than for us."

"And wake to—" He bit off his words. "Oh, God, if only I could *see*!"

Harriet took his arm.

"Do you think you could possibly endure a night on my couch? I'd feel much safer with you here."

"Safer!" His voice was full of caustic irony.

"Very much safer," she said firmly.

And then suddenly he had his arms around her and was holding her with savage tightness.

"Harriet! My poor child! Am I your evil genius, or what?"

She tried to stop trembling, but now she couldn't. She was so utterly exhausted, and it had been so long since she had been held like this. She wanted, in that moment, nothing more than to close her eyes and sleep on his breast.

Suddenly, however, the telephone rang again. After a moment of panic, Harriet snatched at it eagerly.

Had her tormentor relented? But, no. It was only
Fred, apologetic at disturbing her at such a late
hour, but he and his mother were still waiting to
see if anything had happened. Neither of them could
sleep.

"We're not doing much of that ourselves," Harriet
said wryly. "No, Fred, there's nothing you can do.
Just be around."

"I've been that all day, madam. I've watched
everyone who's come in and gone out. Especially
tonight. But there's been nothing you might report
as queer."

Harriet felt impelled to ask whether he had seen
anyone resembling the blonde woman who so haunted
Millie. But at that Fred gave a slight snort and said
he didn't think Millie was very reliable. Look how
she'd behaved with Jamie, letting him follow her
down the street like that. And the other night she had
blamed him for losing a pair of earrings, but never
a word to him the next day as to whether she had
got into trouble or not.

"That kind," Fred's voice came informatively,
"likes to dramatize themselves."

Harriet cut off Fred's talkativeness by saying briefly, "Nothing's going to happen until the morning."

"You know that for certain?"

"Yes, I know that for certain." She couldn't explain and justify herself to Fred as well as to Flynn.
In spite of the sharp curiosity in his voice, he would
have to wait to hear what had happened. "So tell
your mother to stop worrying and go to bed."

Fred, however, could not bear to be left in the
dark.

"Did something go wrong tonight, madam?"

"Slightly wrong."

"But you're not calling the police?"

"Not—just yet."

"You're sure there's nothing I can do?"

"No, Fred, thank you. Good night."

"Don't you think, Harriet," said Flynn in his ironic voice, "that your allies are poor broken reeds. A scared nursemaid, a porter who, if I'm not mistaken, wouldn't be averse to a bribe, a potty old woman who should have been sitting in the Place de la Bastille watching the aristocrats lose their heads, a valet who is besotted with a sick wife and isn't aware of anything much else, and myself blind. Scotland Yard could really do better than that."

"Oh, Flynn, be quiet!"

"Very well. For another eight hours precisely. Now where's this couch where I endure physical discomfort as well?"

"It's really very comfortable."

He smiled at last. "Of course, Harriet. I know it is. Try to sleep, my dear."

Sheer exhaustion made Harriet sleep. In the morning she came slowly out of the fog of tiredness to a strange sound. At first, in sleep-drugged confusion, she thought it was the telephone, and only half awake shot up in bed, tense with apprehension. Then she realized that it was the spaniel puppy crying. Poor little thing, he had not yet had much care, but Jamie would make amends for that when he came home.

She put on a housecoat and went into the kitchen to comfort the puppy and give it milk. It was seven o'clock.

Daylight had not yet lightened the gray sky. There was still a thin scattering of snow on the window-sills and roofs. It was very cold, and no day for children to be outdoors.

Harriet shivered and put on water to heat for

coffee. Then she went quietly into the living room and looked down at Flynn on the couch. The light did not waken him. But of course it wouldn't for he couldn't see.

His dark glasses were lying on the floor, and with his eyes closed he looked young and peaceful, the tautness and strain smoothed out of his face. Harriet suddenly wanted to touch his forehead. As if she had actually done so, he woke.

"You're with me, Flynn, on my couch," she said swiftly, anticipating his dark bewilderment. "It's just after seven and I'm making coffee."

He reached for her hand.

"Wonderful. Did you sleep?"

"Until the puppy woke me."

"The post comes about eight."

"Yes."

He sat up energetically.

"Coffee. Post. Then I go home to shave and avoid scandalizing Jones."

"Because you slept on my couch?"

"Because I slept in my clothes. Jones has the standards of a good valet."

Harriet smiled.

"It's my Mrs. Blunt who'll be scandalized for the other reason. Excuse me, there's the kettle boiling."

"Wonderful girl. Harriet, have I told you you're wonderful?"

"I expect you have. I hardly think many of your female friends escape that little attention."

"I wasn't admiring you for your looks. I haven't seen them. But for your self-discipline."

"Oh!" she went away slowly. "I guess that's a thing one has to learn."

"Yes, one has. Some earlier than others. Some more successfully."

"You're being very successful, Flynn."

"Am I? Am I really?" The eagerness in his voice was deeply touching. Suddenly her eyes filled with tears. Was she falling a little in love? The thought startled her. Joe, darling! she whispered soundlessly.

"Are you standing there staring at me, Harriet? I thought you were going to make coffee."

"So I am."

"What a luxury, after my fumbling efforts. Jones always arrives expecting to find me scalded or the kitchen on fire. Actually, I hardly ever break any crockery now."

"You shall make it for me one day," Harriet said lightly.

"Splendid. That's a promise. What's the time now?"

"Twenty minutes past seven."

"Has that puppy made a mess?"

"I'm afraid so. It's my fault. I didn't handle him very well."

"I must start taking him for walks. I depend on Jamie for that. And we have to name him."

"You're very good to Jamie."

"Harriet, why are we being so polite to one another?"

"We're making conversation," she said bleakly.

"I suppose we are. To pass time. Let's do this another day when time doesn't have to be passed so urgently."

"Of course. Black or white coffee?"

"Black this morning."

"Same for me. I'm not going to wake Millie yet. Actually, in her present state I prefer her when she's asleep. Flynn, you'll have to go before Mrs. Blunt arrives. She thinks the children are in the country."

"And you may be meeting their train this morning?"

"Oh, I *hope so!*" she breathed.

At that moment, as if it were obeying a cue, the telephone rang.

Flynn sprang up. The cup in Harriet's hand clattered against its saucer.

"Shall I answer it?" Flynn asked.

"No, I'd better. Who—what—It's ridiculous being so scared of the telephone!"

But she was. Her hand was shaking so that she could scarcely pick up the receiver.

"Hello," she said tentatively.

And then the unbelievable, the miracle happened. It was Jamie's voice.

"Is that you, Mummy? When are you coming to get us?"

"Jamie! Darling! Where are you? Tell me quickly."

"In a house by the river. I sleep on the floor. I don't like it, Arabella—"

And that was all. His voice was cut off. There was a click as the receiver was put down.

"Jamie! Jamie!" Harriet cried uselessly. She was crying as she left the telephone. "They wouldn't let him speak. They stopped him."

"But he's alive!" Flynn said excitedly. "God, Harriet, if the police were here they could have traced that call."

"They stopped him," Harriet repeated desolately. "I didn't even have time to tell him about the puppy." But a little color had come into her cheeks. Suddenly she laughed through her tears. "He's apparently being a handful, as usual."

"He has always phoned you from my flat. Jones taught him. He knows the number by heart. He'll ring again."

"They'll take good care not to let him."

"He's difficult to stop, when he wants to do a thing."

Harriet nodded, smiling again. The little episode, though it had ended abortively, had heartened them both. The children were alive and well. The unknown voice in the night had told the truth. So perhaps one could trust it today, also.

"Here's your coffee, Flynn. Oh, here's Millie, too. Millie, Jamie has just rung us."

"Oh!" gasped Millie. "What did he say? Where is he?"

"He couldn't tell us. He wouldn't know, anyway. And they stopped him telling, of course."

"And the baby?" Millie asked, wide-eyed.

"Jamie was just going to say when he was stopped. Oh! There's the doorbell. The postman."

"He's early," Millie said nervously. "Shall I go, ma'am?"

"No, I will." Harriet was already halfway to the front door. But now her mouth was dry, her knees weak. In a few moments the suspense would be over. They would know what was in the mysterious parcel.

"Good morning, madam," the postman said cheerfully. "Parcel for you."

"No letters?" said Harriet automatically, taking the medium-sized but curiously light parcel.

"No letters. Good day, madam."

He was gone on his cheerful way, and she was slowly closing the door, holding the parcel gingerly and looking at the scrawled printing of her name.

"Oh, what is it, Mrs. Lacey?" Millie asked shakily.

"I—don't know."

"Take it easy, Harriet," said Flynn. "There can't

be anything very serious in a small parcel."

Suddenly, feverishly, Harriet was tearing the paper off. Inside was a shabby cardboard box. With the same feverish haste she lifted off the lid, then gave a faint stricken cry and dropped everything to the floor.

"What is it? Harriet, what is it?" Flynn was shouting, his face taut with anxiety and frustration. "Don't you know I can't see! What made you cry out?"

Harriet knelt, her hands gently on the spilled sunshine. The spilled London sunshine that once Joe had loved.

"It's Arabella's hair," she whispered. "Her curls. They have been cut off."

Flynn's fingers clenched around his stick.

"Is there nothing else? No letter?"

"It's so diabolical! Poor little Arabella."

"Harriet! Pull yourself together. Is there any kind of message?"

"Yes. Yes, at the bottom. I didn't notice it before."

"Well, read it, for heaven's sake."

"It's printed. It says:

BECAUSE I WAS WATCHED LAST NIGHT I COULDN'T PICK UP THE MONEY, SO THE SAME AMOUNT TONIGHT. PLEASE, DO IT IN A PARCEL AND THROW IT OVER THE WALL OF THE BOMBED SITE ON THE CORNER OF PARKER AND ABBOTT STREET HAMMERSMITH AT NINE O'CLOCK. MAKE SURE YOU'RE NOT WATCHED. YOU'D BETTER BORROW THE MONEY FROM YOUR BLIND FRIEND SO YOUR BANK DON'T ASK NO AWKWARD QUESTIONS. YOUR LITTLE

GIRL'S HAIR WILL GROW AGAIN—IF YOU'RE
CAREFUL."

Flynn spoke authoritatively, "Millie, are you
there? Gather up those wrappings carefully. Don't
handle them more than you can help. Harriet, you
have yesterday's note, as well as today's, I imagine."

"Yes, of course. Why are you asking?"

"Because whether you agree or not, this is when
the police come in."

"Otherwise—"

"Otherwise we wait all day until nine o'clock this
evening, then probably again until midnight—"

"Another midnight," Harriet said dazedly.

"Which would be unendurable, for you as well as
your children. I am able to dial the police, but it
would be simpler if you did it for me."

Harriet got slowly to her feet. They were leaden,
as she walked towards the telephone.

XVI

THE DOORBELL ringing was not to announce the arrival of the police, but merely of Mrs. Blunt, wrapped in her shapeless coat, clutching her familiar string bag bulging with its various sharp-cornered parcels.

"Good morning, madam," she said cheerfully. "Cold, ain't it? That wind would cut you in half. Did you get my message about the soap? I believe the baby ate half the last lot, and of course, Jamie wastes it shockingly. Oh, I beg your pardon, you've got a visitor."

"We're having coffee," Harriet said inanely. "Actually, we're waiting for the police."

Mrs. Blunt gasped. "You haven't had burglars!"

"In a way, yes," Harriet said wryly. "But it isn't jewelry that's missing, it's the children."

Unlike Millie, Mrs. Blunt did not sob and threaten to have hysterics. She listened to Harriet's story soberly, and at the end she said, "I thought you wasn't telling me the truth yesterday about the children being in the country, but it wasn't none of my business. But, oh, madam, why didn't you get the police immediately?" She turned to Flynn. "Why didn't you make her do it, sir?"

"Don't blame Mr. Palmer," Harriet intervened. "He tried his best. And. now—now they're coming."

Mrs. Blunt, stout and solid and reassuring, stood over her protectively.

"You sit down, madam, and I'll make some fresh coffee. You look fair worn out, and no wonder. Kidnapping!" She seemed to be just beginning to realize the enormity of the situation. "My goodness! The nerve of whoever it is! I'd like to lay my hands on him. Where's that lazy Millie? Her carelessness is to blame for this. Wait till I tell her what I think of her! Oh, madam, fancy keeping all this to yourself yesterday. But don't worry, your little ones will come back safe and sound. And the kidnapper will have no soap left in his house! Death on soap, those two! Only I don't suppose he'd have any variety Arabella would favor the taste of."

The loud, astonished voice, which was Mrs. Blunt's way of expressing shock, went on in the kitchen. Harriet could hear her beginning to scold Millie, and Millie's whimpering protests. But now the need for secrecy, and the need to devise her own way of action, was gone, she found she could think no more. She was unbearably tired. It seemed almost impossible to cope with the questions of the police. When Flynn said he must go down to let Jones in and tell him what had happened, she begged him to stay.

"I can't face the police alone. Please! Jones will come up here when he finds you not at home."

"Of course I'll stay, Harriet."

His quiet voice calmed her incipient hysteria, and presently Mrs. Blunt arrived with steaming coffee and buttered toast.

"Now, madam, you're to have this. You, too, Mr. Palmer. You've both had a shocking night, I can see. And as for Millie, she's scared of her own shadow. Wants to know if she'll get sent to jail. I've told her there's such a thing as criminal negligence. But

I reckon the police will decide she's just plain dumb. Oh, Lor', there's the doorbell now! I'll answer it, madam. Then I'll put more coffee on. I've no doubt they're humans, same as us."

When Mrs. Blunt came back, followed by a tall, grizzled middle-aged police inspector, and a young constable, she drew back the curtains and the gray day came into the room.

Harriet stood up to greet the older man who introduced himself as Inspector Burns. She then explained who Flynn was, and the long-dreaded inquisition began.

Fortunately Inspector Burns was a quietly-spoken man who at once inspired confidence. At first he was startled, then deeply interested. He scarcely interrupted at all while Harriet told her story. He made notes and then talked almost to himself. Kidnappings were extremely rare in England, he said. He guessed that they would not now be dealing with the highly-organized and ruthless gangster type, but with an amateur, probably extremely nervous, ready to disappear like a startled rabbit the moment his plans went even slightly wrong. The fact that the presence, even at a long distance, of Flynn and his servant last night had scared him off was evidence of this.

On the other hand, he could be the sort of man Flynn suggested—the greedy blackmailer who, having succeeded once in extorting money from his victim, would go on playing his luck until he made his inevitable mistake.

"In that case, what would be happening to my children?"

"Your guess is as good as mine, Mrs. Lacey. But I'd say it would be regrettable that you hadn't called us earlier." Inspector Burns had kind eyes. He did not intend to waste time in useless recriminations.

He left the room to have a low-voiced conversation with the young constable in the hall, then came back, smiling reassuringly.

"I've sent Reilly to the park to check up on any evidence. If your man was scared off last night that money may still be there. It's early, and it's snowing. Or some honest person may turn it in to a police station. We constantly get surprises in our job. Now, Mrs. Lacey, I want to ask quite a lot of questions. And later I want to interview everyone who has had any part in this affair—the porter and his mother, Mr. Palmer's servant, the nursemaid, particularly the nursemaid."

It was Fred who sprang up from the breakfast table to answer the telephone when it rang in the basement. His mother, listening with concealed alarm, heard him exclaim, "The police, Mr. Palmer! They're there now? But why didn't you stop her from getting them? Now she's upset the apple cart!"

Then he recollected himself, and after listening for a moment said, "Certainly, sir. They can ask me what they like. I haven't got anything to hide."

He hung up and turned towards his mother. His handsome face was flushed with anger, and something else, was it fear? Did she imagine that his eyes did not quite meet hers?

"What do you think, Mrs. Lacey lost her nerve and called the police. At least, she didn't do it. It was that interfering Mr. Palmer. Fancied himself playing the hero, I suppose. He won't fancy himself so much if the kids are fished out of the Thames."

"I think they've done the right thing," Mrs. Helps said stoutly. She was always a little afraid of her big son's flashing eyes and sudden tempers, but she was not going to be intimidated now. The police should have been called at the beginning. If Fred hadn't a clear conscience he would have to face the consequences.

This was what she told herself, even though she knew she would lie to the end to save him.

Fred crossed the room agitatedly.

"You don't know anything about it, ma, so keep your mouth shut. The right thing! Knowing the way a desperate man's mind works. Knowing that now he can't either give the kids up or take them with him when he gets out. So what do you think he'll do?"

With that Fred left his half-finished breakfast and went to put on his working overalls.

"If they come trying to snoop in here, call me."

"Why shouldn't they snoop in here? Or have you something to hide?"

Fred came out of his room.

"Course I haven't. But I don't like cops, see. And I particularly don't like them snooping. Now I got to go and stoke the furnaces, or all the old women will be complaining they're cold." He grinned. He had recovered his breezy good-humor. But in that moment of being caught off his guard his mother had seen his fear, and she couldn't forget it.

If Fred were in any way connected with this shameful thing that was the end of life for her. But surely he couldn't be. He may not have been completely honest in the past, but he had never been unkind or brutal. Even now he pursued his secretive affairs, refusing to tell her where he had been the afternoon the children had disappeared, when she had lied for him and said he was sleeping on his bed, and again last night, when he had come in late, with snow on his shoulders, and a strange excitement in his eyes that he could not hide.

She made herself do her housework, washing the

breakfast dishes, tidying the flat, making Fred's bed.
Presently she would sit down to her wig-making,
and that would calm her.

It was the day for changing the bed linen. If it
hadn't been for that fact she might never have noticed the small trickle of fluff from the mattress
under Fred's bed. That was funny, there must be
a hole in the covering. She turned it over to look.
No, there was no sign of a tear. But wait a moment.
What was this? The stitching along the edge seemed
to have been slit to make a small opening. It had
been stitched together again, but clumsily. It had been
done recently, as evidence the little drift of fluff,
like dirty snow.

Her heart beat suffocatingly as the old lady ripped
open the amateur stitching, and plunged her hand
into the soft wool. She had to grope for a little while
before she found the foreign article. When she drew
it out, her hand was shaking. It was a neat brown
paper parcel. She knew what was in it, even before
she had unwrapped it. Five hundred pounds in crisp
one pound notes.

The ransom for the Lacey children!

On the fourth floor Inspector Burns was saying to
Harriet in his gentle probing voice, "And you're sure
you have no enemies, Mrs. Lacey? What about your
late husband?"

"My husband has been dead for two years."

"I understand that, but before he died. Perhaps
some old score?"

"Joe wasn't the kind to make enemies."

"His parents in Boston then? You tell me they're
wealthy."

"You mean," said Harriet incredulously, "that you
think someone would cross the Atlantic just to find

Joe's children, and steal them, for a miserable five hundred pounds!"

"It's a thousand now, isn't it?" the inspector pointed out courteously. "And it may not stop at that. On the whole, I don't expect it to, depending on what happens this evening.

"You're going to follow the instructions in that note?"

"*You're* going to, Mrs. Lacey. To the letter."

Harriet winced. She did not think she could face another of those solitary trips, in the biting wind, with the feeling that unseen eyes were watching her all the way.

"You believe the same thing as Mr. Palmer," she said unhappily. "That the kidnapper really got that money last night and now is getting bolder."

"Reilly reports that it was gone. Unfortunately the snow has covered any footprints. Not that they would be much use in a public park. We'll be fingerprinting the threatening notes, and the parcel wrappings, of course. But there are eight million people in London. Without some personal clue it's a long job tracking down a criminal of this kind."

"There's no time to waste."

He looked at her reflectively. He did not point out that already thirty-six hours had been wasted. He merely said, "We'll set a trap tonight. If that fails, we shall have to come out in the open. Publish photographs of the children and broadcast for anyone who has seen them. Someone will have, you know. Out of the thousand people who think they have, there'll be perhaps one who has some real information."

"But that means the kidnapper will panic!"

"Perhaps. On the other hand, tomorrow will be the fourth day. It's a long time, whatever way you look at it. By the way, I'm not very happy about the nursemaid. How much do you know about her?"

"Very little. I'm afraid I took her on trust. She seemed young and jolly. For a week it was wonderful. It really was. The children were happy and so was Millie."

"And then what happened?"

"Well, as Millie told you, she began to imagine this strange blonde woman was watching her. Jamie played a trick one day, wearing a blonde wig, and frightened her, but that same night she came home from a dance positively trembling. She said this woman had been watching her from the square gardens. After that, somehow, she was never quite the same. I should have realized, but I'm afraid I didn't. And then it was too late."

"Do you think she has invented this woman?"

Harriet looked surprised. "No, I don't. She was in a state of absolute panic. She couldn't have invented that."

"Something else could have frightened her."

"No, I don't think so. She couldn't have made it up about the woman. She just hasn't enough imagination."

"I'd like to talk to her again," the inspector said. "So far I haven't got much beyond tears."

Harriet smiled wryly. "You'll get plenty of those, I'm afraid."

"She sticks to this rather odd story that she told Jamie to stay home that afternoon. Was that a usual thing to do?"

"Not at all. She'd never done it before, or Jamie would have told me."

"It was cold, and she wanted to hurry. That's plausible enough. But it seems to me there might be more behind it. Send her in again, will you? And after that I'll see Palmer's servant, what's his name,

Jones? The man with the sick wife. By the way, I suppose he has a sick wife?"

"Oh, I'm sure he has. He worries so much about her."

"But you don't know of anyone who has actually seen her? Well, we'll check on that later. I also want to see the porter." Inspector Burns looked up and smiled. "Cheer up, Mrs. Lacey. We're getting on nicely."

It was ten o'clock. Jones had been late for work, and Flynn had bathed and shaved before he arrived. He apologized for his lateness, saying that his wife had had a particularly bad night.

"She got upset because I was late getting home, sir."

"But you rang and told her you would be late."

"I know I did, but it's the first time I've done it, and it worried her. Goodness knows what she really thought I was up to." Jones gave a somewhat hollow laugh. "And after that she couldn't sleep. I was up half a dozen times, making her hot drinks and things. It's her nerves, you see, sir."

"Well, it's a pity you weren't up to something more diverting last night," Flynn said ironically. "If one's going to worry, one might as well have a real cause."

"It was diverting enough in its peculiar way, sir. I've been wondering all night what happened. I was going to ring, but I didn't want to disturb you. If there had been anyone to be with Nell I wouldn't have gone home."

"You couldn't have done anything here."

"You say the children didn't come back, sir."

"The children didn't come back. There was a threatening phone call at eleven o'clock, and this morning at eight a mysterious parcel. At eight-thirty the police arrived. So now it's out of our hands."

"The police! Oh, sir!"

"Confound you, Jones! Don't sound so suicidal."

"But isn't that—I mean, the fat in the fire, and all that? Of course I don't know the whole story since nine o'clock last night."

"No, you don't." Flynn's voice was sharp. "So please keep your criticisms to yourself. Calling the police was the logical thing to do. It should never have been delayed. Criminals are like dictators. A taste of power, and they can't resist more. Anyway, you and I have bungled it badly enough. The police can't do worse."

"I expect you're right sir." Jones was the well trained servant again. "What were you planning to have for lunch, sir? And will you be having guests?"

"Oh, lord—Zoe! She's sure to be in to find out about our impromptu visit. And we must see that Harriet eats. Better get a cold chicken. Ring for it, don't go out because the inspector will probably want a word with you at some time."

"Very good, sir. Dear, dear, what a business this all is. What about the girl, sir?"

"The girl?"

"Millie, sir. She was in a proper funk, wasn't she. I should think the police would just about finish her off."

It was true that Millie was in a lamentable state of funk. Twice she had been cross-examined by the inspector whose mild eyes, in some strange way, seemed to see right into her. She had stuck stubbornly to the story she had told previously, although she had had an uneasy feeling that the inspector didn't believe more than half of it. He kept questioning her about the blonde woman, but there she could be convincing enough because she still got the shivers when she thought of that strange, menacing figure. They all believed it was a man who had taken the children, but she knew it was that woman. She just knew it.

She had only to tell of the threatening voice on the telephone, and the plan to leave Arabella outside Woolworth's, and probably they would trace the children in no time. She was genuinely fearful for the children's safety, but the fear for her own was greater. If she told, she would also have to confess to taking the earrings. And that meant either jail or losing Fred, or both.

She couldn't make that sacrifice. She couldn't really. And anyway the children were all right so far, because hadn't Jamie rung up this morning?

The inspector did keep on saying in his soft persuasive voice that now the police were investigating it might considerably increase the children's danger, therefore it was most urgent to trace them immediately. But why should she sacrifice her life for two kids who had everything—an adoring mother, servants, a lovely home. She'd never had any of those things, only that crowded cottage falling to bits with damp, filled with squalling kids and the sound of her mother and father shouting at one another. It had been time something nice happened to her.

Now it had happened, in the shape of Fred. But no sooner had he appeared than he was to be snatched tantalizingly away. No, she wouldn't let him go, not for all the pampered kids in the world.

If only she hadn't borrowed those earrings. . . . Mum had always said her vanity would get her into trouble. . . .

Supposing the police tracked down the blonde woman and she told about the earrings. . . .

Then it would have been better if Millie had confessed on her own accord.

She had wanted to scream and scream when they had showed her Arabella's curls. Jamie was a holy terror, but the baby had been soft and laughing and sweet. It would be so awful if something had happened to her.

Perhaps she should tell. . . .

She felt as if she had been cooped up in the flat for weeks. It was almost as bad as being in jail. And Fred didn't ring, or come near. It wasn't fair of him to treat her like this, when he knew what she must be going through. If he wouldn't come and see her, why shouldn't she go and see him?

The idea sprang into her mind and grew excitingly urgent. She had stayed faithfully in the flat when Mrs. Lacey had told her not to leave it in case the telephone rang. She had been lonely and terrified for hours, but she had obeyed. Now there was no need to be there, because the inspector and Constable Reilly were shut in the living room, and they could look after the telephone if it rang. She would slip quietly down to the basement and have a word with Fred. If he would just tell her that he still liked her and would be seeing her when this business was cleared up, she would be happy.

It was not difficult to tiptoe quietly through the hall and slip out of the door. She did not take the elevator, but ran all the way down the five flights of stairs, and arrived breathless at the door of the basement flat.

It was a pity that it was Fred's mother who came to the door. The old lady did not like her, and one look at her face showed that she had not changed her mind.

"What do you want?" she asked rudely.

"I want to see Fred."

"He's not here."

"Then where is he? I've got a right to see him, surely."

"That's up to you, young lady. But if I was you, I'd wait first to see if Fred wanted to see you."

"Why shouldn't he want to see me? He wanted me enough the other night," Millie was getting angry. "I believe it's you that's stopping him."

Mrs. Helps gave a humorless smile.

"My Fred does as he likes, I'm sorry to say. And he's not backward about making up to girls if he likes them." Her faded gaze, flicking over Millie, was significant. Millie interpreted it clearly enough. The woman was speaking the truth. If Fred wanted to see her, he wouldn't be backward about it. So he obviously wasn't interested in her any more. But why? Had he thought she was too prudish when they sat in the gardens?

Well, if that's the way it was, there wasn't much point in keeping her secret. She might as well be brave and confess to everything. If she had lost Fred, it didn't really matter if she went to jail.

Disconsolately and wearily Millie climbed the stairs. She had her head down and scarcely noticed where she was going. At the top of the fourth flight she almost bumped into Jones who was coming down from Mrs. Lacey's flat.

He said, "I beg your pardon, miss," in his polite voice.

"It was my fault. I wasn't looking where I was going." Millie looked up into his long, earnest face, and had a sudden desire to keep him there talking. She hadn't talked to anyone for so long, because you couldn't count Mrs. Lacey, or that fault-finding

Mrs. Blunt with her do this and do that. "Have you been cross-examined, too?"

"The inspector asked me a few questions. But I'm sorry to say I couldn't help him much, being an onlooker only, so to speak. It must all have been a horrible experience for you."

The sympathy in the man's voice brought the ready tears to Millie's eyes.

"Oh, Mr. Jones, if you only knew! I've been so scared."

"Scared? What of?" Jones gave an intimate and teasing smile. "You're a little too big to be kidnapped."

"It's not that I'm frightened of," Millie blurted out. "It's the voice on the telephone. And that woman with the long hair who watches me!" Suddenly confession, even partial confession, was such a relief that the words tumbled out. "You see, I lost Mrs. Lacey's earrings, and this woman knows, so she threatens me."

Jones's eyes were narrow and interested.

"Have you told this to the police?"

"No, not yet. I was so scared of being sent to jail. But now—" Millie's tears overflowed once more— "it doesn't really matter. If it's my life or the children's, it ought to be the children's, oughtn't it? They're only babies. Oh, it's all so awful!"

Millie began to stumble away, blind with tears. Jones's voice followed her sternly, "You ought to tell the police everything that you think might help. It's very wrong to hide anything."

"Should I?" Millie faltered, her courage ebbing again.

"I won't give you away, but when the inspector comes back this afternoon you should certainly tell him anything that seems important. You say this woman threatened you?"

"Yes. At least—Oh, if only I could talk to Fred. He'd tell me what to do. But his mother says he doesn't want to see me." The corners of Millie's mouth were turned down like a child about to bawl.

"Cheer up," said Jones. "I'd say the old woman's making that up. She's a bit jealous, I wouldn't wonder. You'll find Fred will be around. How long is it since you saw him?"

"T-two days."

"Two days! Good gracious, that's half a lifetime, isn't it? I wouldn't wonder if he's not on the phone this minute."

"Oh, do you think so?"

"Could be." Jones smiled tolerantly. He was really rather nice, with his sharp, black eyes and his teasing smile. But she had no time to think about him now, because it well could happen that Fred was on the telephone. His mother might have told him she was down, and he'd be ringing to say he was sorry his mother was such an old B—

With resilient spirits, Millie began to giggle.

"I'd better go, then."

"Don't know what Fred's thinking of, a pretty girl like you. But you tell the inspector all you know, miss. You don't know what might be a clue, and there's those poor kids to think of."

"Yes," said Millie hurriedly. "Yes, I guess so. Goodbye, Mr. Jones. And thanks for cheering me up."

XVII

FLYNN INSISTED that Harriet should come down to lunch. Mrs. Blunt was staying on for a while to see if she could be of help, and Millie was there. Either of them could run down with a message if anything happened. Inspector Burns was working on a plan to have Harriet carefully but invisibly screened that night when she made her second bleak trip with the parcel of money.

So there was nothing to do now but wait.

It was impossible to deny that the hours passed more quickly in Flynn's company than when she was restlessly and tensely waiting alone. Waiting for what? The telephone to ring with another sinister message? The postman to come? It was too much to hope that the doorbell would ring, and there would be the children on the doorstep. To see them again now seemed like a radiant and completely unrealizable dream. She was bogged down in the dark nightmare. It was only Flynn who kept her even partially sane.

If the police had been there to trace Jamie's call, all might have been over by now. She should have called them long ago. But if they had been called, something more dreadful than Arabella's shorn curls might have arrived in the post. . . .

If Flynn, in his determination to help, had not fol-

lowed her last night, all might have been over by now.
The kidnapper might really have been honest. . . .

But again how could one know?

The knowledge to cling to was that the children
were still alive. Jamie's voice had been vigorous
and indignant. He was such a grand, tough little
boy. Even this bewildering and frightening thing
that had happened to him had not cowed him. Joe
would have been so proud of him.

"But he needs a father, Harriet darling. He's going to be too much for you to handle. . . ."

The words seemed to come out of the air. They
must have been in her own mind, but for a moment,
fantastically, it seemed as if Joe had spoken them.

She was still thinking about them as she went
down to Flynn's flat on the third floor.

It was foolish of her to have forgotten all about
Zoe, or not to remember that such a constant visitor
would not allow two days to go by without calling
on Flynn. Especially after what had happened yesterday.

She had apparently just arrived. As Jones let
Harriet in, Harriet heard Zoe saying incredulously,
"But you couldn't have thought I would have them!"

Flynn's sharp ears had caught Harriet's footsteps.
"Come in, Harriet. I've just been telling Zoe everything."

"Harriet darling, how dreadful!" Zoe burst out
with complete sincerity. "But surely you couldn't
have thought I'd play a trick like that on you! Oh,
I know I wasn't very polite the other day, but I
guess I was in a bad mood. You shouldn't have tak-
en it seriously."

Zoe's pretty face was so distressed that Harriet
found herself liking her more than she had ever
done.

"I didn't really take it seriously," she said. "But you understand I had to explore every avenue, no matter how unlikely. I wish you had had the children. Then it really would have been only a joke."

"A pretty unfunny one for us all," Zoe said. "Do you think I'd let Jamie loose in my room!"

"What was going on between you girls?" Flynn asked inquisitively. "I didn't hear about this."

"It's time those greedy ears of yours missed something," Zoe said flippantly. "Well, how did you like my room, Harriet?"

Her voice remained light and flippant, but her eyes did not. Those long, sea-green eyes were full of apprehension. Did you see the wedding dress? they were asking. And did you tell Flynn about it?

"Your room was nice," said Harriet. "And I didn't know you were so clever at sewing."

"Zoe sewing!" Flynn exclaimed. "I thought she did nothing but stand in elegant postures!"

"I sometimes make things for my friends," Zoe said defensively. "It helps. Jobs aren't all that plentiful. You don't know."

"I don't if you don't tell me." Flynn reached for her hand. He patted it reassuringly. "You should let me look after you better than that."

Zoe's lip trembled. For a moment it seemed that she was going to fling herself into Flynn's arms and weep. Then abruptly she pulled herself together. She tossed her head and her face hardened.

"I can look after myself, thank you very much. But I'm not averse to some food, if there's any. That dress I'm making is for my cousin. Do you think she will like it, Harriet?"

"I'm sure she will," Harriet said sincerely.

"You know, Flynn," Zoe went on, "I was jealous of Harriet. I thought she had such a lot, two kids, a nice flat, a wonderful career. But now this horrible thing has happened. You can never be certain of anything, can you? Oh, well! I guess one lives and learns. Aren't we going to have a drink? I could certainly use one."

"Help yourself," said Flynn. "Give Harriet one. I'll have a whisky. Don't drown it."

"Isn't there *anything* we can do about those kids?" Zoe asked. Suddenly she began to laugh without mirth. "When I think of me landing them on Mrs. Higgs! Lord! That would be the day. But I don't blame you for being suspicious."

"You were very secretive about your address," Flynn pointed out.

"I'd only just moved there, and I'm not exactly proud of it. I have to walk half a mile to catch a bus. But it's cheap. Or cheaper than some."

"You're a very silly girl," said Flynn. "You know that I'd help you get on your feet. You've only to ask."

Zoe looked at him with narrowed eyes.

"Maybe I could use some help, too."

And in that moment Harriet knew that she had discarded her cherished dream. The half-finished wedding dress would be swept away and hidden in some drawer. The small amount of softness there had been in Zoe would disappear. She would grow astute and mercenary, her lovely green eyes alert for the best chance. She would succeed, too. She might even be happy, since money and success represented happiness to her.

But with the discarded wedding dress went the last fragments of her innocence.

As she said, one lived and learned. It was all enormously sad. . . .

"Where's Jones?" asked Flynn. "We'll have something to eat. Oh, there's the telephone. Wait, he'll answer it."

Jones did not, however, answer the telephone in his usual prompt way. The bell went on shrilling. Harriet, her nerves tensed to that now dreaded sound, went herself to pick up the receiver.

The voice that came into her ear was frail and far off, and somehow curiously unreal.

"Is my husband there, please?"

"Your husband?"

"Yes, Mr. Jones. Have I the right number?"

"Oh, you're Mrs. Jones!" Harriet exclaimed. The sick wife! The one about whose existence Inspector Burns had expressed doubt.

"I said so, didn't I?"

"Wait a moment, will you? I'll get him."

But Jones was not in the flat. Harriet looked in the kitchen, and the bedrooms without success.

"Confound him!" Flynn exclaimed. "I told him not to go out. He'll be back in a minute, surely. Tell the little woman that."

"Is she always ringing?" Zoe asked with amusement.

"Quite often, yes. She clings."

"Jones doesn't look a frightfully strong thing to cling to."

"Thin but wiry."

Harriet picked up the receiver.

"I'm sorry, Mrs. Jones. Your husband will be back in a moment. I'll tell him you rang."

"Yes, do that, will you, dear? I don't know who you are, but please tell him I'm very worried. That Miss Lane, she's my nurse, you know, she's out just now or I wouldn't be ringing, well, anyway, I've discoverd that she's been stealing my clothes. Of course I can't wear them myself, I'm quite bedridden, but all the same one doesn't want one's best coat to be worn by someone else whom one doesn't even *like!* If I'd voluntarily given it to her, that would be quite another thing. A barathea. I had it tailored by a good man. Oh, of course I know it isn't new any longer. But she'll have to go. One can't have that sort of thing happening. You will ask my husband to ring me, won't you? And within half an hour, because after that Miss Lane will be back. Thank you very much dear. I don't know who you are, but I'm sure you're trustworthy."

Harriet put down the receiver.

"What's the bee in her bonnet now?" Flynn called-ed.

"Not in her bonnet, in her coat," Harriet had a mad desire to laugh, with a mixture of impatience and amusement. She visualized a tall, rather thin, bumblebee strolling along High Street in an old-fashioned but good, tailored barathea coat. . . .

Jones came in a moment later, carrying parcels.

"Your wife has just been ringing," Harriet told him.

"Oh, dear! Is anything wrong?"

Harriet remembered the thin complaining voice and was sorry for Jones. He was so anxious, so ready to be bullied. . . .

"It isn't serious. Something about Miss Lane and a missing coat."

Flynn was calling impatiently,

"Jones, I thought I told you not to go out."

"It was just to get some greens, sir. I just slipped around the corner. I thought you'd want some with the chicken."

"It wouldn't have been a major calamity to go without them. All right, cook them and don't waste time. What's the day like out?"

"Cold and dark, sir. It's not snowing, but it probably will."

Flynn walked restlessly about the room.

"Look out of the window, Harriet. Tell me what you can see."

The scene was not reassuring. There were the knotted and leafless branches of the trees in the gardens, a few traces of snow still on the grass. Cars were parked along the street, but there were few people about, a man in a raincoat loitering on the corner opposite, a woman overladen with shopping bags, a policeman carefully taking the number of an obstructing car. It was all quiet and forlorn, with nothing to indicate that the sun would ever shine again, or the trees burst into radiant leaf.

But she related obediently what she saw, and Flynn said, "The man in the raincoat will be a plain clothes man, I should think. I shouldn't be surprised, too, if the car parkers in this square have an unfortunate time today." He rapped his stick on the floor, with restrained violence.

"It's so hard doing nothing," Harriet said, speaking the words for him.

"We can have another drink, can't we?" Zoe suggested. "I've got a modeling job this afternoon, but as long as I can stand upright, who cares?"

"Does that man look unobtrusive, Harriet?"

"He's lighting a cigarette. Yes, now he's strolling on."

"We can trust Scotland Yard to do the best possible job. After all, it's better than sitting helplessly all day waiting until nine o'clock, and knowing nothing's being done."

"Flynn, stop worrying. I helped you call the police, didn't I?"

"Would you have done it yourself?"

"I—I expect so. After that parcel."

Harriet hugged her arms around herself, trying to stop shivering. Zoe handed her another drink. What a fine trio they were, she thought. Zoe, with her shattered dreams (but she hadn't really loved Flynn, she had been thinking of an easy life; it had been a rosy dream of a constant supply of good clothes and champagne), herself with her lost children. Flynn so angrily helpless because of his blindness. . . . Jones, too, to make a quartet, with his anxiety about his strange, ailing wife. . . .

But the hours were going by. It was one o'clock already. Only eight more to that second journey . . .

Flynn picked up her thoughts, for he said suddenly, "What are you going to use for money tonight?"

"The inspector is arranging about that. I don't have to do anything except take a look at the site this afternoon."

"I'll come with you."

"Of course. If you want to."

"You'll have to be my eyes again, dammit."

"Does she make a good pair of eyes?" Zoe asked in her flippant voice.

"Excellent. Except that I don't know their color."

"What a perfectionist you are! Even though you do play at husbands and wives, it's a thing quite a lot of husbands don't know about their wives." Zoe's voice remained flippant, but Harriet caught the suddenly bleak, knowledgeable look she gave Flynn, and that strange unexpected tremor of delight shot through her again. It was connected with the love letters she had read about the unknown Mary Weston, with the feel of Flynn's arm in hers on the staircase of that dreary boarding house yesterday, and the sudden unexpected desire she had had last night to lay her head on his breast. It was a faint thread weaving through the darkness, like the promise of the inevitable spring.

"My eyes are blue," she said flatly. "Unremarkable."

And then the unnerving moment had gone with Jones coming in to announce in the pompous voice he assumed for those occasions that luncheon was served.

It was a little later that the telephone rang again.

"Answer that, Jones, but if it's your wife tell her she must keep off the line today. I'm sorry, but it may be wanted much more urgently."

"I understand, sir," Jones said, and disappeared into the hall, closing the door behind him.

Almost immediately he was back, acutely distressed.

"Oh, sir, I'm very sorry, but Nell's had a bad turn. I'll have to go to her."

Flynn's head shot up suspiciously.

"Did she ring you and tell you that herself?"

"No, it was Miss Lane, her companion, the one I told you I don't trust, sir."

"The one who stole the coat?" Harriet said.

"Yes, apparently poor Nell got out of bed and fell. She's had some kind of seizure. I'm sorry, sir, but I'll have to go."

"Dammit Jones, I wanted you to drive us to Hammersmith. Very well, if it's really serious you'll have to go. We can get a taxi."

Jones looked at Harriet. He was in a pitiful state of agitation, perspiration on his brow, his mouth working.

"I can't say how sorry I am at this time, madam"

"You can't help that, Jones. My troubles aren't yours. Don't waste time. Get away."

"Thank you, madam. I'll keep in touch, sir, and come back later, if I can."

The telephone had been ringing in Harriet's flat, too. This had been an hour ago, and Millie had been able to do nothing but look at it in fear, like a mesmerized rabbit. Oh, if it was that awful voice again she would die. . . .

Mrs. Blunt, however, had no inhibitions.

"What's wrong? It won't eat you," she said scathingly, and picking up the receiver said a brisk, "Hello! Who is it?" A moment later she turned to Millie.

"It's for you. It's your boyfriend."

"Fred!" Millie cried incredulously. She snatched the receiver from Mrs. Blunt and then could scarcely speak.

"Oh, Fred!"

"What's up? You sound out of breath."

"No, I'm not. Well, I am a bit, with surprise." Millie tried valiantly to be laconic. "I thought you'd disappeared off the face of the earth."

"Come off it. It's only a couple of days since I saw you."

"I know, but there've been so many awful things happening, and I've been cooped up here."

Fred's voice softened.

"Been having a bad time, have you? Police been asking too many questions?"

"What do you mean?"

"Well, you were a bit careless, weren't you?"

"If you only knew—" Millie was horrified to find

she had almost said too much. "I guess I was," she said humbly.

"Never mind, love. What can't be cured must be endured. Talking of that, could you endure my company for a couple of hours this afternoon?"

"Oh, Fred! That would be smashing!"

"It's my afternoon off. I've got to go out Barnes way to make a business call. Don't tell Ma. It's something about a bet. She doesn't approve. Meet me on the common about five o'clock and we'll walk across to a sweet little pub I know. Can you make it?"

"I'll make it somehow."

"Good girl."

"But whereabouts, Fred? It's a big place."

"At the bus stop on a 73 bus. If I'm not waiting for you, there's a seat there, facing the football field. But I won't be late."

"Please don't be. It'll be getting dark by then."

"Go on with you. It was much later and darker the other night."

Remembering, Millie giggled pleasurably.

"Fred! Behave yourself!"

"And don't come wearing earrings to lose at inconvenient moments. Understand?"

"Yes, Fred." Millie breathed deeply. "Darling!"

"Have you made a date?" asked Mrs. Blunt severely.

"Just for two hours."

"You mean you can go gallivanting while those poor babies are lost!"

"I'll go mad if I stay in here any longer," Millie cried desperately. "You don't know how awful it's been. Besides, I'm not doing anything, am I? The police are watching everything now, and honestly they give me the willies."

"Guilty conscience?"

"Of course not!" Millie cried indignantly. "But I've told them everything, and I can't do anything more by being here. It's only for a little while. I know Mrs. Lacey won't mind."

"A broken reed to lean on, you are," Mrs. Blunt said contemptuously. "I've got to go now to my other lady. Don't you dare step outside this flat until Mrs. Lacey comes home!"

"No, I promise!" Millie said eagerly.

"And tell her I've left a note in the kitchen about coffee. Things have to go on as usual, notwithstanding."

XVIII

THE WOMAN had been angrier than she had ever been when Jamie had rung his mother on the telephone that morning. When she had heard him she had snatched the telephone out of his hand and then smacked him hard.

"If you do that again," she threatened, "it will be the end of you. Into the river for the fishes to eat!"

Jamie would not have cried because her smacking had hurt. But he had, for that one blessed moment, heard his mother's voice, and when it had been snatched away he was just a forlorn little boy, lost and frightened. He opened his mouth and bawled.

Eve looked at him in complete exasperation.

"Now stop making that noise. Next thing the neighbors will hear."

"I want to go home! You promised."

"Sure, you'll go home today, most likely. But not if you carry on like that."

Jamie, in spite of his distress, had a wary ear for a promise. He managed to stop sobbing and asked suspiciously, "When?"

"Oh, maybe after dinner. But you've got to be good. Your sister's behaving much better now. She's getting to know me, see?"

Arabella was sitting on the floor in front of a smoky fire. Jamie didn't recognize her at first, she looked so funny with her curls cut off. Like a shaved chicken. But she was playing contentedly enough, and when she saw Jamie she gave one of her old joyful gurgles.

"Why did you cut her hair off?" he asked.

"Because it's easier to manage this way. I think she looks cute. Now come and eat your porridge and milk, and don't say you don't want it because I won't stand any of that nonsense. I warn you I'm in a bad mood today. I didn't sleep last night."

"Why?"

"Because I've got worries, that's why. And you're one of them."

Arabella waved her plump fists and gurgled again.

The woman's face softened curiously. "Hi, gorgeous!" she said. "You're one of my worries, too. Oh, hell!"

For a moment her face crumpled up as if she were about to cry. Then she shrugged fatalistically and went to spoon hot, lumpy porridge onto a plate.

"The three bears," she said. "That's us."

"Why wouldn't you let me talk to my mother?" Jamie demanded.

"Full of questions this morning, aren't you? Because it isn't convenient just now. You can talk to her all you want when you get home. And that reminds me, I'll just put the telephone out of reach. I can't trust you not to play that trick again."

"I only know two numbers," said Jamie. "Mummy's and Flynn's. Jones showed me how to ring them."

"Who's Jones?"

"Just a man. I don't like this porridge."

"That's a pity, isn't it? But you'll eat it just the same, or you don't go home today."

It really seemed as if she meant to take them home. But, in spite of his swallowing the nasty porridge, and not trying to get the telephone down off the high shelf where she had put it, and making hardly any noise at all, the morning went by without any suggestion being made about leaving. Jamie moped about, bored and irritable. Occasionally he asked questions.

"Will we go by bus?"

"We might."

"What bus do we catch?"

"A Number 9, maybe."

"Where's the bus stop?"

"At the corner."

She was answering his questions automatically, as she lit one cigarette after another, and kept walking to peer out of the curtained window at the gray day.

"Will you take us right home or just to Woolworth's?"

"Woolworth's?" she spun around.

"That's where you got us from," Jamie said logically.

"No, I won't take you home. I'll leave you in an underground station on a seat in the rush hour, and you'll look after Arabella until your mother comes."

Jamie's eyes widened.

"By ourselves!"

"Why not? A big boy like you can't look after his baby sister?"

Jamie was impressed and excited by this very daring exploit. He had never been allowed to do anything like that before.

"How will Mummy know to come?"

"She'll know. She'll be told. If she behaves herself, the same as you."

Jamie's boredom had temporarily vanished.

But the woman was impatient now.

"There's nothing more to tell. That's all there is to it. Simple, isn't it?"

Jamie watched her curiously as she paced about.

"Why don't you sit down?"

"My heavens, child, is this a twenty questions session, or what? I don't want to sit down because I'm waiting for the telephone to ring. Is that clear?"

But it wasn't the telephone that rang. It was the doorbell.

At first it seemed as if the woman wasn't going to answer it. Jamie flew to the window to try to see who was at the door, but he was grabbed back instantly.

"Stay away from there!" the woman hissed. "And keep out of sight or you know what will happen to you."

Jamie refused to be afraid of the threat about the river, but he did know that she could stop him going home if she were really angry. So he lurked in the background while he watched her reach for the key which was on the ledge above the door and insert it in the lock.

She turned it and opened the door, and as the chilly fog swirled in Jamie heard her saying in a cool voice, "Oh, it's you again, Mrs. Briggs."

"Well, I ain't seen you about, dear. I wondered if the kids was all right. And your sister? How's she, poor dear? I said to my husband last night, if I don't see nothing of the folks next door in the morning I'm going to inquire."

"We're all perfectly all right, thank you."

"Well, I'm pleased to hear that, love. And your sister? Was the operation a success?"

"Yes, thank you."

"You'll be glad about that, won't you? Well, I suppose if there's nothing I can do—"

"There isn't."

"No need to be short with me, dear. I was only being neighborly."

Without further ado the door was banged shut, and the woman, running her fingers through her short dark hair, strode up the passage angrily.

"Nosey Parker!" she muttered. "Just trying to snoop, that's all. Oh, why doesn't that blasted telephone ring?"

The door banging shut had awakened Arabella and she was crying. The woman went to attend to her. Jamie, left in the hall, gazed in fascination at the door. She had left the key in it. It could be opened and he could get out.

On the haphazard and unpremeditated impulse that had made him dial his mother's number on the telephone earlier that morning, he opened the door quietly and stepped out into the fog.

The river ran along one side of the street. On the other there was a row of houses that stretched to the corner. At the corner there was a large red bus. As Jamie stared at it in growing excitement, it moved on. But presently there would be another. He fingered the sixpence that had been in his pocket since his mother had given it to him four days ago, and which he had had no opportunity to spend. He would catch a bus home all by himself. He had never been allowed to do such an exciting thing, but it was easy. The woman had said it had to be a number 9. All he had to do was climb on it, and it would take him home.

Suddenly Jamie, still wary, gave a small whoop of joy and began to run hard to the corner.

The conductress looked in some amusement at the still breathless and rather grubby small boy.

"Where do you think you're going, son?"

Jamie held out his sixpence.

"I want to get out at Manchester Court, please," he said, imitating the firm prim manner that Nannie Brown had used on buses.

"Sure. Meeting your girlfriend?"

Jamie grinned. "You mean silly old Millie?"

"Silly old Millie, or whoever she is. Does your mother know you're out?"

"I'm going home to her now," Jamie said sedately, and settled down to enjoy the ride.

He didn't know what made him go to the back door at Manchester Court. It was probably a reflex action from never being allowed to do so when he was with his mother or Millie. But it suddenly occurred to him, also, that it would be nice to say hello to Mrs. Helps in passing, and see what color wig she was making. The last time he had seen her it had been that pale one that he had naughtily borrowed, and then thrown in the coal bin.

She wouldn't believe it when he told her his adventures. "I was nearly thrown in the river," he would say. "And they cut Arabella's hair off." (Was it Mrs. Helps who had wanted Arabella's hair to make another wig?)

Although he had been away a long time, he hadn't expected her to be quite so surprised to see him. When she opened the door she gave a little scream, and her face went as white as her hair. Then suddenly she took his arm and pulled him inside, and shutting the door hugged him until he could scarcely breathe.

"Oh, Jamie, you're safe! You're safe!"

"Course," he said, in a bored voice. "You're doing a black one. Can I watch?"

The old lady gasped and trembled, as if she were

a thin old tree and someone were shaking her.

"Oh, the wig? Of course you can watch, love. But where did you come from?"

"That house.".

"Which house?"

"The one by the river. I caught a bus all by myself. Who's the wig for?"

"The wig—oh—Lady Kennelly."

"Who's she? Tell me about her!" The old enchantment was creeping on him, the dim room, the strange, faceless heads with their long, shining hair, the old lady weaving her stories about the princesses and the witches and the bad girls for whom she had made wigs. Some of them lived in hovels, she said, and some of them in grand houses with marble staircases and gold ceilings. He wanted to know about this Lady Kennelly. Did she live in a grand house? Or in one with a cold basement, and the sound of the river running by, and a doorbell that rang late at night. . . .

Mrs. Helps was watching him with a suddenly secret and wary look.

"Of course I'll tell you about her love. But tell me all about what you've been doing. Where you've been, and who has been looking after you?"

"I told you, I've been in that house. Arabella's there, too. She cried at first, but now she likes the woman better."

"What woman?"

"The one who made me eat bad porridge."

"What's she like?"

Jamie sighed. He was suddenly very tired.

"I don't know what she's like. She's got black hair, like that." He touched the tresses on the table."

"What's her name?"

"She never told me. She was a cross woman. I

hated her. Someone comes at night."

"At night?"

Jamie sighed again. "You said you were going to tell me about Lady Kennelly?"

"In a moment. Who comes at night?"

"I don't know. I never saw."

"Then how did you know someone came?"

Jamie thrust his fists into his eyes. "I heard talking the night I was sick. I'm going home now."

Mrs. Helps sprang up.

"No, don't go home yet, love. I've got some cookies for you. Besides you haven't heard about Lady Kennelly yet, the one who lives in a castle with peacocks on the lawn."

Against his will Jamie was interested.

"Anyway, your mother won't be home at present. She'll be at the theater. There'll only be Millie, and I expect she isn't very pleased with you for running away. Look, why don't you come into my bedroom and have a rest on my bed. I'll get you a cookie and some milk, and tell you about Lady Kennelly."

"Not milk that makes me sick."

"Of course it won't make you sick. Come along. But first tell me how is Arabella. Is she all right?"

Jamie nodded wearily. He was very tired indeed.

"I told you. She doesn't cry now. She likes the woman better. But I don't. I hate her."

"You don't hate me," said Mrs. Helps, smiling gently, her white hair a cloud around her face. "I'm kind to you. I'm going to give you a nice drink and tell you about Lady Kennelly who lives in a castle. . . .

Jamie was still sleeping, and no one had come prying at four o'clock, which was the time when Millie, upstairs in the fourth floor flat, began to get restless. If she didn't leave in the next five minutes she'd never get there in time, and Fred wouldn't wait, she knew that.

But Mrs. Lacey had been late coming home after going out in a taxi with Mr. Palmer, and then that inquisitive inspector had come back. It looked now as if he meant to stay until it was time for Mrs. Lacey to go on her rendezvous.

In front of him Millie could not ask for permission to go out and meet Fred. There was only one thing to do, and that was to sneak out. She would be back long before Mrs. Lacey had to leave. With luck they wouldn't even know she had been away.

It was surprising how easy this was to do. The living room door was shut, and she was able to tiptoe down the hall, open the door and slip out, unseen and unheard. On the stairs she began to run.

Downstairs she was able to slip out of the building unnoticed by any snooping detectives, because luckily a number of people were just leaving one of the ground floor flats, presumably after a late luncheon party, and there was a great deal of talking and merriment. An inconspicous figure on the edge of the crowd, Millie safely reached High Street and joined the bus line. If she was too late for the appointment, she couldn't bear it.

It was almost five o'clock when she scrambled off the bus into the mist and gathering dark. This must be the place Fred had meant. There was a footpath from the road into the common. A little way off, behind a clump of bushes, was the seat Fred had told her about. It was empty, and so, apparently, was the common. In the distance, just discernible in the gloom, was the empty football field. Beyond it, a long way off it seemed, there were lighted windows, probably from the pub Fred meant to take her to.

She hoped he would hurry up and come. It was lonely here, and cold. Should she walk across the common to meet him, or should she wait here? On the whole, it was probably safer to wait here, because the fog was growing thicker and darker, and she might miss him.

She sat on the damp seat and shivered. Occasionally drips fell from the dark twisted branches of the tree above her. There was no wind, but it seemed, now and then, as if the bushes rustled.

Dogs, or rabbits, or squirrels, she told herself. Goodness, she wished Fred would hurry. What a place to ask her to meet him! It might be private, but that was all you could say for it.

If Fred got a bit fresh, there wouldn't be much she could do about it. Well! Millie shrugged with a certain amount of apprehensive pleasure and succeeded, for a little while, in stopping shivering.

Cars and buses made a faint roar in the distance. The bushes behind her rustled again faintly, then suddenly a pigeon burst out and flapped overhead. Millie was as startled as apparently it had been. She gave a small scream, which changed to joy as at last she heard a footstep behind her.

"Fred!" she cried.

Then the words died in her throat. She shrank back, paralyzed with terror, as she recognized the tall, thin form of the blonde woman, her long hair hanging over her face, her fingers reaching for Millie's throat.

XIX

MRS. BLUNT'S NOTE was propped against the coffee tin: "More coffee, please. Those police are fair devils for it." Harriet read it with a glimmer of a smile. She had just come back from her rehearsal of the evening's performance, and a strange desolate stage it had been, with the fog clinging coldly about the ruined bricks and mortar, the billboards advertising detergents, and the wild wet tangle of weeds growing over the bomb crater. It would not be difficult to hide among that debris, especially when it was dark. Already she could imagine the peering eyes, and the sudden greedy outstretched hands as she tossed the parcel of banknotes down.

It was not a difficult assignment. It merely filled her with horror and distate.

To explain her continued absence from rehearsals she had at last to tell Len what had happened, but had begged him not to talk about it until after this evening, at least.

If this evening failed, every morning newspaper would carry the story, with photographs of Jamie and Arabella. Joe's mother in Boston would have to be told. Journalists and photographers would besiege her flat. It would not be amusing.

So she had to pray there would be that lurking figure near the bomb crater this evening, and that he would walk into the police trap like a fox into a snare.

She went into the children's bedroom for the twentieth time to assure herself that the beds were ready, their night things got out and favorite toys on the pillows. Jamie must have missed his trucks frightfully, but when he came back he would have eyes for nothing but the puppy. . . .

Millie, rather surprisingly, offered to make tea. It was the first voluntary thing the girl had done since the shock of that awful first day. But before they could drink it, the inspector had come back.

So Harriet had to take a tray into the living room and pour tea for the inspector while he talked in his mild, pleasant manner. They had checked on Jones's wife, he said. Her illness was genuine enough. It was one of those forms of slow, creeping paralysis, and early this afternoon she had had a scene with her nurse, which had reduced her to a state of collapse. She seemed very dependeant on her husband, and he, perhaps mistakenly, encouraged this attitude. He had been with her when the Yard men had left, and had sent a message that when he got her sufficiently calm he would come back.

"Poor fellow. Conscientious devil," Inspector Burns said. "You can hardly wonder, can you. Now that porter, Fred Helps, is another matter altogether. He has a police record, did you know? Receiving stolen goods, and earlier than that some kid stuff about breaking into unoccupied premises. His mother says he's reformed, but that may be wishful thinking on her part. I'd guess he's an ambitious young man, and also that he likes to show off, particularly to women. There must be a woman in this, you know. Someone's got to feed that baby."

"Yes," Harriet said soberly.

"Mind you, if the boy hadn't rung you this morning, I'd have been more doubtful—"

"About their needing to be fed any more?"

"I guess that's what I mean. But don't worry. We've got it under control. I've checked the other tenants in this building. Mostly elderly people, aren't they?"

"A good many retired people live here."

"Yes. Eminently respectable. I don't think our man is any of our neighbors. Personally, I still stick to the theory that it's some complete stranger who's simply sorted out a victim, after doing a nice bit of preliminary watching."

The blonde woman, thought Harriet involuntarily, and called Millie to bring some hot water.

Millie did not answer or obey. With an exclamation of impatience Harriet went to the kitchen. There was no one there. Neither was there anyone in Millie's bedroom or in any part of the flat.

"Well, really! she said. "She might have asked me if she could go out, or told me she was going, at least."

"Millie gone?"

"Yes. Taken French leave, apparently."

The inspector went quickly into the hall and picked up the telephone. He spoke for a little while to someone, then came back.

"She hasn't been seen leaving the building. She's probably dropped in on somebody."

"She couldn't drop in on anyone here except Fred."

"My man's checking on that. You know, Mrs. Lacey, I'm still not happy about Millie's story, but I can't shake her from it."

"I know. She's even got the home perm stuff to prove she went into Woolworth's that day."

Where had Millie gone? Harriet, expecting her to come back any moment, full of breathless apology, went to her bedroom and looked in her closet. Just as she discovered that Millie's topcoat was missing, the telephone rang.

The inspector came back from answering it, looking perturbed.

"She doesn't seem to be around. Apparently rather a large party left from the ground floor flat about half an hour ago, and she could have been among them."

"Her coat's gone," Harriet reported.

The inspector said something under his breath, then apologized.

"Never mind, Mrs. Lacey, this may be an interesting development. We'll see what her story is when she returns. Miss Millie isn't that good a liar."

"If she returns," Harriet said involuntarily.

"Oh, she'll come back. She has a reason for what she does, that young lady. Now how long would it take her to reach her home from here?"

"About three-quarters of an hour."

"Very well. We'll check on that later. In the meantime, I'll just have a word with the Yard."

It was hard waiting. Harriet was filled with the most profound uneasiness. It was all very well for the inspector to remain so calm and confident, and it well may be that Millie had felt impelled to go out for some fresh air. Poor kid, she hadn't had much of that lately. But nothing was simple any longer.

Supposing Millie, for all her apparently straightforward story, was hiding something. Supposing she knew too much for someone's safety. . . .

She kept thinking of the blonde woman, the strange creature whom she had never seen, but who was suddenly becoming as fearful to her as she had been to Millie. . . .

"Inspector Burns," she said desperately, "what chance is there of bringing this off tonight?"

"Every chance in the world."

"But he'll know about my having called you in. If he knew that Flynn and Jones were watching last night. . . ."

"Without meaning to be derogatory about your friends, Mrs. Lacey, our fellows are trained to be invisible."

Inspector Burns smiled and patted her hand in a paternal way.

"Don't worry, my dear. I've a hunch we'll bring this off. We have to try it. It's our biggest clue. If it fails, I've made arrangements for an immediate broadcast, and of course in the morning the papers will splash the story."

The telephone rang.

Harriet could still not control her nervous jump of apprehension when this happened.

"You answer it," said the inspector quietly.

She approached it, almost as Millie had done, eyeing it as if it were a snake.

Would it be Millie ringing? Or the strange, husky, unidentifiable voice with its menacing instructions.

"Hello," said a brisk voice in her ear. "Inspector Burns there? It's urgent."

She had to listen to what the inspector said as he gripped the receiver, his pleasant face tightening and growing grim.

"Where? How long ago? Is she badly hurt? Quite. Too late, of course. Right. I'll be there in ten minutes."

He paused a moment before he put the receiver down and turned to Harriet.

"It's Millie?" she whispered. "It's Millie, isn't it?"

"Yes, it's Millie."

"She's not—dead?"

"No. She's been lucky. She was attacked on Barnes Common, but the person who attacked her was interrupted and ran off, leaving the job half done. The witnesses, a man and woman who were crossing the common, came on them suddenly out of the fog, but the attacker got away. The man gave chase, but the fog was too thick. He describes the attacker as a tall, rather slightly built person, but he couldn't swear to the sex. On the other hand, Millie says—"

"She's able to speak?"

"Yes. They've got her in the Hammersmith Hospital, badly bruised and suffering from shock. But she's able to speak. She says—" here the inspector looked angry and frustrated—"it was the person who I thought was a myth. The blonde woman."

He picked up his overcoat and put it on.

"I have to go to the hospital and see her before they dope her too much. I won't be long. One of my men is downstairs. If anything happens, anything at all, ring this number. Right?"

"Right," Harriet murmured dazedly.

Now she was alone. Completely alone for the first time since these extraordinary things had begun happening. She remembered her promise to Flynn when she had left him an hour ago to call on him the moment she needed him. Suddenly the need to do that was very strong indeed. She just had her hand on the telephone to dial his number when her doorbell rang.

It was absurd to be so cautious about everything one did. The telephone could not do one physical harm when one answered it, but whoever stood at the door—

The blonde woman, she thought again, absurdly, and her mouth was dry as she turned the knob.

When she saw Flynn standing there she simply went into his arms.

"Harriet! Harriet, my sweet!"

"Oh, forgive me, Flynn. I'm just so jittery. I can't seem to do without you."

His arms tightened, but his voice was harsh.

"Much use I am to you."

"If you only knew! Flynn, kiss me, so that I can know you're real and alive."

"Is that the only reason?" But without waiting for her answer he found her mouth, and for one wild sweet moment nothing else existed.

Then he pushed her away.

"Now?"

"It's Millie. She's been half killed. Just as quickly as that. Almost before one has turned one's back."

As soon as Flynn had listened to her rather incoherent story he told her why he had happened to arrive at that moment. His own telephone had just rung, and when he had answered it a woman had asked for Jones.

"I told her Jones was out, and she just said, 'Tell him I'm so lonely.' "

"Who was it?"

"That's what I want to know. She hung up before I could ask."

"The blonde woman," said Harriet breathlessly.

"That's jumping to a quite unjustified conclusion. You have the blonde woman on your mind, the way Millie had. No, I don't think that's who it was, I think it was Jones's wife."

"His wife!"

"It was a thin, weak voice, and whining, the way an invalid would speak."

"Yes. That's the way she sounded when I spoke to her earlier. But how could it be her? Jones is with her. The police checked."

"Harriet, I want you to go down and look in my telephone book for the number Jones said he left there. Then I want you to ring his wife and see what she has to say."

"Yes." Harriet was excited, and, all at once, no longer afraid. "That's a wonderful idea. You wait here for me, in case my telephone rings. I won't be long."

Strangely enough, however, there seemed to be no number in Flynn's telephone book, as Jones had promised there was. There were varieties of other numbers, some business firms, some under the cryptic headings of Sally or Kate or Nobby, but nothing under Jones, nothing under the letter "J" at all. Indeed, it rather looked as if a page of the looseleaf book had been slipped out. That was interesting, but baffling, and extremely disappointing. Harriet, in despair, went to the telephone to see if by any chance Jones had left a number written anywhere else.

But the little pad was virgin white, no scribbled messages, no doodles. Although—wait a moment! There were faint marks that had come through the upper sheet which had been torn off. It looked like a number, written several times, in a doodling way, as Jones had spoken on the telephone.

Rapidly she carried the pad to the light. It was not easy to read. In one the first three letters FUL were quite clear, but none of the following numbers were decipherable. In the next, she could read 5, but nothing else. Ah, here the figures were clear. She could read all four of them.

But how mysterious, for Jones to make such a secret of his home telephone number. She would dial it and see what happened.

At first, nothing at all happened.

Then a woman's voice, with a sharpness that seemed apprehensive, said, "Yes? Who is it?"

"I want to speak to Mrs. Jones, please," Harriet said. Then, when there was no answer, she repeated clearly, "Mrs. Jones. Have I the right number?"

There was a brief pause. Then the voice said curtly, "You have the wrong number."

But before she could hang up Harriet called, "Wait! Wait! I can hear my baby crying! It is my baby, isn't it?"

There was an audible gasp, then a silence, save for Arabella's distinctive and vigorous wail in the background.

The woman suddenly said rapidly, "If you're the mother, come quickly. Don't tell the police, or he'll kill the baby. Just come."

"But where? Where?" Harriet cried.

"14 River Lane, Hammersmith. Don't tell the police! Promise!"

"Then hurry. . . ."

"I promise."

She was quite calm. She wrote on the telephone pad, "I have gone to 14 River Lane, Hammersmith. If I am not back in an hour tell the police."

Flynn could not see the note, but whoever else came in would. It was a small safeguard, at least. Because she had to go alone. She couldn't even take Flynn. He was blind and might get hurt. And the police might provoke some dreadful accident to the children.

She believed the desperate, frightened voice of the woman on the telephone. She would give Harriet her children.

She had neither overcoat nor money. But a quick look in Flynn's wardrobe produced a tweed coat that would serve the purpose, and she apologized silently to him as she opened his writing desk and found a few odd coins in it.

In the too large tweed coat, and with a scarf tied around her head, she looked quite anonymous. Even Fred at the doors did not recognize her as she slipped past, with her head down. It was a cold enough night to be going out well muffled up. Little more than her nose was visible.

She might be any small anonymous woman, she thought, and had a fleeting pang for the trick she was playing on Flynn, left alone and unseeing in her flat. But Arabella's crying was still echoing in her ears, and she had only one thought, to get to this house as quickly as possible. Alone and defenseless, so that the blonde woman would take pity on her.

It was not a long taxi ride. The driver, peering into the fog, said, "It's hard to see the numbers, madam. This isn't a way I come much. There's a six. Fourteen won't be far. Afraid I'll have to let you out here, madam, I can't turn further down."

Harriet got out and paid the man. She stood a moment in the swirling fog. Then she walked briskly down the narrow street, peering at numbers, until she came to number 14 on the door of a narrow, shabby house that showed no lights.

She felt for the bell and rang. No one came. She could hear the hiss and ripple of the river, unseen in the fog. The air was full of a clammy cold damp.

Was there no one home? But there must be. It

was less then twenty minutes since the woman had answered the telephone. Harriet rang, again, impatiently.

Still no lights appeared. There was no sound of footsteps within.

But this was the right address, unless the woman had played a trick on her. This was where, such a short time ago, she had heard Arabella crying.

Suddenly, losing the remains of her patience, Harriet rapped sharply on the door and then turned the knob.

To her surprise, the door opened. She found herself facing a narrow dark hall. Groping her way inside, she felt for a light switch. When the light flashed on she saw the dreary place, with its peeling wallpaper, its uncarpeted floor.

"Is there anyone home?" she called.

There was no answer. The house had a forlorn look of being completely uninhabited. But the door had been unlocked, and in the tiny living room there were the remains of a fire in the gate and a vague lingering warmth. Here was the kitchen, a dank, molding place, with dishes in the sink. Unwashed dishes, used recently. There was a saucepan with remains of porridge. Porridge! Children!

In a state of tense excitement and apprehension, Harriet hastened up the narrow stairway. She switched on more lights and found a bathroom and two small bedrooms. In one the bed was unmade and there she found Arabella's fuzzy wool beret. And there also was the note, roughly penciled:

HE'S JUST RUNG TO SAY HE'S ON HIS WAY. I'M TOO SCARED TO STAY. AM TAKING BABY FOR SAFETY.

Harriet was still on her knees, clutching the scrap of paper, tears of desperate disappointment running down her cheeks, when she heard the sound in the next room. There was someone there! Someone who had obviously been listening and waiting.

There was only one doorway. Whoever was in there had to come through this room to get downstairs.

Harriet looked at the dark doorway.

"Who is it? Who's there?" she whispered. And when there was no answer, but only another furtive sound, she shouted passionately, "Who is it, tell me!"

A tall figure appeared at the door. There was a faint silver shine from the long thick hair. The face was strange, beige-colored, horrible.

"Why, it's me, my dear," came the throaty voice that last she had heard on the telephone that morning. "Weren't you expecting me?"

XX

MILLIE LAY in her bed repeating her story incoherently but stubbornly.

"It was Fred who rang me, but it was the blonde woman who—did this." She touched her throat tenderly. "She just suddenly sprang at me. O-oh! It was awful!"

"But Fred asked you to meet him in that particular spot?"

"Yes. I thought it was a funny place. But he said he had something to do out there. Some business." She opened her eyes in weary puzzlement. "He wasn't there at all. I didn't see him."

"Only this woman?"

The inspector leaned forward. He looked kind and paternal, not in the least the sort of person of whom one needed to be afraid.

"Now, Millie," he said briskly. "What about telling me the whole story from the beginning. . . ."

In Harriet's flat Flynn began to grow impatient. Harriet was taking a deuced long time over that call. Was she all right? But surely nothing could happen to her between here and the third floor. She had asked him to wait there in case her telephone rang. He was reluctant to leave. But how much time had gone by? Half an hour? This was absurd. He must go down and see what she was doing.

He made the now familiar journey safely, and
opened the unlocked door of his flat.

"Harriet! Harriet, where are you?"

There was silence within. He crossed the hall into
the living room.

If she were there she would speak to him. She
would not stand motionless, concealing her presence
from him.

But if she were not there, where had she gone?

Millie had suddenly disappeared earlier this afternoon and then had been discovered on Barnes Common, half dead. Millie, of course, must have had an
assignation. But supposing Harriet, in the last half
hour, had also made an assignation. If it were to
recover her children she would plunge into it blindly
and impulsively. He knew that by her previous behavior when she had kept the whole terrifying thing
to herself.

Surely now that the police had been called in she
would not do a reckless thing like that, at least not
without leaving a message.

But probably she had left a message and he could
not see it!

It was a long time since he had had one of his bitter, useless rages about his blindness. Now one swept
over him, irresistibly, and he stood rigid, gripping
his stick, wanting to destroy things, wanting to
plunge about the room breaking down his carefully
erected facade, stamping on phonograph records,
tearing up the carefully preserved letters of his great-
grandfather, hurling the typewriter with its Braille
lettering out of the window. All these things,
these carefully nurtured compensations, were useless
in the wilderness that faced him. Harriet had disappeared, she may have left a message, and he
could not see. He was helpless. And he loved her.

He had loved her from the beginning. At first it had been guiltily, because of his inadvertent part in her husband's death, and secretly, for how could he, a blind man, burden her with unwanted love?

So the façade of Zoe and the other girls, gaiety, music, extravagance, had been built up. He had even been almost contented, knowing that she was near, that she might walk in at any moment, that one day his fingers would explore her face.

But it was no longer possible to skim lightly and facetiously on the surface when this trouble had come. It had been so difficult, from the moment of his first suspicion that something was wrong, not to take her in his arms and comfort her.

He, a blind man, helpless to her!

And now she was gone off somewhere without telling him, no doubt because she was too kind to admit to him his uselessness.

But he did not need to be entirely useless. He could ring the police. Someone would come up and search to see if there were any clue as to where Harriet had gone. She may merely have slipped out to the shops, improbable as such a thing seemed at this moment. But one could do something about that. It was not difficult for him to dial the police. If the inspector thought he was fussing like an old woman it could not be helped.

He had scarcely picked up the receiver, however, when the door opened behind him.

"Harriet!"

"It's only me, sir," came Jones's apologetic voice. "My wife was better, so I came back. Has anything more transpired, sir?"

"Thank God you're here, Jones. Have a look and see if Mrs. Lacey has left a message anywhere."

"A message, sir?"

"Yes, she went out rather suddenly, without an explanation."

Jones moved about, searching. "There's nothing here, sir. Isn't she in her flat?"

"I've just come from her flat, you fool! I want you to ring the police."

"But mightn't she just have gone shopping, sir?"

Flynn tried to control his impatience and apprehension.

"Millie went out a couple of hours ago, and she was picked up on Barnes Common, half strangled."

Jones gave a horrified gasp. "That's isn't very nice, sir."

"An understatement, Jones."

"Who did it, sir?"

"If we knew that we'd know a lot, wouldn't we? Now get on to the police."

"Excuse me, sir, but shouldn't I inquire first if Mrs. Lacey is in the building? She might have called on someone else, or gone down to see Mrs. Helps in the basement. Listen, there's someone coming now."

Flynn, too, had heard the footsteps pause at his door, and then the urgent ring of the bell.

Jones opened the door, and then exclaimed in his flat voice, "Talk of angels! It's Mrs. Helps, herself." His voice grew concerned. "Is something wrong, Mrs. Helps?"

The old lady seemed to be gasping for breath. She got out, in a wheezy whisper, "I went up to Mrs. Lacey, but there's no one there. I thought she might be here."

"She isn't," said Flynn curtly. "What's wrong?"

"Oh, sir, they've arrested my Fred!"

"No!" ejaculated Jones.

"It's that Millie—I told him she was no good

after that I had to confess everything. Oh dear, oh dear, what will become of us now?"

"Sit down, Mrs. Helps," Flynn said. "Try to tell us clearly what happened. What did you confess?"

"About the money. I found it hidden in Fred's mattress this morning. The five hundred pounds. But I still couldn't believe it. Fred isn't that sort. Oh, he might be a sharp one, now and then, but he wouldn't do anything to innocent children. I know he wouldn't."

"Now listen," said Flynn calmly. "If he's innocent he can prove it. You confessed about the money because of what happened to Millie this afternoon. Do the police accuse Fred of that?"

"They said he lured her," the old lady gasped. "She told them so. But Fred wouldn't criminally assault anybody. It's a lie. They shouldn't believe what she says."

"But you believed her or you wouldn't have confessed about discovering the money. Would you?"

"I had to do that, Mr. Palmer. Because of Jamie."

"Jamie!"

"He's asleep in my bed at this minute."

Flynn was incredulous.

"Mrs. Helps, you haven't had Jamie here all the time!"

"Oh, no, sir! Of course I haven't. He only came back this morning. It was just after I'd found the money in Fred's mattress, and it made me panic, seeing him there, knowing Fred must have done it. I couldn't think of anything except that I had to hide him until Fred came and explained. I put him in my bed and gave him one of my sleeping pills in a glass of milk. He's still asleep." The old lady snuffled noisily. "Poor lamb."

"Where's the baby?" Flynn demanded.

"In that house with the woman, I suppose."

"The blonde woman?"

"No, Jamie said she had black hair. And he'd know. He notices things like that, after watching my work. The house must be near the river because she talked of throwing him in. But a five-year-old can't tell you much. And now we've got to wait till he wakes up."

"Can't he be wakened?"

"The sergeant tried. But he was too dopey. I suppose one of my pills was rather a large dose for a child."

"Mrs. Helps, do you realize how very foolishly you have behaved?"

The old lady snuffled again pathetically.

"Yes, sir, I do now. But if you had an only son you'd try to save him, wouldn't you?"

"At the expense of two little children?"

"Oh, sir! I'm that upset. They've taken Fred away to try to make him tell them where this house with the dark woman and Arabella is. But he keeps saying he doesn't know anything about it. He says he never rang Millie up this afternoon and never saw her."

"If he wasn't on Barnes Common he can prove it, surely."

"But he can't. Because he says he was taking a look at the bombed place in Hammersmith where the money is to be put tonight. No one saw him, he said. And that's guilty, you see, being so interested in where the second lot of money is going. And what Mrs. Lacey will say when she finds out I've got Jamie! Oh dear, oh dear! I must go now in case Jamie wakes. But if you can do anything to help Fred, you will, won't you?"

"If he deserves it, yes."

When the old lady at last had gone Flynn said softly, "Fred! I suppose he always was the obvious one.
Do you believe it, Jones?"

"Can't say I'm surprised, sir. And he was leading
Millie up the garden path. With ulterior motives, as
you can now see."

"The thing is whether he's been able to warn this
woman who's got the baby. If not, she's still in that
house by the river. Waiting. . . ."

"Yes, sir."

"And when she doesn't hear from Fred . . ."
Flynn began pacing up and down. "You know, I can't
altogether reconcile Fred with this. A petty crime,
perhaps, but not this. He liked women too much. He
wasn't likely to kill one, or even attempt to."

"I wouldn't be surprised, sir," Jones said in his
flat voice. "Stranger things happen. It was more
likely Fred than the blonde woman, like Millie
said. . . ."

Flynn frowned suddenly in concentration.

It was then that Inspector Burns arrived. He came
in briskly, apologizing for being away so long, but
they had made important progress. Fred, whom Millie had said had made an assignation with her on
the common that afternoon, had been taken away
for questioning. It was thought he could help a good
deal in their inquiries.

"He's not arrested?" Flynn asked.

"No, we've made no charges yet. There are some
strange aspects to this case. For instance, Millie
insists it was this mysterious blonde woman, and
not Fred, who attacked her. She swears to that. On
the other hand Fred had the ransom money, and his
mother has been hiding the boy. By the way, Mrs.
Lacey's with you, is she? I've been up to her flat but

there's no one there. She'll want to know the boy's safe."

Flynn quickly and clearly told him what had happened. Harriet had now been gone for more than an hour, with no explanation whatever. She had come down here to try to ring Jones's wife who had been complaining that she was lonely, and that was the last Flynn had seen of her.

"So your wife recovered?" the inspector said to Jones.

"Yes, sir. She was much better. And the neighbors promised to keep an eye on her so that I could come back. I was worrying about things here. But I didn't know she had been ringing up. That was naughty of her. It must have been just after I left. You see, she's a sick woman, sir, and she sometimes resents the time I give to Mr. Palmer, not realizing it's my job."

"Yes," said the inspector thoughtfully. "I could see she was not in a normal condition." He pulled out his watch. "It's now seven-thirty. We can't do much about the baby until the boy wakes up and we get some sense out of him. A house by the river. Imagine! From Greenwich to Richmond! But Mrs. Lacey can't be far away. I'll get onto that."

"Nothing I can do?"

Flynn heard the kind but firm refusal with a resurge of his bitter rage.

"Afraid not, old man. Just be around in case we want to ask you things."

He hadn't seemed unduly agitated about Harriet's absence. But if he were, he would hide it from Flynn, a blind man, who could do nothing to help.

With a tremendous effort Flynn made himself overcome his hot rage and become calm and constructive in his thoughts.

There happened to be just one thing that perhaps he could do.

It was quite dark, blacker than coal, beneath the closely growing yew trees. The path was only a glimmer, but beyond the yews a street light caught the tombstones, and shone like moonlight on them. The woman's foot caught in the uneven paving and she stumbled, the baby in her arms giving a murmur of protest. Suddenly she stopped and pressed her face against the little round one, muffled in blankets.

"Sweetie!" she whispered.

The baby gave a small crow of pleasure.

"Little shaven head! But it'll grow again. You'll never know."

The woman went around the curve of the path and came to the dim arched porch of the church. It was very dark inside, and smelled of cold stone, but it was sheltered from the wind. And it would not be for long.

She carefully laid the baby on the thick mat in front of the door.

"Don't cry!" she admonished. "It won't be for long."

The baby immediately began to wail. The woman looked around in panic.

"Don't do that, lovey. I'm saving you. Don't you understand?"

Then, without another word, and without looking back, she hurried out of the porch and down the dark path. At the gate she gave a fleeting glance at the street light shining on the old mossy tombstones. Then she hurried down the street, as if she were being pursued. At the corner there was a telephone booth. She went into it quickly. Her hand was trembling as she dialed the police. . . . She spoke for a moment. Through the window she saw a bus approaching. She hung up, and running hastily to the stop, scrambled onto the bus just as it was moving off.

The time was seven forty-five. It was funny, thought Harriet, but now she couldn't remember why it had been so important to try to get out of this room. Something about Jamie and Arabella. . . . But it was late. They would be sound asleep in their beds by now, with Nannie Brown. . . . No, not Nannie Brown, someone else, what was her name?

Not the woman with the long, untidy blonde hair. The one with the curiously beige-colored flat face, like a Chinese. But whoever had heard of a Chinese with blonde hair?

And even that woman, so obscurely, no longer seemed important.

She only wanted to sleep. . . .

XXI

THE CHIMING CLOCK in the living room struck the quarter hour. It was only ten minutes since Inspector Burns had left. Much too early to expect any news, though time for him to have ascertained that Harriet was not in the building.

With Millie the news had come astonishingly quickly. But even then it had been some time since they had discovered her absence.

"Excuse me, sir," said Jones. "That puppy—"

"Never mind the puppy, Jones. We'll get Jamie started on training him tomorrow. Jones, I've been trying to put myself in this man's shoes."

"Man's?"

"The kidnapper's. You don't honestly think it's a woman, do you?"

"Well, sir, the evidence points that way."

"No doubt he has an accomplice, of course, to whom he seems to be leaving the dirty work. But there's a man in it, of course. Now, if you were he, how would you react, having progressed this far with your diabolical plans?"

"I'm sure I don't know, sir. I think I'd want to call it off. What with the police on my tail, and all."

"What, and get nothing out of it at all, after all the risks you'd taken?"

"Well, sir, I'd have one lot of five hundred pounds, wouldn't I?"

"Ah, yes, assuming the man is Fred. But supposing he isn't. Supposing Fred, snooping inquisitively, just as we were the other night, came upon that little windfall and couldn't resist collecting it? Then, you see, you'd have precisely nothing. I really think you would make one final desperate attempt to get something. After all, Jamie has escaped somehow, but you've still got the baby. A very strong card. And you don't know for sure the police are on the watch. You probably do, of course, but you can't be everywhere at once, and Millie certainly didn't have time to talk this afternoon. Personally, you know I think you might show up at that rendezvous tonight. Early, of course, to be sure of being concealed, and yet with a good view, before the package of money is tossed down into the ruins."

"Maybe you're right, sir," Jones said reflectively.

"I may be entirely wrong." Flynn got up briskly. "It's a long chance, but it's better than sitting here doing nothing. Willing to come with me and have a shot at it?"

"A shot at it, sir?"

"Yes. We'll put the clock forward. Assuming our man will get himself concealed in ample time before zero hour. Why don't we get the money from Harriet's flat now, and do Harriet's part for her."

"You mean—leave the money in the bomb ruins!"

"And see if this fellow shows himself?"

"I'm only guessing he may be there. And, as you realize, at that time undisturbed by the police."

"I think it's a fantastic plan, sir."

"Are you afraid, Jones? I admit I won't be of

much use. But I can't do it without your eyes, you understand."

There was a short silence. Then Jones said, "Would we take the car, sir?"

"Of course. Leaving it well out of sight when we come to the spot. But you can't tell me that if that fellow is concealing himself somewhere he will be able to resist collecting that parcel when he sees it tossed in."

"He resisted it the other night, sir."

"Ah, maybe Fred got there first. Maybe it was Fred. But are you willing to give it a trial?"

"Yes, sir, certainly, sir," Jones said smartly.

"Good man. Want to ring your wife first?"

"No, sir. Mustn't pamper her too much."

The Bentley, guided by Jones, turned slowly through the Hammersmith bottleneck.

"Where are we?" asked Flynn.

"Almost there, sir."

"All right, turn down the first narrow quiet street you see."

"Yes, sir."

Flynn, sitting tensely beside Jones, felt the big car drawing to a standstill. He was not afraid. He was just filled with the most urgent desire for haste. Even now it might be too late. But somehow he didn't think it was.

"That's it, sir," said Jones in his correct voice. Then, in surprise, "What are you doing, sir?"

"I am merely sticking my revolver in your ribs. Now take me to the house by the river, the house where the dark woman or the blonde woman or whoever she is, has Arabella and Harriet."

"*Sir!*"

"Drop that hypocrisy, Jones, I know who you

are. I was right, wasn't I, when I said you'd finally go to any desperate lengths to get that money, even to falling for that colossally stupid plan of mine. Now don't waste time. The house is near here. If I'm not with Harriet in—I'll give you fifteen minutes you're a dead man. If you think I'm bluffing, you're mistaken. I haven't got that much to lose. Have I?"

"Mr. Palmer—"

"Drive!" barked Flynn, prodding the gun harder against the man's ribs. "And if you make one unexpected move I fire."

After what seemed an endless pause, the car began to move.

Flynn felt it turning. He tried to control his exultation. His wild scheme had succeeded so far. He still lacked sight. There were a thousand tricks Jones could play on him. But he had a hunch the man was almost all in. It had been a long day. And, as Harriet had said at the beginning, the criminal could so well have been some timid almost honest person, succeeding because of the sheer unlikelihood of his plans, or crumpling when attacked.

"Where are we now?" he said curtly.

"C-coming to the river."

He had dropped the deferential "Sir" Flynn noticed with grim amusement. If he played any tricks now . . .

"Fifteen minutes is all, Jones. I know it isn't far from here. Barnes Common, the bombed site, the house by the river. They're all in the same area, aren't they?"

The car turned another corner. Flynn detected a faint smell of oil and mud and salt, the smell of the Thames at low tide.

"Harriet must be there, remember. If you don't take me to her, I shoot."

Above the purr of the car he could hear the man's heavy breathing.

"Are you taking me straight there, Jones?"

"Gawd help me, sir"

"Keep going. Nice little revolver, this. I got it in Germany, and I've kept it since the war. Against regulations, I fear. All law-breakers are not so lucky. I'd hate to have to break the bad news to your wife, Jones. . . ."

The car swung violently around a corner, slowed down and came to a stop. Simultaneously, Jones had opened the door and gone.

Flynn fired. It was too late, he knew. Curse it, he hadn't wanted to kill the man. But to be foiled at this last moment, his wild scheme failing as completely as had that other wild scheme of the kidnapper's.

There was the sound of running footsteps, a woman's voice shouting. Flynn fumbled his way out of the car. He stood helplessly, the perspiration chilling on his brow. Then suddenly a woman cried vigorously. "It's all right, I've got him. I can hold him. Sammy will help me. Dad, go and ring the police."

Flynn, with his stick, felt his way along the road. There were numbers of people shouting and talking now. But the woman's strident voice rose above them all.

"I knew from the start something funny was going on in that house. I wanted to ring the police a dozen times, but Dad always stopped me. Sammy, don't sit on his head quite that hard. Don't want to smother him. Cor, there's the gent that fired the gun."

Flynn stopped. There was a sudden silence. He was able to speak quietly and clearly.

"I'm blind. I want to go into that house, but I can't do so alone. I shall probably fall over something. Will someone come in with me?"

"Bill!" said the strident-voiced woman, "come and hold this man down. I think he's passed out, but he might be shamming. I'll take the gentleman into the house. He's looking for the kids, no doubt. I always said they weren't hers."

"Actually," said Flynn politely, "it's the children's mother I want. I think we ought to hurry."

He felt his arm gripped firmly by a large plump one.

"Cor! Not that dark hussy!"

"No. But I'd like to find her, too."

"We'll find her all right, and without waiting for the police. I've been waiting for an excuse to get in that house and tell her what I thought of her, keeping the kids shut in, no fresh air, no nothing. *And* a visitor late at nights. Mind the step, love. Fancy being blind, you poor dear. The war, I suppose. We won't waste time knocking. Just barge in, says me. Cor, the door's not locked."

It was then that he smelled the gas.

"Quick!" he cried. "Find her for me!"

The woman stopped talking. Flynn heard her running heavily through the rooms, and then up the stairs. There was the sound of a door being unlocked. Then a great shout.

"Dad! Come and help. Open all the windows! Oh, the poor, poor lady!"

It was probably not long before the police and then an ambulance arrived. Flynn only knew that he had seemed to have Harriet's heavy head in his lap for an age.

Afterwards, he had asked if there had been anyone else in the house, and he had been told that there was no one at all. Not even a baby. Only, strangely enough, a woman's light gray coat, a rather grisly wig of long blonde hair, and half of a nylon stocking. These had all been thrust into the boiler in the basement, ready for burning.

XXII

FLYNN OPENED the door of his flat. He heard someone move.

"It's me," came Zoe's voice. "Don't make a noise. She's just dropping off."

"She?"

"The baby, Arabella." Zoe began to laugh. "You should have seen Constable Reilly bringing her home. He was so embarrassed. Flynn darling, you look exhausted."

"I am."

"How's Harriet? Is it true that she's recovering?"

"They say so. Apparently we were in time."

"You were," said Zoe admiringly. "Gosh, that was a clever piece of work."

"Not clever. Just lucky."

"So you say."

Flynn flung around, his nerves raw.

"Do you mind if I don't talk about it just now?"

"Of course not. You're all in. Why don't you go to bed? I'm staying in Harriet's flat with the children tonight. But Mrs. Blunt will have to take over in the morning. I've got a job. Full time and permanent. It's the old story of the new leaf being turned. Not much time for dropping in on you, but I guess that's a good thing." Zoe's voice was slightly ironical, slightly regretful. But she was, surprisingly enough, a good loser. "Get some sleep, Flynn. Harriet will want to see you in the morning."

"Zoe thank you very much."

"What on earth for? Planning to marry you when I didn't love you? I'm a low type."

"Not the lowest."

She laughed shakily, and coming up to him brushed her cheek against his.

"Tell Harriet Arabella hasn't a mark on her. And her funny little shorn head is cute. I think that woman really cared about her."

"I believe that's what happened in the end. She determined to save the baby. So it ended in a melodrama. The baby on the church steps. Funny to think of old Jones having a passionate love affair."

"Not so funny when you think his wife's been an invalid for ten years."

"Yes, the poor devil!"

"Don't think of it, Flynn. Get some sleep. We'll be upstairs, if you want us."

In the end, it was Len Brinker, Harriet's producer, who identified Jones as Leo Lunn, who, with his wife, Nella, used to do a comedy act, years ago, in variety. Then the wife had fallen ill and Leo hadn't been able to get a booking on his own. He didn't know what had happened to them, but he did remember Leo's gift for mimicry. It would have been no trouble to imitate a voice, especially one with a Cockney flavor like Fred's.

But all this no one knew until the next day. By that time Harriet was home. They had wanted to keep her longer in the hospital, but she had got up and walked out. She had a lot of things to do at home, she said. The first ones were to buy soap and coffee, or Mrs. Blunt would be leaving an irate note. She didn't like her messages to be ignored.

"I have to be a better housekeeper," she said apologetically. "I've been careless."

Of course she had been careless, wrapped up in her memories of Joe, and her desire to succeed as an actress, as if that would be compensation for having no husband. She had allowed Jamie to become wilful and difficult, and Arabella had been growing sweetly and almost unnoticed, like a primrose in a shadowy wood.

Her children! And all her life ahead! She must go home at once to get on with it.

Fred was there to open the taxi door and welcome her. He was still handsome in his uniform, but curiously deflated and quiet.

"Glad to see you home, Mrs. Lacey."

"Thank you, Fred. And you, too."

He was embarrassed. "Oh, Ma put up my bail. They say I'll get a sentence, but it won't be a long one. I don't know what came over me. When I saw that parcel of money lying on the seat I just couldn't resist it. Seemed silly, kind of, to leave it there. But that's all I did, Mrs. Lacey. The other things when ma covered up for me, I was just out at a place I know, doing a little gambling. I only didn't tell Ma because she worried about it. And Millie—I didn't know those earrings were real diamonds, I swear I didn't."

"I didn't even know I had lost them," Harriet said. "And yet they seem to have been at the bottom of all this trouble. I can't have Millie back, of course. She'll have to get another job."

"Lucky she's alive to," Fred growled. "Your kids are waiting for you upstairs, Mrs. Lacey. Jamie's had that puppy around the garden six times already."

That was how she was greeted, with Jamie pushing the fat puppy into her arms and shouting, "Look Mummy! He's mine and Flynn's. I have to take him for walks and train him, you know."

His square, bright face, lit with the excitement of the puppy, showed no trace of his ordeal. Nor, indeed, did Arabella's as she sat on the floor, gurgling with delight at seeing her mother. She was rosy and healthy and sweet.

"My darlings!" whispered Harriet.

Mrs. Blunt bustled in.

"They look well enough, don't they, madam? Almost as if they *had* been in the country. But lordy, madam, you look like a ghost yourself. Sit down and I'll make some coffee. Oh, there isn't any! Those guzzling policemen drank it all."

"Just slip out and get some, Mrs. Blunt. And as you're passing, tell Mr. Palmer to come up, if he's in."

"Oh, he's in, all right. Had me ringing the hospital six times this morning. Are you sure you're all right, love?"

"Perfectly all right, Mrs. Blunt, thank you. Just a little weak. Gas never was my favorite anaesthetic."

"Did he *really* tie you to the chair?"

"Well, he didn't want me to escape out of the window, naturally. Take Jamie with you, Mrs. Blunt. The puppy might like a walk."

"He's just been," Jamie said loudly.

"Never mind. It won't hurt him to go again."

So there was only Arabella, contentedly playing on the floor, when Flynn came. He knew his way about in her living room now. As she spoke he walked unhesitatingly towards her.

"Harriet! My darling!"

There were just the two of them as she went into his arms.

"Harriet, I have no eyes."

"And I have no life without you."

"Because of yesterday?"

"If you hadn't come in time, yes. But in every other way, Flynn. Every other way."

She felt the tautness go out of him. His hands came up to explore her face.

"I've wanted to do this for so long."

"How long?"

"From the first time I met you. But especially from the day you bought a new hat. You walked gaily."

"I was gay, that day."

"You will be again, my sweet."

"We both will."

"Do you remember my great-grandfather's letter, 'You might be any small anonymous woman.' "

"In a way I am anonymous. You can't see me."

"I see you the way great-grandfather saw his Mary, only there's a difference. I have you, haven't I?"

"You have me, Flynn darling."

"No shadows any more?"

"No shadows."

Mrs. Blunt came bursting in noisily.

"We weren't long, were we? Now, Jamie, come and help me in the kitchen. Mr. Palmer wants to tell your mother things."

"About the nasty porridge and the night I was sick?"

"And other things," said Mrs. Blunt firmly.

"Sit down, Harriet," said Flynn. "The inspector will be telling you all this later, but I'll tell you first. Because I think I understand Jones better. He really is crazy about his sick wife, you know. Certainly he had a mistress. He's no saint, after all, and he is an actor of ability. I believe he made an amusing and dashing lover, another role he could play, of course. Anyway, this woman Eve adored him, and was ready to do his slightest wish. She thought going to live in the house by the river was exciting, and promised much better things for the future.

"But for years Jones had fretted about his inability to give his wife the comfort and care she should have. It was a case of water wearing away stone. This year he cracked. Some way, any way, he determined to get money. I believe he pilfered from me, in small ways but what he wanted was a lump sum. Just enough to get a better flat and get out of his dreary rut.

"Then you came to live here. A wealthy American, he thought. Two small children. What way did crooks have of making money quickly? Kidnapping, of course.

"He made his plans carefully. He rented the empty house by the river, giving Eve false ideas. He planned, shamelessly, to use her. He also planned to use whatever nursemaid you had for the children. When Millie came he could see that she was vain and stupid, and exactly the type he wanted. He only had to watch until he had some means of blackmailing her. He saw her burying the odd earring in the garden that night, and later dug it up, and realized it was a diamond, and yours. He also found the one Millie had lost. So he had the best kind of threat to make to her.

"But, as you suspected at the beginning, he meant to play fair. If he had been able to collect the money that first evening you would have got your children back in the morning, left on a seat in an underground station during the rush hour, with a telephone message to you as to where to pick them up. But I upset that plan by asking him to drive me to the park that night. He couldn't collect the money at the right time. When he finally got there it was gone, lifted by Fred, as we now know.

"He became a little desperate then. He thought Arabella's shorn hair would give you and me warning enough not to call the police. But as you know, we did call them. So there began a frantic day for Jones. He was still determined, if possible, to bring off the thing; he didn't quite know how. But Millie threatened to confess to the police about the lost earring and the threats she had had, and he had to deal with her. He slipped out of my flat, if you remember, presumably to buy sprouts, but really to ring Millie, impersonating Fred when he did so.

"He didn't mean to kill her, he said, but just to give her a good fright. But then Eve rang my flat yesterday afternoon to say Jamie had escaped, and he was in a panic. He invented his wife's collapse, which, as it happened, was real enough, as she had accused her nurse of stealing a gray coat which actually Jones had been wearing in his impersonation of the blonde woman."

"He was the blonde woman, of course," Harriet said, rousing herself from her fascinated absorption in the story.

"Yes. A theatrical touch which came to him the day Jamie borrowed one of Mrs. Helps wigs and frightened Millie. It really was a touch of genius on Jones's part to follow that up, lurking conspiciously when he knew there was a chance of Millie seeing him."

"The beige face?" Harriet queried, shivering a little.

"A nylon stocking drawn over it, flattening his features."

"It was quite horrifying."

"I can imagine it was. As you see, Jones was drawn always to the theatrical, as also in the grisly gesture of Arabella's hair. But here is the nicest part of the story. The woman, Eve, after a nightmare couple of days trying to cope with the children and feeling all the time that she was spied on by the neighbor, Mrs. Briggs (it was Mrs. Briggs who came to our rescue last night), found she was growing very fond of Arabella. She was, by this time, extremely frightened—Jones, in his best Frankenstein manner, had been pretty effective. When Jamie escaped, she was panic-stricken. The only thing in her head was to save the baby. Then you rang, accidentally, and she seized the opportunity to ask you to come. But before you could get there Jones had rung, saying he was on his way, and she was terrified that he would kill the baby. So she ran away and later left Arabella on the church steps, to be picked up by the police. Jones arrived. There was no one there. He was rather at his wits end, I think, and would have thrown the whole thing up, and probably no one would have been any the wiser.

"But you walked in. You surprised him upstairs. He couldn't get out without you seeing him, and anyway you must have had some inside knowledge to have come there. So in that moment, from being an amater, rather nibbling at crime, he became a desperate criminal. He genuinely tried to kill you. It was, he told himself, you or his wife. And you had had so much, Nell so little. There was no choice.

"He left you there, tied to the chair, slowly inhaling gas, and came back to the flat to see if you had left any clues. You had, of course. Your note saying where you had gone.

"That was easy to get rid of, and almost immediately the news came that Fred was arrested. So Jones got over confident and made his fatal mistake."

"What was it?" Harriet asked breathlessly. "How did you know so certainly that he was guilty?"

"Because he insisted that, although Fred denied it, it probably had been Fred who had attacked Millie, and not the blonde woman, as she had said. At that stage no one, *no one,* had told Jones that Millie had said she was attacked by the blonde woman. In that moment I understood everything."

Harriet put her hand on his. She didn't speak for a little while. Then she said, "The woman? The one who grew fond of Arabella?"

"They picked her up late last night. Poor little scrap. She'll get off lightly, probably. She didn't seem to mind a lot. As long as the baby was safe, she said. I don't think she had ever handled a baby before."

"And Jones's wife?"

"She'll be cared for until he comes out. Probably do them both good. She had him worn to a frazzle."

"Oh, Flynn! How sad it all is."

"Yes, but it's broken an unhealthy spell for them."

"It's so wonderful not to be afraid of the telephone any more. That deadly little bell! It was like listening to danger."

Then Jamie came in, the puppy bundled fatly in his arms.

"Here's one of the reasons things went wrong for Jones," Flynn said. "He never meant to get himself saddled with a five-year-old."

"The unpredictable," said Harriet. "The uncertainty of the human element."

"Flynn, do you suppose now you haven't got Jones

we ought to look after you?" Jamie asked, with the air of producing an original and brilliant idea.

"I'd appreciate it," said Flynn, and Jamie's face lit with his wide warm smile.

"Coffee's ready," called Mrs. Blunt. "I'll have to go now, Mrs. Lacey. It isn't really my morning here. I've left a note about floor polish. Don't get that scented kind. It gives me hay fever. Funny how good things are bad for you, and bad things are good."

Harriet leaned over to touch Flynn's eyelids lightly with her fingertips. He seized her hand and kissed it.

"Let's look at it that way," he said cheerfully.

The Novels of
Dorothy Eden

$1.75 each

Available wherever paperbacks are sold or use this coupon.

ace books, (Dept. MM) Box 576, Times Square Station
New York, N.Y. 10036
Please send me titles checked above.

I enclose $.................Add 35c handling fee per copy.

Name ....

Address ....

City...................... State............. Zip........